wood's Spies, volume 1: Archer

ooks that you just have to start talking
e finished (and I did). The concept is
incredible and unique, and will keep you on the edge of your seat!"
—Nicole Sager, author of *The Heart of Arcrea*

"Camille Elliot's regency romance has always been top notch;
but this time she combined it with a hint of Marvel Comic's The
Incredible Hulk, and the action never stops … Throw in some
astonishingly evil villains, and you certainly have a read you can't
put down and will leave you screaming: When is the next book
coming out?"
—L. Ertelt, Christian Fiction Devourers Moderator

"Mysteries, homeland agents operating in disguise, then the
appearance of 'Incredible Hulk' or Dr. Jekyll/Mr. Hyde-type
characters wreaking havoc and death, the story developed into a
complex kaleidoscope, wherein every chapter presents a new
permutation or another aspect of one of the character's past life.
To me, this was a riveting read from the beginning."
—J. Stone, Amazon reviewer

"This story was truly captivating and captured my attention
right from the beginning. This is Regency romance at its finest
with not only the culture and mannerisms of the time, but also
with intrigue, espionage, and drama which all make this quite the
page-turner."
—Anonymous5, Goodreads reviewer

Lady Wynwood's Spies series
Recommended reading order

The Spinster's Christmas (prequel)
The Gentleman Thief (prequel novella)
Lady Wynwood's Spies, volume 1: Archer
Lady Wynwood's Spies, volume 2: Berserker
Lady Wynwood's Spies, volume 3: Aggressor
Lady Wynwood's Spies, volume 4: Betrayer
Lady Wynwood's Spies, volume 5: Prisoner
Lady Wynwood's Spies, volume 6: Martyr
Lady Wynwood's Spies, volume 7: Spinster (coming soon)

Standalone novels

Prelude for a Lord
The Gentleman's Quest

Devotional

Who I Want to Be

Lady Wynwood's Spies, volume 2: Berserker

A Christian Regency Romantic Adventure serial novel

Camille Elliot

Camy Tang
P.O. Box 23143
San Jose, CA 95153-3143
www.camilleelliot.com

Publisher's Note: This is a work of fiction. Names, characters, places,
and incidents are a product of the author's imagination. Locales and
public names are sometimes used for atmospheric purposes. Any
resemblance to actual people, living or dead, or to businesses,
companies, events, institutions, or locales is completely coincidental.

Lady Wynwood's Spies, volume 2: Berserker/ Camille Elliot. — 1st ed.

eBook: ISBN-13: 978-1-942225-23-2
Print book: ISBN-13: 978-1-942225-24-9

Some trust in chariots, and some in horses:

but we will remember the name of the LORD our God.

Psalm 20:7

Chapter One

The house on Park Street was quiet again. It was not so very late in the evening, especially considering that many events during the Season ended in the early morning hours. But London was still a little thin of company at the moment, with the exception of mothers with daughters to launch, who had arrived early to get shopping and dressmaking done before the feverish rounds of balls and parties.

Laura Glencowe, Lady Wynwood, peered through a slit in the drawing room curtains to glance at the houses across from her townhouse and to peer up and down the street to see the lights from her neighbors' homes. Most of the houses were still dark. Her right-hand neighbor was a retired admiral who was probably still fishing in Scotland, while her left-hand neighbor was a wealthy banker who had become a baronet six or seven years ago and still had the habit of retiring early. There was no one to remark upon the activity of her servants entering and exiting her house, but everyone had used the small lane that ran behind her tiny garden, and so her home appeared nothing out of the ordinary.

Except that the occupants of her house had had a most extraordinary evening. The man who had just that evening caused considerable damage to several streets in the Long Glades lay slumbering on a cot in what had once been her storeroom, with the door locked and bolted in the event that he awoke as the same mindless monster. And the ones who had put the beast to sleep were her coachman, her eleven-year-old twin servants, her old friend Sol Drydale, and two young ladies of society, one of whom was her niece.

In the years since her husband had died, she cared less and less about the opinions of the fashionable world, but in this case she needn't worry at all. If she told the absolute truth to her friends among the *haut ton*, they would smile and suggest a repairing lease to the countryside to escape her vivid nightmares. Then they would gobble up all her tea cookies and escape her house as fast as possible.

The street was quiet, but she still felt that tremor of unease in the pit of her stomach. She had first felt it when her niece Phoebe told her about sedating Mr. Coulton-Jones and using up all of the medicinal paste she had concocted with her friend Miss Gardinier.

They still didn't know why Mr. Coulton-Jones had been taken by those mysterious men. Had they been seeking him? Had it been purely by chance?

But it had not been by chance that he had been turned into that monster. They had done that to him deliberately, for reasons that she could not fathom.

And now Mr. Ackett was missing. She had no reason to think he had been captured, but the uncertainty quickened her heartbeat like a shadow just out of her range of vision.

Earlier that evening, while they were setting up the storeroom as Mr. Coulton-Jones's sickroom and prison cell, Calvin had very earnestly come to her.

The young boy looked down and bit his thumbnail. "M'lady, I want to go searching for him."

"For Mr. Ackett?"

"Yes, m'lady. There are dangerous men out there. What if they find him and hurt him? I wish I had stayed with him."

"If you had, we might not have saved Mr. Coulton-Jones."

Calvin looked up, his eyes wide, his expression worried. "Please let me go look for him. Mr. Havner will go with me, if I ask him."

When he stepped into the drawing room, she had known what he would ask. She had also known she wouldn't be able to refuse him.

What she hadn't expected was what she saw when she looked in Calvin's eyes. She suddenly saw another man's face floating in front of Calvin's, like a vision. "Help me," the man begged. And then suddenly the vision was gone, and it was just her eleven-year-old pageboy, looking more anguished than she had ever seen him before.

The vision made her feel a nameless urgency, similar to that unease in her stomach earlier when speaking to Phoebe about the medicinal paste. She didn't know what it meant. Instead, she focused on Calvin, with his mouth pulled wide in pleading and regret.

She also hadn't mentioned that if he hadn't come to her, she would have asked him if he wanted to go.

The coachman, Mr. Havner, had been quick to offer to accompany him. Sol had been quick to object.

She and Sol had the most fierce row they had ever had, and Sol stormed out. Although he also promised—although it sounded more like a threat—to return shortly.

Her gaze was drawn again to the scene outside the window. Her coach had suddenly come clattering down the street, going at a much faster pace than it had left. Since her coachman was preparing to leave for the Long Glades tonight, she had been forced to ask Fred to drive Keriah to her sister's home to pick up her things so that she could stay at Laura's home for a few days, but she hadn't expected her footman to be quite so hamfisted with the reins.

Barely a minute had passed before footsteps thundered up

the stairs and Keriah burst into the drawing room. Laura couldn't understand how such a delicate frame could make such a racket.

"My lady! It's terrible!"

Laura blinked. She had no idea how to respond to a proclamation like that.

Luckily, only a few seconds later, she could hear softer, steadier footsteps on the stairs and soon a short, slightly balding, middle-aged man appeared in the drawing room door. He did not enter immediately, but he peered inside and his eyes darted nervously from the marble fireplace to the brocade drapery to the delicately carved tea table before alighting upon Laura.

What surprised her was that he promptly shoved Keriah aside, making her stumble a few steps.

He entered the drawing room and bowed. "My lady, I beg you will pardon the intrusion and excuse my rudeness in introducing myself. I am Dr. Augustus Shokes."

Laura smiled, not only because she recognized his name, but also because Keriah looked startled at being shunted aside so brusquely. "Dr. Shokes, I am well acquainted with you by reputation thanks to Keriah and Phoebe. You are more than welcome in my home."

"Please excuse my visit at this late hour. I am afraid the matter was urgent. Although Keriah had no need to be quite so melodramatic." He eyed the young woman with asperity, although Keriah studiously looked away.

Keriah's startling proclamation had caused tension to creep up the back of her shoulders and into the back of her skull, but something about Dr. Shokes's calm manner made the panicked atmosphere relax. "Please do sit down." She gestured to the sofa.

Behind him through the open doorway stood her butler, who had belatedly followed the pair and was obviously distressed that he had not been able to properly announce the visitors. He sighed and Laura could have sworn he rolled his eyes as he turned away.

The housekeeper, standing beside him, nodded at Laura's significant look, then quietly closed the door before going downstairs to gather what refreshments they could find at this time of night.

Laura sat across from Dr. Shokes. "Doctor, what did you need to tell me?"

Keriah also sat down next to the doctor, and it was she who answered. "My lady, it would be best if you let Phoebe and I return with Dr. Shokes to the apothecary shop tonight."

Laura sighed. "Keriah, I already explained to you that I am not sending genteel young women into the Long Glades at this time of night."

"But now there are other circumstances—"

Dr. Shokes laid a hand upon Keriah's arm, and gave her a look like a father admonishing a child. Keriah closed her mouth.

Dr. Shokes addressed Laura. "I apologize that I must ask this of you, but a situation has arisen at my brother's shop tonight. Although I am not intimately acquainted with the events that happened this evening, everyone in my neighborhood is aware of the crazed man who created havoc along several streets in Jem Town and the Long Glades. However, there are rumors that a group of people attempted to lead him away toward Harding Lane, the area the last crazed man had appeared only a few days ago, and then he disappeared without a trace. Since I am aware of what your niece and Keriah have been doing in my brother's stillroom, I can hazard a guess as to what might have happened."

At times like this, Laura wished she had better control over her facial features. She only hoped she wasn't revealing to Dr. Shokes her fervent desire to jump up and go into hysterics.

At that moment, the door opened and Phoebe came in

bearing a tea tray. "Dr. Shokes, Mrs. Rook told me you had arrived, and here I am with jam tarts we found in the kitchen," she said cheerfully. She set the tray down as she sat next to Keriah.

"Oh ... you mustn't ... jam tarts ... well ..." Dr. Shokes spoke to the plate of tarts.

Laura was never more grateful for a cup of tea. She nodded to Phoebe to pour, and Dr. Shokes continued speaking around a mouthful of jam tart. "Unfortunately, I believe my brother, Mr. Farley Shokes, has his own suspicions about what they have been doing, especially since they left quite suddenly earlier tonight. An hour ago, I found him in his stillroom, looking through the equipment that Keriah and Miss Phoebe left out this evening, even though he had previously said that he would respect their privacy. He responded to me quite guiltily. He may already suspect that they were analyzing a sample of the infamous serum that Jack Dix is known to be distributing to his men—a serum linked to extraordinary strength, quite like the extraordinary strength displayed by crazed men in the Long Glades recently."

Keriah couldn't hold herself back any longer. "So you see, my lady—"

Still with that gentle smile on his face, Dr. Shokes reached over and clamped his hand over Keriah's mouth, then continued as if she had not spoken. "I scolded my brother and sent him back to his wife—who had asked me to find him for her—but she will retire soon, I fear, and I do not trust Farley not to return to his stillroom later tonight. I would like to suggest that the young ladies return to take down their equipment and secure any samples they don't wish him to find. I would have done so myself, but I admit I am quite a disaster in a stillroom."

Keriah's face was turning bright red, so Dr. Shokes finally released her. She gave a squeak but remained silent this time.

Phoebe set down her teacup a little too carefully, and her

shoulders twitched as she deliberately did not look at Keriah. "Aunt Laura, we could put away all the equipment in an hour or two."

"Another option would be for me to remain awake to guard the stillroom," Dr. Shokes said.

"You mustn't do that," Laura said quickly. "You have patients to see in the morning, do you not?"

"I have had my fair share of babies born in the wee hours." Dr. Shokes sighed. "But I do admit those nights are more and more difficult as I grow older."

"Aunt Laura, I know you did not wish for Keriah to return tonight, but it may be even more dangerous if Mr. Farley Shokes is able to deduce the ingredients in the Root sample based on our experiments." Phoebe had a tightness to her jaw and a straightness to her brows that indicated she was ready to counter any resistance.

But Laura simply said, "If you are not tired, then yes, you should leave with Calvin and the coachmen."

Phoebe opened her mouth as if to argue, but then closed it when she realized Laura had agreed. "What?"

Keriah stepped on Phoebe's foot to tell her to shut up.

Laura pretended not to notice.

She didn't want to send them back to the Long Glades at all, but Dr. Shokes was probably correct to worry about his brother. She also remembered the strange vision she'd seen. Since then, she had noticed a dark feeling in her head, in her body, which she could not explain and could not ignore.

But was not ready to trust her visions enough to tell the two young women to do the action to which the vision seemed to point—to make more of the sedative paste posthaste. She also suspected Keriah would decide to do just that once they arrived at the apothecary shop.

Heavenly Father, she prayed, *I am unsure if this is Thy Holy Spirit speaking wordlessly to my heart, but I pray this decision is in line with Thy will.*

Almost to herself, Laura muttered, "Don't misunderstand me. If I felt that it was wrong, I would not allow the two of you to march into danger, no matter how much you wanted to do so. But right now, it would be wrong for me *not* to send you out to do what you do best."

Phoebe's expression turned from surprised to perplexed. "What we do best?" But then Keriah's hand whipped out and backslapped her arm to silence her.

Laura continued, "And there is also the chance ... I have a sense that the Holy Spirit may be speaking wordlessly to my heart that you must go."

Something in Phoebe's face became both alert and calmer at the words, but Keriah's eyes flickered away. Unlike Phoebe, she was not as accustomed to Laura's frank mention of God's influence in her life, but her reaction always made Laura wonder if her discomfort had a deeper reason.

"Dr. Shokes, you will accompany them back to the Long Glades?"

"Of course, my lady."

"My coachman is just about to set out. He shall drive you to the apothecary shop and set you down, but you may need to remain until he returns in the early morning hours. I will send my footman, Fred, to help guard you while you are there. Fred is not as intimidating as Mr. Havner, but he is a good enough bodyguard, I should think." Laura rose to her feet. "Well then, you two should prepare to leave. Oh, and I am expressly forbidding you from helping Mr. Havner and Calvin with their errand tonight."

Both Keriah and Phoebe tried to look innocent, but they must have realized or been told what Calvin would be doing and couldn't hide their rebellious reaction.

Laura sighed. "If you think clearly about it, you will realize that two young women in disguise would be more likely to be a hindrance to a search party in the unsavory areas of London in the middle of the night."

"Quite so, my lady," the doctor said.

"But Aunt Laura—"

"But my lady—"

"You aren't attempting to argue with my logic, surely?" She eyed the two girls sternly.

After a moment where they made inarticulate grumbling sounds, they shook their heads.

"Just so. Be glad I am not making you sit at home and embroider seat cushions."

Chapter Two

Laura was alone at last, but she felt the need to peer out the windows of the drawing room onto the dark street again, as if to assure herself. The rest of the servants were bustling about with tasks that had been interrupted by the appearance of the unconscious man in the locked storeroom.

Only Aya understood her need to look through Wynwood's old ledgers, an unusual pastime considering the events of tonight.

She crossed the drawing room and opened the double doors into the library. At the desk, she lit a lamp and opened the top ledger of the stack of books.

As she suspected, she hadn't been able to find the jeweler's receipt. She might have thrown it away when she was cleaning out his desk after he died, but she suspected that Wynwood wouldn't have left evidence of that particular purchase anywhere. However, this would have been a sizable order, which he could not pay in cash, and so there must be a record of it somewhere. He would have hidden it in the ledgers in such a way that it would appear vague, but he would know immediately what it was. She could only hope that she would also recognize that entry if she saw it.

She should have told Sol … No, she was not ready for that yet.

She was not nervous, precisely, but she was not relaxed—how could she be, when two of her servants and two young women were heading toward the Long Glades at this time of night? But it was not merely her worry that made her restless. Even as she searched the ledger, her heart felt weighted down with iron manacles. She thought perhaps that a part of her did not want to know the truth, and she was afraid and ashamed.

She was so focused on the ledger that when Aya knocked and entered the library without waiting for an answer, it startled her.

Aya was unusually flustered. "My lady, you have visitors. Mr. Drydale and ... Lady Aymer."

Laura shot to her feet, making the wooden chair rattle against the floor behind her. "Did Sol bring her?"

"Yes, my lady."

"So she knows about her brother?"

"I don't know, my lady."

Laura clenched a fist to counter the trembling in her hand. What was Sol doing? She had expected him to return, although not this quickly. In light of Mr. Coulton-Jones's condition, she would never have expected him to bring his sister. Unless she was the person Laura had dared him to find, as impossible as that seemed.

"Bring them to the drawing room, and ask Cook for refreshments." Despite the late hour, and the fact that her household was at sixes and sevens, she could at least fall back upon the conventions of polite hospitality.

But before she had finished speaking, there was a footfall outside the library door, and Sol entered, followed by Lady Aymer in a dark traveling cloak. "There is no need to stand upon ceremony with me or Lady Aymer, Laura."

She slammed the ledger shut with more force than she intended, but she was composed when she faced the two of them. She gave a polite smile and curtsy to Lady Aymer, and a lancing glare at Sol. "Won't you join me in the drawing room? It is better lit than the library."

"If you don't mind, I would like to see my brother," Lady Aymer said.

"Of course." Laura led the way to the back of the house, down a narrow corridor to the locked storeroom. Graham and Aya had followed them, and he moved to unlock the door, but not before listening at the door to ensure that all was quiet within. Only then did he turn the bronze key in the heavy padlock and remove the metal fastenings that bolted the door closed. He opened the door gingerly, but there was no response from the man inside.

Lady Aymer made to enter the room, but Sol held her back with a hand on her arm. He opened the door wider and accepted a lamp that Aya had brought with her, holding it high as he peered inside.

Mr. Coulton-Jones lay on the cot exactly as they had left him, and his slow, deep breaths could be seen in the dim light from the lamp.

With the cot filling most of the storeroom, there was barely enough room for two people to stand, so Sol retreated in order to allow Lady Aymer to enter the room. She sat on the side of the cot and laid a hand against her brother's still cheek, then reached for Sol's lamp, which he handed to her.

Laura could not see her face as she gazed down at her brother, but there was a droop to her shoulders that had not been there when she and Phoebe had visited Lady Aymer's mother a few days ago. She said nothing, but she held her brother's hand and stroked the back of it.

The moment was very intimate. Laura retreated further down the corridor, and Sol and the two servants followed her. Aya and Graham nodded to her as they continued toward the back of the house and to their other duties.

Laura remained standing in the corridor several yards away

from the open door. Sol sighed and leaned against the wall across from her. There was silence between them for several minutes, but then Laura gave in to her curiosity. "Does she know about her brother's former association with the Home Office?"

Sol's face tightened at the frank mention of Mr. Coulton-Jones's activities. His eyes darted up and down the corridor, and then he nodded to her.

Her mouth thinned with irritation. It was ridiculous to keep this information from her servants. It was what she and Sol had argued about earlier this that evening—in the entire time of their friendship, they had never exchanged such heated words. He hadn't wanted her to involve civilians in this matter anymore, which she thought was ridiculous since they were already involved. She had refused to wait around when Mr. Ackett was missing and had fully intended to send Calvin and the coachman out again to the Long Glades to look for him. She also knew she couldn't have stopped the two of them from going out on their own to search.

Laura had argued that Sol had no other choice unless he could produce another agent from out of his pocket at that moment.

But apparently he had.

"Is she your...?"

"No, but he will be arriving shortly."

"You really did pull one from out of your pocket."

"Actually, it was Lady Aymer who did that. She is here to vouch for me when he arrives."

"Why did you instruct him to come here?"

"I assume you already sent Calvin and the coachman to try to find Sep?"

She nodded warily.

"Then Mr. Rosmont will need Clara."

"Ah, I see. To find Calvin and vouch for... Mr. Rosmont, did you say?" And it was Lady Aymer who knew him, and not a personal acquaintance of Sol. "I believe I know who he is, but … *what* is he?"

Sol glanced down the corridor again, setting Laura's teeth on edge. "Let's adjourn to your drawing room."

She cast one last glance at the open door to her storeroom, then led the way upstairs. A tea tray had already been set up on the low table.

It was as Laura was passing him a cup of tea that she spotted the twigs in his hair. She reached over to pluck them out of his thick, wavy locks, and saw a small, creamy colored rose petal lodged in there, also. The scent of rose mixed with his natural musk, a warm, green, woody scent that brought to mind ivy basking in autumn sunlight. She hastily sat back down and tossed the vegetation into the fire nearby.

A flush glowed on Sol's ears as he watched her. "I used unconventional methods to enter Mrs. Coulton-Jones's house." He seemed a bit defensive. After a pause, his eyes flickered to the closed double doors to the library. "Doing accounting at this time of night?"

She kept her face impassive. "My youngest pageboy, my coachman, my niece, and her friend are out in the Long Glades right now. I could not get my mind or body to rest."

She noticed her fingers fidgeting, so she reached out to put a lemon biscuit on her plate and changed the subject. "I didn't realize you were so close to Lady Aymer." She sipped her tea calmly, because she was *not* irritated at Sol's relationship with a young, beautiful widow fifteen years younger than herself. Not at all.

"I was only distantly acquainted with her, but … I was made aware of her interesting connections."

Which of course, said nothing at all about her. Laura was not surprised that Lady Aymer had been aware of Mr. Coulton-Jones's activities as a spy, since during the brief visit to Mrs.

Coulton-Jones, the two siblings had seemed very close. But Sol had gone to her despite his argument with Laura over involving civilians, and Lady Aymer had known of another spy who could help Sol immediately, at this late hour. There was something else about her beyond her knowledge of her brother's secret life.

"So, why did you not use your own special connections to find someone?"

His face became set and hard. "Because any connections that I may have would require a full report, and they would take a week to dither about and decide who they could spare. I am responsible for Sep. I owe that to his uncle. I do not have a week to waste. I was not certain Lady Aymer would know of anyone who was in London right at this moment, but I had to take the chance."

"So she summoned your new knight in shining armor?"

"She sent a message and a servant to Mr. Rosmont's townhouse to wake him or find him, and to ask him to meet her at your house. I was lucky he was in London and not at his estate."

"He is like Mr. Coulton-Jones?"

"He has the same skill set, yes."

Laura tried again. "How is it that Lady Aymer has knowledge of someone like this?"

Sol was uncomfortable but trying not to show it. However, there was a tightness to his hazel eyes as he struggled to not avert his gaze. "Because of her brother, she has knowledge of things that a normal society widow would be ignorant of."

Laura had to admit that was a clever answer, and it still gave her no information about Lady Aymer. "But you know nothing of Mr. Rosmont?"

A cultured voice rang out in the drawing room. "Lady Wynwood, I assure you that Thorne Rosmont is an old family friend of the Coulton-Joneses." Lady Aymer entered the room and sank gracefully into a chair.

Laura admitted she was duly chastised for speaking of someone who was not in the room. She poured Lady Aymer a cup of tea. "I hope you will forgive my curiosity, since he will be working with my servants and my niece."

Lady Aymer paused in reaching for the cup that Laura held out to her. "Your niece?"

"Sol, I had assumed you told her about everything that happened tonight."

"He did, but I had thought Miss Sauber's role was done with the rescue of my brother."

"Dr. Shokes arrived at this late hour to tell us that he found his brother looking through the girls' equipment," Laura said. "He worried that his brother suspected they were analyzing the Root."

Sol's brows furrowed. "That would be an untenable situation. I specifically approved their analysis of the Root because I knew they would have no outside agenda, but any other man ..."

Laura nodded. "I felt uneasy, in a way that I cannot explain. I sent them back to the apothecary shop to clear away their work as soon as possible."

Sol frowned. "At this time of night?"

"Lady Wynwood, was there really a need for such urgency?"

Laura hesitated. Phoebe and Keriah had been more than eager to return to the apothecary shop, but she had not told them about the vision she'd seen, nor of the restless tension she had been feeling. If it had been simply Sol, she would have openly shared about both her unexplainable feelings, because he was used to her speaking about the stirrings she felt from a higher power. She was not ashamed of these workings of God in her life, but she still hesitated because Lady Aymer was a stranger. Yet, she was also entrusting her family friend to Sol and Laura. "It might appear foolhardy to you both, but over the years I have learned to recognize these premonitions from the Holy Spirit."

Sol reacted as he always did, by leaning away from her slightly, and making his face politely blank. They had had long discussions about religion, and she had explained how her experiences had thrown her into a more intimate relationship with God, but he simply could not fully understand her way of thinking. To him, God was who he prayed to on Sundays in church, and as the occasional expletive.

But to Laura's surprise, there was an answering light in Lady Aymer's eyes and a smile hovering on her lips. She nodded firmly. "If God has spoken to you about this, then of course you must listen. It might be of vital importance that they prevent Dr. Shokes's brother from discovering the sample."

Laura blinked at Lady Aymer. Then the two of them shared a smile whose warmth went beyond politeness, and worked instead as a bond between kindred souls.

"It seems a waste of time, because the young women were intending to return to the Long Glades in the morning to continue making more of the sedative." Although Laura did wonder if perhaps they would decide to remain at the apothecary shop to make more sedative tonight. "Depending upon how quickly they work, they might be of aid to Mr. Rosmont, and he to them."

"I can assure you that if they need him, Thorne is trustworthy. He has worked with Michael several times overseas."

Lady Aymer had been completely earnest when speaking her first sentence, but for her second, there was something about her face and her hands that came to Laura's notice. She thought that perhaps Lady Aymer's second sentence was not entirely truthful, or perhaps there was something about Mr. Rosmont that she was withholding. Laura hesitated, but it did not seem that Lady Aymer spoke with any malice, so she let it go.

Laura did not always hear her door knocker, but tonight the

sound boomed through her tiny townhouse under a firm hand. She jumped at the sudden noise.

"That would be Thorne," Lady Aymer said serenely.

Laura's eyes automatically went to Sol's face, and they exchanged a look that expressed their wariness, curiosity, and surprise. It was such a familiar action, and at the same time it seemed foreign, because they were now working together in an area that had previously been solely Sol's secretive life. Laura looked away quickly.

Thudding, long footsteps sounded on the wooden floors and drew closer to the drawing room. The door was open, so Laura immediately saw the figure that appeared and filled up the entire doorframe.

He was very tall, a few inches taller than Mr. Coulton-Jones, and he moved with an athletic grace that somehow reminded her of Mr. Coulton-Jones, as well. But he had a more powerful build, with wide shoulders and muscular legs that were obvious even though his coat and breeches were rumpled and loosely fitted. His large hand gripped the edge of the doorway while his green eyes scanned the occupants of the room. They landed first on Lady Aymer, flickered warily over Laura and Sol, then returned to Lady Aymer again.

"I came as soon as I received your message." His voice was low and slightly husky.

Lady Aymer rose and crossed the room to him, laying a hand on his arm. While he hadn't been moving in any way, somehow her touch stilled him.

"Thank you for coming, Thorne. Let me introduce to you Lady Wynwood and Mr. Drydale. This is Mr. Thorne Rosmont."

He bowed to them.

"We have met before, I believe, at occasional society functions," Laura said.

"Yes, my lady." There was an infinitesimal pause, and then he said, "You most likely know my father, Mr. Kane Rosmont."

Laura felt her face tighten, although she tried not to. The man's father had the honor of being the most unpleasant man she had ever met—and that included Phoebe's insufferable prig of a father. She couldn't imagine what it must have been like to grow up as his son.

"Please, won't you sit down? All will be explained." She sent a pointed look at Sol.

As Sol related what had happened in the past evening, Laura took the opportunity to observe Mr. Rosmont. His entire body was tense, like a spring that had been too tightly wound, and a part of her was afraid of the moment he would suddenly fly apart. He was about the same age as Mr. Coulton-Jones, and his skin was lightly tanned, indicating that he spent long hours outdoors. It could be that he was an attentive landlord of the estate that Lady Aymer had mentioned. His eyes on Sol were intense and sharply intelligent.

"And so, we would like you to help us find Septimus Ackett," Sol said.

Mr. Rosmont nodded, then he looked at Laura. "Might I speak to your pageboy, Calvin, I believe his name was? I would like to know what happened when he last saw Mr. Ackett."

Laura explained about Calvin and the coachman taking Phoebe and Keriah back to the apothecary shop while they went searching for Mr. Ackett in the Long Glades. Then Sol added, "Calvin's sister, Clara, can accompany you to the Long Glades. She will help you find Calvin and she will vouch for you when you do."

Laura rose and pulled the bell pull. "I will call for Clara."

The butler scratched on the door almost immediately, and she gave him a quiet word of instruction.

But as she turned away from the drawing room door, she was surprised by the deep frown that darkened Mr. Rosmont's face. His glance at Sol was faintly accusatory. "I do not work with civilians," he said curtly. "I work alone."

Strangely, Lady Aymer's mouth opened as if she were about to say something, but then she closed it and her face became as smooth as glass.

"Calvin will never speak to you if Clara is not with you." Laura reseated herself on the sofa. "And you may not find him without her, either."

Mr. Rosmont's face went through various shades of frustration. Laura could almost see the scales in his head as he weighed his normal procedure against the needs of this mission.

Her impression of his stubborn nature was confirmed when he did not acknowledge Laura's argument, nor explicitly agree to take Clara with him. With a clenched jaw, Mr. Rosmont turned to Sol. "What kind of an agent is Mr. Ackett?"

Sol hesitated in confusion. "I'm not certain I understand what you are asking."

"There are different types of agents, and they make different decisions based on personality and beliefs. If I better understand Mr. Ackett, I can better guess what decisions he might have made last night."

"I have known him most of his life," Sol said slowly, "for I am friends with his uncle. He has always been quiet—observant, rather than taciturn. His body is strong and flexible, and he has been best suited for missions of infiltration."

A different way of saying that he was skilled at breaking into houses, Laura surmised.

Sol continued, "He is smart, and weighs the facts and situation carefully before making a decision. But he has an unusual propensity ..." Sol scratched the back of his head. "He prefers running across rooftops to riding a horse or taking a carriage."

Laura had to stop and think back over what he had just said to make sure she had heard him correctly. It was a rather boyish habit for a man whose expressionless face seemed to look out upon the world with a serious mien.

There was another soft knock upon the door, and Clara entered the drawing room. When she returned to the house, she had changed back into her normal dress, but now she had again donned the boy's clothes that Laura had provided for her. Since her brother had left the house, she had probably assumed she would now be sent after him.

Her eyes widened when she was introduced to Mr. Rosmont— perhaps because of his size, towering over her, or perhaps because of the glower on his face as he stared at her. But when Laura explained what Clara needed to do for Mr. Rosmont, he gave her a small, firm nod, as if he were confident she would find her brother.

Laura rose and placed her hands on Clara's shoulders, then faced Mr. Rosmont. "When you have found Calvin, please send him and Clara back to the apothecary shop."

If it had been Calvin, there would have been an explosion of protest. Since this was Clara, she simply turned and gave a wounded look at her employer.

Mr. Rosmont nodded, and seemed pleased by her request.

"M'lady," Clara said in a whining voice, "Calvin and I could help them."

Laura knelt down so that she was more at eye level with Clara. "I have complete confidence in your ability to ferret out information. Which is why I want you and Calvin to get some rest so that you can take up the search in the morning, if Mr. Rosmont is unsuccessful."

Mr. Rosmont frowned again, no doubt objecting to her trust in a pair of eleven-year-old twins contrasted with her doubt of his abilities.

However, the hurt on Clara's face melted away, although there was still a bit of sulk on her bottom lip.

Mr. Rosmont's expression suddenly softened, but was no less worried. "May I see Michael?"

"Of course." As she had with Lady Aymer, she led the way to

her storeroom and Sol cautiously opened the door. However, Mr. Rosmont did not enter the room, but instead stood in the open doorway and stared at his friend. Laura hadn't thought it was possible, but he became even more tightly drawn, his muscles bunching visibly even though his coat was old and loose. Muscles popped along his jaw, but he said nothing.

Then he suddenly squeezed his eyes shut and drew in a sharp breath. When he opened his eyes and exhaled, he turned to her with a focused gaze. "We shall depart."

Trailed by Lady Aymer and Sol, Laura escorted Mr. Rosmont and Clara to the back door of the house, where they would traverse the garden and exit by the laundry house in back, so that no one would see them leave her house. "May the Lord God watch over you."

Clara seemed heartened by her mistress's words, but Laura caught the curl of Mr. Rosmont's upper lip just before he turned away.

The three of them watched until she could no longer make out their figures in the shadows of the garden, then returned to the drawing room. She had hardly preached a sermon to him, and yet his disdain had been sharp. It did not offend her, but the fact that the slight mention of faith had caused such a reaction in him made her think that he possibly had some deep personal anger against God.

She was not certain how she felt about the choice of Mr. Rosmont. He was like the lid on a boiling pot, and she was especially wary of instability. She spent a minute fretting about Phoebe and Keriah and her servants, but then she remembered to send a prayer up to the One who could keep them safe better than the finest agent of the Crown.

Lord God, please protect them. She hesitated, then added, *And enable them to do Thy will, and to resist the evil lurking in London.*

Sol and Lady Aymer had walked ahead of her to the front

foyer, where they accepted their outerwear from the butler.

"Pray, do not stand upon ceremony, but call upon me early tomorrow," Laura said. Or rather, today since it was already past midnight. "I am uncertain if Mr. Rosmont will have sent word of his progress, but you are welcome to remain here while we wait for him."

"I would be much obliged," Lady Aymer said. "I will come later in the morning, because I am to attend to my mother at breakfast."

"I will come early," Sol said.

Graham opened the door for them just as Lady Aymer's coachman drew up with her carriage, which they had ridden to Laura's house. Lady Aymer preceded Sol out the door, and he paused to turn back to Laura.

He had a deceptively mild look in his hazel eyes as he commented, "I can only imagine how difficult it must be to do accounts with old ledgers."

Laura could not stop herself from reacting with a slight jerk of her shoulders.

Sol merely tipped his hat to her and then followed Lady Aymer out the door.

As Graham closed the front door, Laura wanted to sink to her knees and thump her fists several times against the marble floor. She might be clever at detecting lies, but she couldn't deceive others.

How had he suspected there was something she was hiding from him?

Chapter Three

Thorne was not intimately familiar with the Long Glades, but he had traversed enough overcrowded cities across the continent that he could recognize the ebb and flow of people, the tales they told with their body language. He was also forced to admit that Clara was extremely valuable in navigating the streets, not only because she had apparently grown up on them, but also because she had a knack for knowing who to approach, what types of questions to ask in order to get the information she needed.

They started in the seedy area where Mr. Coulton-Jones had first begun wreaking havoc. Calvin had probably started his own search at the building where he last saw Mr. Ackett, but Thorne did not know where that was. He would have to search for clues along the trail that Mr. Coulton-Jones had left, backtracking and hoping that he would find the origin point.

Thorne had thought that after the destruction of earlier this evening, the streets would be more empty, but it seemed there were even more people wandering about where Mr. Coulton-Jones had destroyed the most property. A large number were completely foxed, sprinkled with a few street-walkers who were trying to take advantage of the men in their inebriated state. Alehouses and coffeehouses alike were brightly lit. Thorne had expected more shopkeepers to be bustling about to protect their stock, but there was a disheartening amount of looting with no one to object—officers of the watch were absent, not even bothering to enter the area and try to interfere.

Thorne had to remind himself not to grab at Clara when a man came too close, because she was dressed as a boy not a girl. But she proved very adept at avoiding people who might be tempted to deliver a drunken clout for coming too close. When necessary, she could give a scathing set down, peppered with extremely colorful language, to anyone who approached her.

Mr. Coulton-Jones's path had been very erratic, so Thorne had a difficult time trying to determine from which direction he had come. At a crossroads, when he was about to turn right, Clara tugged at his sleeve.

"Sir, I think we should go left."

The left side of the street was not much different from the right. "What makes you say that?"

"Calvin already knows where Mr. Ackett was, and so he'd be looking for where Mr. Ackett would think to run to. There are some places to hide down this way."

Thorne wasn't entirely certain that a grown man would choose the same hiding places of an eleven-year-old, but at the moment he was more interested in finding Calvin. He nodded and followed Clara to the left.

He was right to follow the advice of his guide. Within five minutes, Clara had suddenly burst into a run and skidded to a halt next to a young boy ahead of them. Thorne wasn't even certain how she had been able to see him, since the sidewalks were dark in this section of the street, and Calvin had just slid out of an alley.

When Thorne approached, Clara was in the midst of explaining everything to her brother, and then she introduced Thorne. The young boy looked up at him with shrewd eyes that seemed to search his face for something. Then he pointed back down the alley. "Mr. Havner is still down there. You'll have to explain it all over again to him."

Clara groaned. "I'd forgotten about that." She bopped him in the shoulder with her fist. "Why didn't you stop me sooner?"

"I couldn't get a word in, because you were gobbing like a chicken."

Mr. Havner lumbered into view. Thorne was relieved that the man was wide and strong, looking more like a blacksmith than a coachman. He walked with a deceptively fluid looseness to his muscles, which indicated he was on the alert at the sight of Thorne, despite the relaxed demeanor of the twins standing next to him. "Who's your friend, Calvin?"

Clara went into a repetition of what she told her brother.

"Did you find Mr. Ackett?" Thorne asked, although he suspected the answer was negative.

"We started searching in the opposite direction that Mr. Coulton-Jones went," Calvin said. "We scared away a man from the warehouse. Mr. Havner said the man probably had a friend, and Mr. Ackett was fighting him."

"Since Mr. Ackett had sent Calvin for help, he might have led his opponent away so he wouldn't see our group arrive."

Thorne nodded. It's what he would've guessed, also, and Mr. Drydale had mentioned the same thing to him. "Show me where you last saw Mr. Ackett."

It was an empty brothel that looked as if an entire carriage had crashed into the front of it. The door and part of the wall it had been attached to were in splinters on the ground, and three-quarters of the front room of the shop was open to the street. Candles broken until they looked like creamy gravel littered the floor because most of the wooden shelves along the walls had also been smashed, along with the furniture in the room.

There was also a door on the side of the front room leading to a narrow set of stairs to the floor above, but the door had been smashed into the stairwell. Thorne looked at the pieces, and they seemed smaller than what he would expect if a man had simply been thrown into the door ... as if the wood had been trampled upon by two men engaged in a fistfight.

Thorne turned to Calvin. "You mentioned that Mr. Ackett approached the building from the roof?"

"Uh-huh."

Several of the lower steps of the stairs had been broken, so Thorne had to back up a few steps in order to leap. He rested one foot briefly on the far right edge of the stairs, which boasted only a few inches of wood still attached to the wall, then pushed off so that his other foot could land solidly on the lowest unbroken step. Calvin looked like he was going to try to make the same jump, so Thorne ordered him, "Stay down there."

Calvin's face turned mulish. "What if you need help?"

Only after he had voiced the question did Thorne notice the anxiety the boy was trying to hide. This probably reminded him of when he had watched Mr. Ackett leave him behind. At the same time, Thorne did not want Calvin rushing into a dangerous situation. He might've been helpful to Mr. Drydale in the warehouse earlier tonight, but for Thorne, having him there would be a distraction. "I'll be back in fifteen minutes."

Calvin opened his mouth to protest again, but Thorne turned and headed up the stairway, and his footsteps sounded over whatever the boy said.

He heard the coachman behind him at the bottom of the stairs. "Listen to the man and stay here, Calvin." Thorne was relieved that Mr. Havner reaffirmed his order, but the relief lasted only a few seconds. The sound of muffled footsteps made him turn around and see that the coachman had leaped up to follow him onto the stairwell.

One room on the second floor was empty except for a wooden chair toppled over in the middle of it. There were no lamps, no ropes that might have tied a man to the chair, but the window set high against one wall was open and large enough that a slim man could slip through. Thorne peered through the window and saw the distance to the closest rooftop. The danger of the jump made him blanch a little, but after Mr. Drydale had described Mr. Ackett's rooftop running, Thorne didn't dismiss the possibility.

He and the coachman returned downstairs, where Calvin was still at the base of the stairs, shuffling from foot to foot. He was relieved to see the two of them, although he tried to hide it with a casual expression as he turned to once more enter the front room of the building.

Outside the brothel, Thorne turned to the twins. "Lady Wynwood instructed me to send you both back to the apothecary shop."

Calvin sent out a loud protest. Clara did not, but her face settled into disapproving lines, a more feminine version of the mulish expression that Calvin had showed to Thorne only a few minutes ago.

"Yes, yes, I realize that you want to help, but I am under orders from your employer." He imagined Lady Wynwood's face, calm and patient, but he had sensed the steel behind her polite words. He had instinctively known she was not someone to cross without severe consequences. "I received the impression she would happily slit my stomach if I did not do as she asked."

The twins' protest melted into caution, and they glanced at each other.

"Fine," Calvin said in a voice as if someone asked him to eat a scorpion.

"I'll be staying with you, sir," Mr. Havner stated.

Thorne opened his mouth to protest, suddenly feeling like one of the twins, but Mr. Havner continued, "Don't know if you've noticed, sir, but there are more pickpockets on the street than normal. Probably more robbers, also. Another man with you would deter the more aggressive ones from attacking you for your purse."

He had been alone in cities far more dangerous than the streets now, and he knew he could handle himself if he was attacked. But there was a new dimension to the threat now, if he was attacked by one of the men in Apothecary Jack's gang who possessed the strength given to them by the Root.

The coachman turned to the twins. "Get on with you, the pair of you. I'll stay to watch out for Mr. Rosmont, so you go back to the apothecary shop to protect the two young misses."

The man's words seemed to lighten an invisible burden that Calvin was carrying. He straightened his shoulders, gave a firm nod to the two men, then he and his sister turned away. Thorne was impressed at the way they melted into the darkness edging the street.

For the next several hours, Thorne and Mr. Havner tediously wound through the maze of streets of the Long Glades. Thorne had worked diligently to develop a good memory, and so he was able to conduct the search without backtracking or becoming lost. However, he was not strictly methodical and sometimes decided on paths based on his instincts, or on his guess as to where Mr. Ackett's instinct would take him.

The two men also managed to extract information from the people on the streets, although that number decreased as the hours went by. They asked about two men who may have been fighting, or one chasing the other. They heard that the larger man in pursuit had a ruined ear, which suggested he might be the man named Silas who had fought Michael and Mr. Ackett before.

Unfortunately, many people comfortable on the London streets at night also knew to keep their mouth shut about anything they might have seen, so as to avoid becoming entangled in anything troublesome. If his instincts told him they were hiding something, he would shake his purse, and sometimes that would loosen tongues.

They managed to get a slovenly-looking woman standing in the doorway of a boarding house to speak to them, and she mentioned a nearby orphanage with a large basement with three or four entrances. Thorne doubted Mr. Ackett would lead his pursuer anywhere near so many children, but they checked the large space anyway, which served as a storeroom for the orphanage. All they got for their trouble were spiders in their hair.

However, outside the building, a street urchin who may or may not have belonged to the orphanage told them about two drunks who liked to wile away the evening outside of a closed fishmonger's shop. They kept their eyes open and would occasionally be induced to open their mouths in exchange for coin.

The coming dawn was turning the fog near the river to gray when Thorne and Mr. Havner lost the trail of the two men again. Their last clue had been from the pair of old drunks, but no one with whom they had spoken since then had seen either Mr. Ackett or Silas.

Thorne also began to get more narrowed looks from people along the street. In the darkness, the quality of his clothing hadn't been as noticeable, but now he could tell that he was starting to stand out, even though he had donned his oldest coat, shirt, and breeches. He hadn't known much about what Isabella had wanted him to do, so he had simply opted for plain, nondescript clothing from his normal wardrobe. It was not unusual to see a nobleman in these sorts of areas at night, but this street hadn't any gambling halls and only one dingy brothel.

He had some working men's clothes in the back of the wardrobe at his townhouse, however, so perhaps now would be a good time for him to return and don a disguise.

There was another reason for him to postpone the search. Thorne had been trained to observe the people around him, so that he could blend in—whether a drunkard, a fisherman, or a working man, he could imitate their gait and speech if he had the right clothing.

So he was able to notice the ones on the street who did *not* blend in—men walking confidently, arrogantly sometimes, inciting fear from others who scuttled away when they drew near.

One thin man in particular was closest to them. Other men who were clearly heavier than he would give way for him on the sidewalk and turn away so as not to meet his eyes.

Thorne and Mr. Havner began sauntering away in the opposite direction of the thin man. They shivered in the fog, but Thorne began picking his way back the way they had come.

"It's getting a bit crowded around here." The coachman looked back over his shoulder quickly, then turned around with his head bent forward. "I don't need to pretend to be scared of them. I've never seen men like that before."

"Keep your voice down," Thorne cautioned him. They were walking in the middle of the street and there didn't seem to be anyone nearby, but he didn't want to take any chances. Mr. Drydale had warned him about the dangers of being overheard by those men when he least expected.

"They're still looking for him. There's hope," Thorne said.

"But how long can he remain hidden?"

"Then we had better find him soon. Just be careful who you speak to."

They continued down the river until they reached a section that didn't seem to have any of those swaggering men walking about.

Thorne almost didn't see the too young, too painfully thin prostitute huddled in a darkened doorway. The coachman's path veered toward her, and he said in a gentle voice, "Slow night for you, dearie?"

The girl was obviously exhausted, but she made an effort to

shake the hair out of her eyes and rise shakily to her feet. She gave him a thin smile. "I'm available if you're wanting some company, sir."

"Don't need that. You ought to be getting to bed."

"I got none, unless I bring Ferbin enough money from tonight."

The coachman's face suddenly hardened, although he was not angry at the girl. "You'd be better off getting away from the likes of him."

"That's impossible." Her voice was defeated and tired. It was as if her soul was simply an empty vessel by now.

"How much do you need?"

The eyes that looked up to him were pale blue, almost silver, and they were wary. "Sir?"

"I can pay you for something other than a tumble," he said. "Were you here all night?"

"Mostly." The girl's dirty hand rubbed her nose as she looked down at her feet. "Can't go to the more popular places, the other girls are protective of their territory."

"We're trying to find our friend. He's slender, black hair, might be injured. He was being chased by another man, big, with a mangled ear."

Fear flowed down the girl's face like a bucket of ice water dumped over her head. She shook her head back and forth, and twisted her fingers together. "Never seen him, didn't see nothing."

"You won't get in trouble," Thorne said. "We'll speak of this to no one."

"It doesn't matter. They'll hear."

"They won't from us."

"You won't need to worry, if you get out of town," the coachman said.

Thorne gave the man a sharp glance. He felt for the girl's sorry state, but it was impossible to help every poor, beaten-down drab in London. What was the man doing?

But the girl kept shaking her head. "I told you, it's impossible."

"You've no reason to trust us," the coachman said, "but what do you have to lose? Ferbin will beat you if you come back tonight with your purse too light, and from the looks of you, you won't last many more of those."

The girl stopped shaking her head, but she still wouldn't look up at the two men. She said nothing.

"Tell us what you saw." Thorne glanced up and down the street, but the fog was still thick, and the buildings here were tall enough that the first gray streaks of dawn hardly reached the ground. He strained his ears but could hear nothing. He turned back to the girl. "Our friend is slender, black hair, injured. We have to find him."

"I didn't see him." The girl bit her lip so hard that blood stained her teeth, which were an unusual pearly white. Then she said in a soft voice that Thorne almost didn't hear, "The man after him was Silas."

At that moment, Thorne heard the strike of a boot heel against the ground, far away down the street.

He clapped his hand over the girl's mouth, and motioned to the coachman, indicating the direction he'd heard the footsteps. Mr. Havner looked in that direction, taking a few steps back. Even just those few feet made the coachman's figure become indistinct in the fog, which seemed to have suddenly grown thicker, darker.

Thorne spoke in a low voice, "Come with us." If the man was close enough to hear them, it would sound like a simple proposition, common enough when spoken to a woman in this part of London.

"She won't be going anywhere with you." The voice was a man's voice, but high-pitched. It was also still far away. It had been difficult for Thorne to hear him at all, but apparently the man had heard them clearly.

It was the same man as before. He was almost as painfully thin as the prostitute, with large ears that stuck out from the side of his head almost as far as his narrow shoulders, and he had a long, knobby neck, like a turkey. Or a vulture. His gray hat was shapeless, but there were tufts of straight, red-gold hair that peeked out over his ears.

His eyes were not quite as hard as some of the other men that Thorne had seen—there was frustration, doubt, and a touch of fear that lingered behind the confidence in his gaze. Thorne had known men like this, men who were on the outskirts of a group, wanting to fit in, not quite living up to expectations.

It surprised him, but he should have known better. Gangs were not made up of only one type of man. Even among the men Apothecary Jack had gathered around himself, there would be some who struggled to please their employer.

"What were you saying about Silas?" the man asked as he walked closer. His footsteps weren't extraordinarily soft, and they weren't loud, either. But the sound of his boots hitting the cobblestones was the same sound that Thorne had heard. He had been extraordinarily lucky to hear the man's footstep.

And now it became obvious that the man had clearly heard their conversation, despite being so far away he should have barely been able to make out the words.

The prostitute had begun to shake violently at the sight of the man. Her mouth opened and closed soundlessly, and her skin had turned as white as her eyes. "P-p-please ... Please, Nick ..."

Nick's gaze on the girl was sharp like an ice pick. "You're one of Ferbin's girls, aren't you? You should know better than that."

"It's not what you think ..." The girl stuffed her fist into her mouth in fright.

Nick shifted his attention to Thorne, and his gaze became harder, but there was also a gleam of excitement. "He said someone would come looking for him. How lucky for me that I get to bring you in."

Thorne's entire body vibrated with tension, and he felt the familiar boiling sensation through his veins. Mr. Drydale's logical injunctions to avoid engaging with these men receded to the back of his mind, muted against the roaring of his heartbeat in his ears. If the man wanted a fight, Thorne would give him a fight. Thorne weighed almost twice as much as he did, and was taller. He could snap that neck between his hands. How much strength could a potion really give to a man?

Nick smiled, and Thorne saw that the same excitement rising in him was mirrored in his opponent. It made him burn hotter, and his vision became crystal clear.

He attacked faster than Thorne could see.

The fist flying at him wasn't even a blur, just a twitch at the edge of his vision. He didn't have time to react before the impact slammed into his stomach. He felt the blow all the way to his spine, felt the pain of bones creaking, reluctantly curving, and then suddenly pain exploded all the way from the top of his head down to his tailbone. He belatedly heard the sound of his impact against the wooden door behind him, saw splinters flying around in the air.

There was movement on his right. In his pain, he grabbed at that movement out of self-defense. But his hand latched onto a thin arm.

The prostitute. He needed to get her to safety, he needed to make sure she was out of the range of this fight.

His head was still spinning, the edges of his vision filled with stars, but he stepped out from the doorway on wobbly legs, still holding onto the girl's arm. Then he flung her away, toward where he thought the coachman had been. "Get out of here!" he roared at her.

But as he tried to shove her away, he suddenly felt the bones under his hand snap.

That tiny sensation, the evidence of his strength, made the memory of another tiny set of broken bones engulf his mind. The memory sobered him faster than a dunk in the Thames. Only when he blinked did he realize that there had been a reddish haze over his vision, and the pain in every part of him came screaming to life. He felt as if Nick had punched a hole straight through his gut, and the back of his head throbbed from where the blow had shoved him three or four feet back into the wooden door.

Nick was taking his time, which was the only reason Thorne was still alive. He was struck with amazement by the man's strength. If he had not let his reason fade, he would've realized that Mr. Drydale would not exaggerate about something like that.

He wanted to see how the prostitute fared, but his opponent attacked again, this time with the other fist aimed at Thorne's head. He managed to tilt his head to the side to avoid most of the blow, but it caught on his ear. It felt as if his entire ear had been torn off. After a strange moment of silence, there was a sudden ringing that seem to be sounding right next to his head.

Thorne tried to counter with a fist of his own, but compared to Nick's movements, he looked like he was moving through water. The man almost negligently swatted his arm away as if Thorne's fist was a willow branch, then countered with another jab to his stomach. It didn't hit the exact spot as the last blow —instead, Nick's fist buried itself on the opposite side of Thorne's torso, but there was the same pain as his spine absorbed the impact.

Thorne was too close to him. With an opponent so impossibly fast, he had no chance in close quarters. But his back was to the doorway the prostitute had been hiding in. When he tried to shift to his right, he was lucky enough to stumble and avoid another fist that the man threw at him.

Thorne's knees bent from his misstep, his arms thrown out on either side of his body, so he used his lower stance to his advantage. One hand was close enough to the wooden wall that he could flatten it firmly, then he planted his right leg like a tree trunk and kicked out as fast and hard as he could with his left leg.

He wasn't entirely certain why Nick didn't dodge. He was fast enough that he could have, but perhaps Thorne's kick took him by surprise. His boot cut the man in the stomach and thrust him several feet away. Thorne unbent quickly, ignoring the screaming pain in his middle, to try to predict what his opponent would do next.

But the attack never came. Instead, a blur came out of the fog, a thin black wisp that was nearly invisible, and it cracked inches in front of Nick's nose with a sound like a gunshot. A horsewhip. Thorne knew of only one man who would have that in this place, at this time.

He could see a shadowy figure in the fog, but not the coachman's features. However, Thorne recognized his movements and the tall, solid build of Mr. Havner. He could barely see, and he wondered how Mr. Havner had managed to aim at Thorne's attacker. Then again, perhaps he had been aiming for the body and had only hit the space in front of him because of his obscured vision.

Whatever his intentions, the whip startled Nick, who jerked his head and stumbled backward a few more steps. But he didn't hesitate for a long. His eyes darted toward where the whip had come from, then back to Thorne. He took a step toward him, but the whip cracked again. This time a scarlet line appeared across the thin man's thigh. He howled and grabbed at his thigh.

"Run, man!"

Only when he heard the coachman's voice did Thorne realize he had frozen. He obeyed, sprinting down the street. Footsteps began to follow behind him, but when he glanced back, Nick was simply a ghostly smear in the fog. Matching that image, a voice roared at them with all the fury of a spirit haunting the mortal plane in search of revenge. "You can't get away from me! I'll find you! *I remember your face!*"

Not only had he failed to find Mr. Ackett—now one of Apothecary Jack's men knew Thorne's face.

Chapter Four

Behind him, the dogs had gathered, nipping at his heels.

Nick had called out again, but not to Thorne. Within minutes, several booted feet sounded softly in the darkness and the fog.

He remembered the streets from the hours wandering them earlier. He took a twisted path through dark alleys, running as fast as he could, that kept the pursuers from catching up to him too quickly. He thought perhaps some of the men were led astray, missing a turn here or there, but enough remained on his trail. Soon, they would be close enough to see him, despite the fog.

His hand gripped his chest over his heart and squeezed tightly, feeling his fingers claw into his flesh. He recognized the irony that he owed his life to a civilian he had not wanted to bring with him. Had he always been so arrogant?

But then again, he hadn't liked himself for a very long time.

He turned down another small street. He had to get them off his scent. But how?

Then he remembered something he'd seen when he'd passed this area several hours ago. He veered left, scanning the houses, until the found the one he was looking for.

He entered an open doorway that suddenly loomed up out of the fog. The scent of ash and mold surrounded him when he ran through the blackened open doorframe, flanked by two small shutterless windows that stared sightlessly out onto the street. His footsteps thumped hollowly against wooden floorboards that bounced under his weight and made the smell of charcoal even stronger.

As he moved through the shell of a house, he scanned the southern walls as best he could in the dim light. Finally he ducked into what might have been the kitchen, an area that appeared darker than night because of the pitch-black color of the burned floors, walls, and ceiling.

Thorne went to the southern wall and found the remains of the hearth. Stones had broken and fallen to the floor, and a set of wooden shelves had become a blackened jumble of splinters barely held together. He eased aside the debris until he could expose the corner.

When he touched the wall, soot flaked under his fingers like sand and rained upon the floor, where it disappeared in the black color. Yes, it was soft enough.

He searched the room, and found the remnants of an old wooden chair. Pulling off a large piece of wood, he began digging at the wall, low and close to the floor. He worked quickly, and the wall obliged by disintegrating easily.

As soon as the hole was large enough, he crawled through into the neighboring house. Reaching back through the hole, he pulled debris and rocks into place in front of it to hide it.

He finally straightened and looked around. He was in a pantry, empty of foodstuffs and holding only a few old, cracked pieces of pottery and stained wooden spoons.

When he and Mr. Havner had passed through this street, he had seen the burned house but also that the house next door, while darkened and obviously empty, had not been badly burned. He had hoped that there would be some areas where the fire damage would enable him to dig a hole through.

The smoke smell was strong in this house, since it had been

closed up rather than aired out. It looked like it had been another brothel, which was probably why it had been evacuated. Clients would be put off by the smell.

He headed upstairs to a small front sitting room. Peering out the window, he had a view of the entire street.

Within minutes, two men turned into the street and begin heading toward him.

They jogged along, rather than the ambling—or staggering—gait of a man heading home after a long night, and they seemed to be peering at the houses closely.

Thorne became still as one of the men approached the burned-out hull of the house next to his. He entered the wrecked doorway.

Had he remembered to bring with him the piece of wood he'd used to make the hole? Would the man see the hole, even though he'd made an effort to dig it in a hidden corner? Had he scuffed his footprints enough in the soot of the floor?

Thorne had kept the brothel's doors open and listened now for any noises from below-stairs, from the pantry where he'd entered.

Then motion outside the window drew his attention. The man had exited the burned house and gave a mighty sneeze. His friend laughed at him and said something. Thorne couldn't hear, but he could just barely make out the other man's reply.

"… smoke smell is too strong …"

Mr. Drydale had told Thorne everything Michael had said about Jack's men, including how a large man named Silas had been able to smell his face paint. If these men also had enhanced senses, Thorne had been hoping that the smoke would irritate and overwhelm their sense of smell.

The two continued down the street and away from where he hid.

He had a reprieve, but he couldn't remain here. He had to leave the Long Glades while Jack's men were searching for him.

He had to hope he didn't run into Nick, who had seen Thorne's face.

It had been too long since he had been in the field, and he hadn't been as alert and observant as he could have been. Had he already failed before he'd even begun? A sneering face began to rise up in his mind, and he deliberately wiped it away with the abrasiveness of his anger.

Anger at the faces in his past. And most of all, anger at himself.

He didn't have time for recriminations. How could he meet up with the coachman and the girl? And that was assuming they hadn't been captured. He didn't think they would be—even he hadn't seen where the coachman had been in the fog, and Nick had seemed more provoked by Thorne than the faceless whipster.

But if they had been captured, after Mr. Havner had saved Thorne and he had abandoned the two … He didn't want to think about it.

He knew where Mr. Havner would go. The coachman had pointed out the direction of the building when they'd first started searching earlier than night, and it was the most logical haven for the girl.

But how for Thorne to get there without being spotted?

The answer came as he recalled yet more of what Mr. Drydale had told him. Mr. Ackett enjoyed running on rooftops.

Well, Thorne had done that himself a few times.

Thirty minutes later, in a different section of the Long Glades, he headed down a long street. At the far end, the front of the apothecary shop was dark. Thorne walked past the building first with his head down, apparently as uninterested in it as in the other buildings. When he turned the corner, he glanced behind him at the empty street. He hadn't heard footsteps behind him, either. He didn't think he'd been followed.

Well, it would have been difficult to hide a man's presence if one of Jack's men had been following him atop the building rooftops. There had been a couple—to be honest, more than a couple—heart-stopping moments as he jumped from one roof to another, and he'd slipped three times. Dogs had barked at him twice, and he'd interrupted a vicious cat fight on one roof, although the two startled felines went back at each other as soon as he'd passed by. He'd been grateful to find low-slung eaves not too far off the ground where he could swing down.

He had to search for a backdoor to the apothecary shop, uncertain if it had one. Eventually he thought he discovered it along a tiny back alley behind the row of buildings. He unlatched the door, hoping it was the right building and not one of its neighbors.

One whiff of the air from within told him he was correct—bitter, grassy herbs, the strange and sweet mixture of chemicals.

The hallway beyond the door was dark. Thorne was about to enter when he hesitated, then opened the door wider and held his hands up in a gesture of surrender. He counted his heartbeats.

When he reached ten, a whisper of sound from the darkness warned him before a hand roughly grabbed his arm and jerked him inside. "Get out of sight, fool," growled Mr. Havner's voice, rough and yet sounding almost relieved to see him.

"The girl?"

"She's here."

"Where are the two children and the, er, young ladies?"

"Gone, although not long before we arrived. The fireplace in the back sitting room was still warm. They probably found a hackney cab."

That seemed impossible at this hour, but then Thorne thought of the two young scamps, and changed his mind.

The coachman led the way to the back sitting room, where a

small fire burned in the fireplace—not too large, so as not to alert someone on the street. The young prostitute sat on the sofa with weariness covering her like a shroud. She cupped her left elbow in her right hand. Thorne clearly saw the bruise purpling her skin and the unnatural shape of the bones under it.

The sight struck him like a blow stronger than any from Nick, and he felt a tightness and trembling in his gut. He had done that. *He* had done that to her.

He had done it *again*.

"I'm sorry," he said in a hoarse voice. "I had no idea what I was doing."

She did not look up at him, instead staring at a carpet made of various mottled colors. Her entire body was shaking, her teeth chattering.

"We must get you medical attention. The doctor upstairs—"

The coachman shook his head. "Dr. Shokes and his brother left several hours ago, according to Mrs. Shokes. A sick child. Mrs. Shokes looked at Hetty's arm, but the break is bad, and she didn't want to injure the girl further by inexpert doctoring. She's upstairs, getting her something to eat."

"So we either wait for Dr. Shokes to return, or try to find another doctor."

The young girl, whose name was apparently Hetty, looked up at him with eyes that were hollow and rimmed with shadows. "I don't want to see anyone. They might speak to Mr. Dix."

The coachman turned to her. "Dr. Shokes won't do that."

But Thorne didn't know any other apothecary who might be trusted. "We must treat your injury as soon as possible."

"We shall have to wait for Dr. Shokes, then," the coachman said.

"How long will that take? The longer she remains—" Thorne cut off his words, not wanting to upset the girl. But the truth was that they had to help her leave London. Nick had seen her face and had known which pimp she belonged to.

The girl looked away, but there was a paleness to her cheeks that hadn't been there a moment ago. She likely knew exactly what Thorne hadn't said.

"Hetty, child." Mr. Havner sank onto his haunches before her shivering form on the sofa. "If you'd like, I can help you leave London. Unless you have ties here …" His voice was tentative, unlike his gruff exterior.

"Even if—" Thorne began, but a sharp look from the coachman silenced him. Even if she had loved ones keeping her here, it would be safer for her to leave. And yet, Mr. Havner seemed to understand that those ties might be strong enough to bind her to danger and poverty.

Hetty continued to shiver for a minute or two, but then she nodded her head. "I'd like to leave London."

"Then once Mrs. Shokes has fed you, and the doctor has seen to your arm, I'll take you with me back to my employer's home."

"Back to the house?" Thorne hadn't meant to sound so harsh, but was surprised by the coachman's suggestion. He had thought Mr. Havner would simply give her money for a seat on a mail coach leaving today.

"Your employer?" Hetty's body tensed.

"You have nothing to fear, child. She is a good woman. She can hide you and find you employment so you needn't do this anymore."

This was a side of Lady Wynwood that Thorne had never heard about, probably because it would surely scandalize polite society. She had a carefully cultivated reputation for frivolity as she enjoyed the Season each year and gallivanted around the countryside, visiting her numerous relations.

He then realized he shouldn't be surprised, since her actions tonight were hardly those of a social feather-head. He knew all about hiding his true self from others.

A bustling on the narrow stairs preceded Mrs. Shokes, carrying a tea tray. Her face seemed to naturally always form a no-nonsense frown, and her movements were quick and efficient, but her hands as she tucked one of her shawls around Hetty were gentle and tender.

She was about to leave the room when Thorne straightened and bowed toward her. "Ma'am—"

"None of that," she said sharply. "If I won't let Blake Havner thank me, I certainly won't let your high and mightiness do it, either." Her steps back up the stairs were quick and forceful.

Thorne had never quite been treated that way before, even as a young boy raised by cold servants. But Mr. Havner cracked a smile. "She takes some getting used to, but she has a good heart."

"I suppose I expected a doctor's wife to be different."

"Mr. Farley Shokes isn't a doctor, just an herbalist. He tried to train as a chemist, but hasn't the knack for it. He supports his brother well enough with his teas and tinctures."

There were hot scones on the tray and a crock of butter, and Thorne found himself eating ravenously despite a slightly strange flavor to the scones. So did Mr. Havner, although Hetty seemed to have little appetite.

Light now reached the small sitting room window from the high, narrow alley outside. Thorne couldn't tarry any longer.

"Mr. Havner, er ... Hetty, I must leave you. Will it be safe to remain here until the doctor returns?" Thorne asked.

"I believe so. Mrs. Shokes will not betray her. And I can remain with her."

But Thorne could see that the man was exhausted. He had been up all night, since Mr. Coulton-Jones's rampage yesterday evening. He didn't even know where the man had stashed the carriage and horses, although Thorne could find other means of transportation.

Also, if he were to continue his search in the light of day, he needed to take the necessary minutes to change his clothing and perhaps obscure his face and hair.

Thorne now knew the general area of where he could start searching for Mr. Ackett again—bounded by the river, Tate Street, and the orphanage. There had been no sightings of two men fighting, which suggested that Mr. Ackett had lost his pursuer and found somewhere to hide. Jack's men had apparently been looking for something or someone, so they hadn't captured Mr. Ackett yet. But they wanted to find him, and they would not stop until they did. So if he returned to Lady Wynwood's house, Thorne could ask Mr. Drydale and the twins if they may have any ideas of where Mr. Ackett would hide in that specific area.

Thorne drew Mr. Havner aside. "Will it be safe for *you*?"

He paused before answering, "That man who attacked us—Hetty said his name was Nick—I didn't see his face clearly, just a shadow in the fog. So I doubt he saw me enough to recognize me. Although if he's taking the Root ..."

"From what Mr. Drydale told me, the man who tried to approach the empty factory last night did not have superior vision."

"That's assuming all men who take the Root are like that."

Thorne couldn't answer that. "The fog was heavy. Maybe we had a bit of good luck."

Mr. Havner studied his face for a moment. "It wasn't luck. The good Lord was watching over us."

Thorne couldn't prevent the grimace of distaste that flickered across his face.

"You have quite a grudge against God, man." Mr. Havner looked amused rather than offended.

Grudge? He hadn't thought of it in that way, and yet the word seemed to fit the tightness in his chest. However, put in those terms, it made him feel rather petty.

"Then I suppose all the things that went our way tonight was

LADY WYNWOOD'S SPIES, VOL. 2: BERSERKER

an unbelievable bit of *luck*. We might have used up all our luck for the year." Mr. Havner turned back toward the girl, who was now nibbling at another scone.

There had been a great deal that had gone wrong tonight, but Thorne also couldn't ignore the fact that there had been a great deal that had been extraordinarily lucky.

"The good Lord was watching over us."

Thorne didn't believe in Him any longer. Every time there had been a kind hand in his life, he had been slammed with rejection and disappointment in even greater measure. Anger had taken root and festered. So yes, he did have a grudge against a God who would keep beating a man.

But he was also a logical man, and logic did not favor coincidence. He couldn't explain why he'd been able to hear Nick approaching in the fog, which had at that moment suddenly thickened to help blanket them. He couldn't explain why Nick had decided to chase Thorne and not the coachman, who had been wielding a whip.

And so, despite himself, the thought that Someone was watching over him was like a soothing drop of comfort on the smoldering fire in his soul.

Chapter Five

It was her punishment, to stand here and watch him. To feel the nervous flutter under her breast bone, like the wings of a trapped moth, with every rise and fall of his chest.

There was no one awake in the household, not even a servant, to be alarmed that Phoebe stood watching Mr. Coulton-Jones as he slept. She admitted she felt a bit reckless to have the door open, but he was clearly asleep and unlikely to jump up to attack her from a drugged stupor, so she had time to slam the door shut and lock it if he so much as twitched.

She knew she ought to sleep, since they had returned to her aunt's home only two or three hours ago. Once they had arrived at the apothecary shop, Keriah had immediately decided—as Phoebe suspected she would—to stay and make more sedative rather than putting all their equipment away only to set everything up when they returned in a few hours. Fred had made a token objection, but Keriah easily argued over him. Dr. Shokes had been concerned, but then he had been called out to care for a sick child, and he took his brother with him. Without Mr. Farley Stokes in the building, even Fred could see that it was an ideal time for them to work.

Based on how the sedatives had worked (or not worked) on Mr. Coulton-Jones, Keriah had formulated stronger medicinal paste and another powdered option, since that was easier to deliver. Phoebe had helped. They had finished earlier than expected since they had done the procedure once already and they knew what was needed. There was enough for Mr. Coulton-Jones if he awoke, and also enough for one or possibly two crazed men if they should appear. But they ran out of mandragora root and needed more, which was why they had stopped.

She and Keriah had cleaned the stillroom until it was pristine, to make it difficult for Dr. Shokes's brother to be able to determine what they had been concocting. Fred woke Calvin and Clara, and the twins managed to find them a hackney at that hour to return them to Park Lane.

Keriah fell into an exhausted sleep in the hackney. Fred carried her to a bedroom upstairs while Calvin and Clara stumbled to their own room in a stupor. Phoebe fell into a light doze for a couple of hours, but she awoke to stare at the darkened ceiling of her room.

How could she sleep when the man she had followed like a ghost across London ballrooms was unconscious in a storeroom below and may not ever awaken, much less return to his right mind? When Mr. Ackett was out there in the darkness of the street, possibly injured?

She could not do anything about either of those things, but the guilt and the anxiety warred in her stomach. Her heartbeat rose to a canter and her breathing grew faster, which made sleep impossible.

Which was why she had dressed in an old gown and snuck downstairs to stand here staring at Mr. Coulton-Jones.

His peaceful sleep should have eased her. He was not uncontrollable with rage, slave to the poison that had been fed to him. He was not destroying property and injuring people. When Calvin had been out searching, he'd listened to conversations in the aftermath of the events of tonight, and from what he could gather, no one had been killed or even seriously harmed. Mr. Coulton-Jones had vented his energies on destroying buildings and objects, but he hadn't engaged in fights with anyone, unlike when Antonius Dunmark had rampaged through the area a few days ago. Mr. Dunmark had sometimes focused on a particular victim and beat on them until they were unconscious or dead before moving on.

Perhaps that moment when Mr. Coulton-Jones had seemed to recognize her hadn't been her imagination. Perhaps his mind had been fighting the effects of the Root and attempting to regain control. The lack of seriously injured victims had been too coincidental, indicating that he may have been trying to choose the objects of his destructive anger.

If he woke, would he again be wild and raging? Would the sedative work again? Would the rest of his life be a cycle of waking and a dose of sedative?

She shuddered. She knew he would rather die than live a life like that.

What could she do for him? Nothing.

She had helped to make the sedative, acting as Keriah's assistant. She had even been able to give insight into the properties of various roots, seeds, and leaves that they considered. And she had been more than willing to administer the drug, although Uncle Sol had insisted on being the one to fling the powder that they had first tried, since he would need to get close to Mr. Coulton-Jones. Keriah had explained very specifically where she had wanted Phoebe to aim her arrows, so as to administer the drug but not cause a fatal injury. Without being arrogant, Phoebe knew she was one of only a few people who had the skill to aim with accuracy.

So she had not done *nothing*. But now that they had a batch of sedative prepared, she felt adrift. When they had first prepared the medicine, the process was challenging, but they were hopeful. Her heart quivered within her when she was firing arrows at a man she might care about, but her determination lent her strength. When he fell unconscious, but was still alive, she knew relief, and then the slow dawning of realization that they had succeeded.

For the past twenty-four hours, her emotions had run the gamut, but through it all ran a thread of purpose that even now gave her a strange, calming sense of satisfaction. She had helped a man. She was helping Uncle Sol with important work that could influence the war. She was helping her aunt dig into the mysteries surrounding her late Uncle Wynwood. She was doing something beyond making an estate successful, beyond putting money into her father's pockets.

But now, what could she do? Was she only useful in assisting Keriah and shooting arrows?

She wanted to help find Mr. Ackett, but her frustration felt like shackles. She was a young, single woman of a genteel family, and he was lost in a part of London darker and farther removed from her normal existence. She was not afraid to venture into the Long Glades, but she was frustrated with the knowledge that she would be useless. The average man or woman on the street would not speak to someone like her. She had seen Mr. Coulton-Jones disguise himself to match the social class of the man he had been meeting on the Heath, but she did not have that skill.

Or did she?

None of her aunt's servants spoke in the cultured tones of traditionally trained men and women who would fit into the runnings of a noble house. There was a lilt to Aya's speech that spoke of her country background, and Calvin and Clara had a dialect that sounded ... scruffy to her ears. She could hear it in her head even now. Could she mimic that dialect?

If she could adjust her speech, then a rough gown, a simple hairstyle, and her old hunting boots half hidden by a rough cloak would transform her into someone else.

But what would she do? Tramp through the Long Glades,

searching in alleyways and abandoned buildings looking for Mr. Ackett? Would anyone tell her the truth if she asked if they had seen him?

There were many people who would not speak to her, a stranger. Most would probably assume she was a whore if she were alone. Even if she took a footman, dressed appropriately in plainclothes, for protection, would anyone be willing to speak to a woman who wanted information about another man?

She was not a master of disguises like Mr. Coulton-Jones, nor did she have experience in intrigue like Uncle Sol, but she had interacted with the tenants on her father's farm, especially the women. And while country women were very different from the women of the city, she suspected that if she told the right story, presented the right appearance, the women of the Long Glades might be willing to speak to her.

If she took Calvin and Clara with her ... and, say, if she said she were looking for her brother, who had been lost since the chaos of last night ... there may be women who would tell her if they had seen Mr. Ackett. She could search in a different style from Mr. Rosmont, and perhaps uncover new information.

When Calvin and Clara had arrived at the apothecary shop, sent there by Mr. Rosmont, Clara had given her impressions of the man. From how she had described him, Phoebe was not at all certain Mr. Rosmont would welcome a civilian who wanted to help search for Mr. Ackett.

She had been surprised to hear that Lady Aymer had arrived not only to see her brother, but also to introduce Uncle Sol to Mr. Rosmont. He may have had similar "employment" as Mr. Coulton-Jones, and it was possible Lady Aymer knew about her brother's clandestine work.

Phoebe did not feel she needed Mr. Rosmont's permission to help in the search, but he may have found Mr. Ackett already. At the very least, he would know where Mr. Ackett was *not* hiding, and may even have narrowed down an area where he might be found. But she did not know when he might return.

She stared at Mr. Coulton-Jones and felt the buzz of anxiety in her bones. As soon as Calvin and Clara awoke, Phoebe would make plans to take them with her to the Long Glades. They may even find Mr. Rosmont and be able to trade information, if he was willing to share.

She had to do something. Not because she was restless so much as her burning desire to be a part of this particular problem. She wanted to help Uncle Sol, and Mr. Coulton-Jones, and Mr. Ackett, even though she was a woman, even though she was nothing but a piece of fluff in the social circles of London, even though her only talents were her bow and her knowledge of growing plants. Even if those men only saw her as useless, she wanted to try to do something.

Except that they wouldn't see her as useless, because they weren't like her father.

She knocked her head hard against the wooden doorframe. Why did she always return to him? The thought of her father was like a scab she kept picking at. No, that was too mild. Instead, it was like jabbing splinters into an open cut.

But it wasn't solely the pain. There was also an anxiety in the pit of her stomach, an unease at the mystery of her father's actions. He was planning something with her life, without a thought to her wishes. Her feelings smoldered, reigniting every time she tried to put out the burning.

Her father was sly, but not always intelligent. He hadn't given Lord Wynwood's attorney a logical reason for why he would refuse the request for her to remain in Aunt Laura's home in London. It was obvious he was hiding something, and she hated knowing it had something to do with his desire to control her life for his own selfishness.

She wanted to thwart him. She wanted to retrieve her mother's jewels from his safe and worried that she was running out of time.

She heard a whisper of sound that was not the scurrying of a rat.

It was a bit early for the servants to awaken, although it would not be impossible for one of them to start their day sooner than normal. Graham was usually the first at work, since he and Mrs. Rook did not tolerate laziness in the household.

But the sound was not that of the butler's step, even when he was trying to be particularly quiet. Was she being overly suspicious? Would Apothecary Jack have discovered Mr. Coulton-Jones's location so quickly?

The sound whispered again. It was the footfall of someone who wanted to remain undetected in the sleeping house.

She considered closing the door on Mr. Coulton-Jones's room, but the creak of the wooden door and the clinking of the iron lock would alert whoever was there. But if their destination was this room, it would be safer for the door to already be locked rather than trusting that she could fumble the lock closed after she saw who was there.

She grabbed the door and swung it shut. The hinges squeaked only a small amount—Graham wouldn't dare allow noisy hinges in his household—but the heavy wood made a moan and then a cracking sound in protest. It closed with a thud that echoed through the narrow, low-ceilinged passageway, and the iron padlock clanked as she locked it.

The soft footsteps had hurried at the first sound of the noisy door. She now could tell that they were from some soft footwear —slippers or perhaps felt mules—rather than the leather boots she would expect an intruder to be wearing. But by the time she realized that, she had already locked the door and turned toward the far end of the hallway.

Keriah appeared, recognizable even in the dark from the pale color of her hair tumbling around her shoulders. "Phoebe? What are you doing?"

She glanced at the door she had just shut. "Penance."

"What?" Keriah approached, pulling a shawl closer around her shoulders. "You shouldn't have opened the door to the storeroom."

"He's still asleep."

Keriah gave her an admonishing look. "You wouldn't have known that when you first opened the door."

"It was perfectly quiet inside." She touched the old wood, feeling the rough vertical grain. She added softly, "I wanted to see him."

Keriah had no answer for that, and simply stared at her with eyes that looked large and black in the dimness.

Phoebe turned to face the closed door and bowed her head. "Heavenly Father ... please heal him."

When she looked back up, she caught the twist of Keriah's mouth and knew what her friend was thinking. It was an argument they'd had many times before, but right now it caused a flare of annoyance. "Would you have me not pray? It will help."

Keriah's mouth tightened for a second before she finally burst out, "God allowed that to happen, didn't He?"

"You say that as if it were not Jack's fault for giving him the Root in the first place. Are you exonerating Jack so you can blame God?"

Phoebe was usually not so sharp in her words with Keriah when they discussed religion, and Keriah was usually not so vocal about her anger at God. They glared at each other for a moment, but it was Keriah who turned away. "I am not ... blaming God, exactly," she finally said, "but I am rather put out that He didn't stop Jack from doing this."

Phoebe herself didn't understand where God had been when Mr. Coulton-Jones was captured, just as she'd been feeling betrayed by God for allowing her father to treat her like chattel, so a part of her felt hypocritical for arguing with her best friend.

Finally after a moment of awkward silence, Keriah said, "Aren't you cold?" She unfolded her shawl, a large square of sunset-colored wool, and flung it about the two of them. Phoebe automatically grasped one corner while Keriah kept hold of the other and threaded her arm through her friend's. "Let's go to the kitchen. You can make me some tea."

That suited Phoebe's plans very well, because then she would know as soon as the twins were awake.

"So," Keriah said as they walked toward the back of the house, "how will we go searching for Mr. Ackett?"

Chapter Six

It was barely dawn when Laura woke, but when she headed downstairs to the kitchen, she wasn't surprised to find Phoebe and Keriah already seated at the center table, enjoying a pot of tea. It may have even been their second pot, because the cook, Minnie, was scolding them for eating most of a loaf of bread she'd baked the night before and had intended to use for breakfast. However, despite her scolding, Minnie removed some piping hot scones from the oven and set them on a plate in front of the two ladies, along with a crock of butter and another of preserves.

"Aunt Laura, you're awake early." Phoebe had quickly begun slathering a scone with butter, handling it gingerly because of the heat.

"You two are making my servants distraught." But Laura smiled at them as she seated herself.

She didn't remain seated for long, because Mrs. Rook entered the kitchen and let out a yelp. "M'lady, it's one thing for the two young ladies to sneak in here and steal food, but it's quite another for you to sit down as if you're about to share a meal with the servants. Please make your way to the morning room so Minnie can work in peace." To emphasize her words, she removed the plate of scones, the butter and preserves and marched out of the kitchen with them.

Phoebe rose, juggling her hot scone between fingers already sticky with preserves. Keriah had had more self-control and free hands, so she found a plate for Phoebe to drop her scone into and a tea towel to wipe her hands.

Before leaving the kitchen, Phoebe said, "Minnie, please excuse Clara this morning. She and Calvin were out with us quite late last night, so I told them to sleep in."

Minnie smiled. "I doubt they'll stay asleep for long. They'll come tromping in as soon as they smell the—"

She was interrupted by rushing footsteps hurrying down the servants' stairs only moments before the twins rushed into the kitchen. "Good morning," they announced to the room before Calvin exclaimed, "Minnie, I could eat a horse! I walked all over London last night."

By then Laura was out of range of the kitchen, but she heard the gentle tones of Minnie's answer and had no doubt the cook was unearthing the sweet biscuits she'd made especially for them last night before retiring.

Laura had only intended to nibble at a scone, but she found herself eating more heartily than she expected to. The two young ladies ravaged through the scones as though they had not eaten for days.

To be honest, Laura had not expected to see all of them awake. She knew that Calvin and Clara were used to waking up early, and they would forgo sleep so as not to miss breakfast. But when she went down to check on Mr. Coulton-Jones, she had been shocked to hear Phoebe and Keriah's voices filtering down the hallway from the kitchen. There were purple bags under their eyes since they had arrived back at her home several hours after midnight. She knew, because she herself had been lying awake when she heard them climbing the stairs.

She had known that it would accomplish nothing for her to remain awake while so many of her household were in the Long Glades, but she had not been able to soothe her anxiety, which felt like pins and needles constantly prickling in her chest cavity. She had paced in the drawing room, staring out the darkened windows even though there was nothing to see, and then when Aya had scolded her, she had gone to her bedroom, where she had paced and again stared out the windows.

Were the two girls safe at the apothecary shop? Even if they locked the doors, even though Fred was with them, even though Dr. Shokes, his brother, and his brother's wife were upstairs, it was still in the middle of the Long Glades. Why had she felt such urgency that she would send two young women into a dangerous neighborhood in the middle of the night? Why had she given in to Calvin and allowed him to accompany the coachman to wander the streets? And Calvin would not have wanted her to allow his sister to lead Mr. Rosmont along those streets.

She berated herself and second-guessed each of her decisions over and over, until her eye happened to fall upon the leather-bound copy of Psalms and the New Testament lying on her nightstand. And she remembered that she was not alone. With a prayerful apology for becoming too caught up in her own thoughts, she climbed into bed and set the lamp on the nightstand to illuminate the pages of the Bible as she opened it. She had not been looking for any passage in particular, but she happened upon the Book of Luke, chapter 12:

And he said unto his disciples, Therefore I say unto you, Take no thought for your life, what ye shall eat; neither for the body, what ye shall put on. The life is more than meat, and the body is more than raiment. Consider the ravens: for they neither sow nor reap; which neither have storehouse nor barn; and God feedeth them: how much more are ye better than the fowls? And which of you with taking thought can add to his stature one cubit? If ye then be not able to do that thing which is least, why take ye thought for the rest?

Consider the lilies how they grow: they toil not, they spin not;

and yet I say unto you, that Solomon in all his glory was not arrayed like one of these. If then God so clothe the grass, which is to day in the field, and to morrow is cast into the oven; how much more will he clothe you, O ye of little faith? And seek not ye what ye shall eat, or what ye shall drink, neither be ye of doubtful mind. For all these things do the nations of the world seek after: and your Father knoweth that ye have need of these things.

But rather seek ye the kingdom of God; and all these things shall be added unto you.

She did not immediately feel peace soothing all her nervousness like water over a fire. But she did manage to remind herself that while she could not keep hold of everything in the palm of her hand, the God she trusted saw everything that happened, knew about her worries, and heard her prayers.

She prayed for everyone whom she had sent, and for Mr. Ackett's safety, and for the unconscious Mr. Coulton-Jones. And when she was done, she felt a little better after sharing the burden with the Lord. But she had still lain awake until she had heard the two young ladies return home.

Once Mrs. Rook arrived with tea and bacon, she applied herself to a good breakfast. Not because she was as hungry as the two girls, but because she was steeling herself for an errand she must undertake today.

Indeed, it might crush her heart, but it must be done, because they all needed answers only she could unearth.

The door to the morning room had been left open, so they all heard when the front door knocker resounded in the entrance hall. Surprisingly, Keriah was the first to her feet and out the door, followed by Phoebe. Laura found herself following them with more alacrity than she would have thought herself capable of after such a horrid night.

But at the top of the stairs, her heart fell when she recognized the footsteps and then the polite murmur of Sol's voice. It was not simply that she had been hoping for Mr. Rosmont or even Mr. Ackett to have arrived—although when she thought more logically about it, they would not draw attention to their connection to her by knocking upon the front door when they could send a note.

It was because Sol would be a thorn in her plans for today. Allaying his suspicions was going to be difficult, because while she could spot a lie at twenty paces, she couldn't deceive others very well.

The two girls were speaking to Sol even as he gave his cloak, hat, and gloves to the butler.

"Uncle Sol, did Mr. Rosmont return?"

"Did Mr. Rosmont find Mr. Ackett?"

"He did not find him yet," Sol said. "But he arrived with me. He is dressed rather disreputably, so he posed as my coachman."

It took a moment for those words to sink in, but then Laura realized with horror that she needed to rescue Mr. Rosmont right away. "Good gracious! He is driving your coach to the mews right now?"

Sol looked perplexed. "Yes. Is that a problem?"

"Of course it's a problem. Mr. Havner is not here." Laura was already running down the stairs and toward the kitchens at the back of the house. "Calvin! Run to the mews at once! Mr. Rosmont is driving the coach!"

Calvin appeared immediately, although there were crumbs dotting his mouth like a beard. He raced out the back door of the house, through the tiny garden, and disappeared into her laundry house, which had been her mews before she acquired the second, unmarked carriage. Laura followed him and exited the laundry house, turning down the small lane that ran along the back of Park Lane and ducking into a narrow alleyway to a side street. She had only been wearing house slippers, which were soaked through with mud and cut by gravel.

Laura entered the mews to the sound of raised voices. She

was greeted with the sight of Mr. Rosmont atop Sol's carriage, stopped in the middle of the open doorway. He was shouting at her stable boy, Moses, who was facing down Mr. Rosmont with a musket in hand.

"You're not Mr. Drydale's normal driver," Moses was saying, even as Calvin was shouting uselessly that this was Mr. Rosmont.

Mr. Rosmont was shouting, "I am working with Mr. Drydale."

Moses retorted, "When did he hire you? Because I've never seen you before."

Laura came up behind the stable boy and placed a gentle hand on his shoulder. "It's all right, Moses. Mr. Drydale introduced Mr. Rosmont last night."

"You would have met him if you hadn't been holed up with the horses," Calvin said.

"Well, someone had to guard the horses while Mr. Havner was gone." But Moses lowered the musket.

Mr. Rosmont visibly relaxed when he was no longer in the sights of a teenage boy with a gun. He swung down from the coachman's box and handed the reins to Moses. The stable boy still looked at him with distrust, but took the reins. Laura thought she might have seen a gleam of approval in Mr. Rosmont's stern eyes as he watched Moses unhitch the horses and lead them away.

"Where is Mr. Havner?" Laura asked him.

"I'll explain," he said. He looked pale, and there was an anxiety behind his eyes that had not been there a few hours earlier.

"Come, you must be famished." She led the way back to the house.

Sol was in the morning room with Phoebe and Keriah, helping himself to eggs and bacon. "What took you so long?"

Laura picked up a roll and lobbed it at his head. He yelped and ducked.

"You should know better than to send a stranger with the carriage," she said. "Poor Moses nearly shot Mr. Rosmont's head off."

Understanding dawned on Sol's face. "I had forgotten about your overprotective servants."

"Things are especially tense right now, after the events of last night and with Mr. Havner gone." She gestured toward the food and told a slightly scandalized Mr. Rosmont, "Please help yourself." She rounded the table to pick up the fallen roll that she had thrown.

"Did you really need to throw that?" Sol asked. "I was going to eat that."

"If I don't miss my guess, Minnie is making fresh scones just for you," Laura said with disgust. "My chef is clearly trying to woo you through your stomach."

Mr. Rosmont was uncomfortable when Sol gestured for him to explain the events of his search with Laura and the two young women present, and he related the events in as few words as possible. But pain flashed across his face when he explained about Hetty and how he had accidentally injured her.

Laura nodded. "I have the resources to find her a position as a maidservant in the country. She need have no fear of being found if she leaves London."

Mr. Rosmont looked at her in confusion, but Laura had no inclination to explain to him her secret activities with the young women of Rachey Street.

"I did not find Mr. Ackett, but I know where to look," Mr. Rosmont said as he shoved bacon and muffin into his mouth between sentences. "I was hoping, sir, that you might have insight into where Mr. Ackett may have hidden in the area bounded by Tate Street, St. Osmund's Orphanage, and the river."

Sol shook his head. "I don't know. I have not worked much with Septimus on these shores."

"It might be more useful to ask Clara and Calvin," Laura said. "They know that area well, and they would be familiar with places where an injured man might find refuge. But that is still a very large area."

"We would like to help," Keriah said, as Laura knew she would.

"More people searching would be better, don't you think so?" Phoebe added.

Both Sol and Mr. Rosmont began to protest loudly. But Phoebe explained an idea of posing as sisters looking for their older brother, who disappeared amongst the confusion last night, which would explain why they were asking about him.

"I promise, Uncle Sol, we would not do anything foolish." Her gaze was calm but firm, unlike Keriah, who seemed earnest but a little emotional. "I am friends with my aunt's servants. I know full well the dangers of a young woman in the wrong area."

Laura had been hoping that encouraging her niece to hear the stories of the suffering of women in these dark areas in London would make her more cautious, not more daring.

Sol only frowned more deeply. "Then you know why this is folly."

"I know that I have to help. I cannot remain safe. I am not unafraid, and I am not unaware, but I cannot stay home. We will do what we can to help." She glanced at Keriah, then back to Sol. "And we will obey any orders given by Mr. Rosmont. But we *must* help find him, Uncle Sol."

At first, Laura was horrified at the thought of sending them back there, even if they were guarded by the twins and Mr. Rosmont. But then she remembered words often spoken by a rich, smoky voice, weighted with the knowledge of a pained and suffering lifetime: *"You would be surprised at what men will say to a clever woman."*

"Mr. Rosmont, I think it would be a good idea," Laura said.

Sol glared at her. "I am surprised you would approve of such a madcap scheme."

"Phoebe is better at playacting than I had known before. I don't believe she is overestimating her abilities. But if you think about this clearly, you will realize that two women looking for their brother might solicit more favorable responses from strangers than a single, rather large and intimidating man looking for another man."

Mr. Rosmont still looked opposed to the idea, but understanding began to dawn on Sol's face. He glanced at Phoebe, then at Keriah, then back at Laura. "I don't like it," he said, but with less heat than before.

"I had not known Phoebe could play act so well under pressure, but she acquitted herself well at Mr. Farrimond's party. Even you must admit that."

"I could do it, Uncle Sol," Phoebe said.

"Not with an accent like that, you won't," Mr. Rosmont retorted.

"What accent?" And suddenly, subtly, her voice had changed. "A girl from the country ha'n't an accent." Even with those few words, she had perfectly taken on the same lilt of Aya's country dialect.

Sol was visibly surprised. Mr. Rosmont, however, simply glowered more fiercely at her.

"Mr. Rosmont," Laura said, "one thing you have likely never experienced is the contrast in the way the same person will react to a young woman asking for a favor as opposed to a young man. There will be a handful of people who would answer Phoebe's question about a missing brother, but who will ignore your requests for information about a man you are searching for."

"That's as it may be," he said, "but I've been trained to find information even in difficult situations."

"What will you do if Mr. Ackett is injured?" Keriah asked.

"I have experience treating battlefield wounds."

"And what will you do if you are attacked by a man on the Root, or out of control like Mr. Coulton-Jones was last night?" Phoebe asked. Unlike Keriah, her voice was calm, reasonable. "You will not be able to administer the sedative if you are fighting."

"I beg leave to argue that you don't know what I'm capable of doing while I'm fighting."

There was a flash of challenge in Phoebe's eyes. "Perhaps you are correct, but I have seen these crazed men. Unless you are skilled enough to beat two men of Mr. Coulton-Jones's caliber, you will not be able to get close."

"I can shoot an arrow—"

Keriah interrupted, "Phoebe didn't simply shoot an arrow. She administered the sedative into the body's humors without tearing any vital arteries."

"Mr. Rosmont," Laura said, "just one of those men on the Root defeated both Mr. Ackett and Mr. Coulton-Jones. However, if you would like to take him on alone, be my guest. I will look for your body floating in the Thames next week."

He threw her an irritated look, and she returned it with a steely gaze. But her words, or her expression, made him blink and look away. The deep lines between his brows smudged a little as he reluctantly said, "I could not defeat him. That man I fought, Nick ... I could not defeat him."

"Going by yourself is a little reckless, Thorne," said a new voice from the doorway to the morning room.

Lady Aymer stood there, her fine reddish-brown hair twisted into a casual knot unlike her normal fashionable hairstyles. Her dress, also, was not her typical elegant ensemble, but a modest front-fall gown in light green with dark green embroidery.

Laura jumped a little, because not only had her butler failed to announce Lady Aymer, but she herself had not heard any footsteps on the stairs.

Behind her, in the hallway, Graham stood anxiously. He

bowed an apology to Laura, saying, "Lady Aymer insisted I need not announce her."

"I do apologize, my lady," Lady Aymer said as she entered the morning room and sat down next to Mr. Rosmont. She was markedly shorter than he was, but when seated, the top of her head rose over the slope of his shoulders. "I heard raised voices —or rather, I heard Thorne's raised voice, and thought it might be best for me to intervene."

Mr. Rosmont gave her a sour look. But similarly to last night, something about her presence made the harsh lines of his face soften.

Lady Aymer continued, "As I understand it, the young women wish to help Thorne with the search?" She turned to Mr. Rosmont. "You are accustomed to working alone in dangerous situations. But the difference is that here, you might encounter Apothecary Jack's men, who are not like the men you have faced before."

"This is the same as any other time," he replied. "I am not afraid of the danger. I understand the risks."

"I am not saying you do not," she said, "but your chances of success are greater if you have people to help you. That is only logical, Thorne. You must see that."

He glanced at Laura before answering, "I had already come to that conclusion as you arrived."

Phoebe and Keriah straightened with pleased expressions.

Lady Aymer gave Laura an amused look as she said to Mr. Rosmont, "Yes, I had heard that. But I also know that you are a stubborn fool who occasionally needs a corrective blow to the head in order to see reason."

He frowned at her teasing, but his eyes were smiling. He shoved the last piece of bacon into his mouth. "We must leave quickly."

Phoebe and Keriah shot to their feet. "We won't be a moment." They whisked out of the morning room.

Perhaps because they feared Mr. Rosmont would change his mind, the two girls were ready in a few minutes, dressed in old gowns borrowed from Laura's servants. It was Phoebe who also thought to borrow ill-fitting shoes, since the fine leather of even their oldest footwear would be out of place.

Mr. Rosmont conferred with Calvin and Clara about the area. Speaking more to her brother than to Mr. Rosmont, Clara said, "Wouldn't he try to hide at Stony Pete's?"

"Naw," Calvin replied, "Pete's not good with blood, remember?"

"Oh, you're right. How about that lean-to next to the factory?"

"That would be a good place if he could find it." Calvin turned to Mr. Rosmont. "It's off of Greaves Street. The second one, not the first Greaves Street. There are two."

"It's the gray factory, not the gray-brown factory," Clara added unhelpfully.

Mr. Rosmont's face was looking more and more perplexed the more they tried to describe the area.

"Perhaps it would be more efficient to take Clara and Calvin with you?" Laura suggested.

Mr. Rosmont's glare was highly irritated, but he grunted assent. She thought she heard him grumble something about "women and children" as he turned away.

They agreed to leave from the back of the house and trickle out onto the narrow alleyway. Calvin raced ahead to flag down a conveyance.

After they saw the motley group off, Lady Aymer asked to see her brother, and so Laura and Sol stood farther down the narrow servants' hallway from the open storeroom door while Lady Aymer sat inside.

"What happened with your interest in Mr. Farrimond?" Laura asked in a low voice.

Sol glanced up and down the hallway before answering her.

"Normally I would want a more thorough search for the note he received, but Sep is the only agent I have who is able to sneak into a person's house, and he was injured even before he disappeared. I may ask Mr. Rosmont to search his smoking room, as Phoebe suggested, but he will need a means of conning his way into the house. However, the fact that Nick and that other man were there indicates that this group expected someone to come search, so likely the note is gone by now."

"That must be disappointing for you. It is a shame you haven't more bodies to command."

He gave her a sarcastic look. "I assume you are suggesting your niece and servants? And Miss Gardinier as well? I am surprised you would willingly allow them to run headlong into danger."

"That is assuming I have control over Phoebe and Keriah. I do *not* like them running headlong into danger, and I would do all I could to stop them if they were simply being silly girls, unaware of the seriousness of the situation." Sol opened his mouth to disagree, but she interrupted him. "They saw Mr. Coulton-Jones in that state, Sol. And they did not run away."

His mouth settled into grim lines, and he seemed to be recalling the night before.

"And you managed to find an agent to take charge of them. You must be so relieved."

He raised an eyebrow at her facetious tone.

She continued, "Are all agents like this one? So ... independent."

"Mr. Rosmont is perhaps more solitary than others I have known. But I cannot fault him for not desiring to take along women and children in such a dangerous area."

"I would have agreed with you if those particular children hadn't grown up on those streets. And Keriah has spent a great deal of time helping Dr. Shokes with his patients in that area."

"And Phoebe?"

"She has hidden talents that will surprise even you."

"She *has* surprised me. But she is also a gently-bred young lady."

"Your agent is quite gently-bred himself. His cousin is the Earl of Essedon, I believe?"

"Mr. Rosmont has undertaken many missions to find people. He'll find Septimus."

"And if Mr. Ackett is captured by Apothecary Jack, what was your solitary agent intending to do? Rescue him all by himself?"

"Unlike civilians, Septimus is too well-trained to be captured."

Chapter Seven

Mrs. Pam Wright was the first person to arrive for her charity group, as usual. The door to Brannon Church was difficult to open, and she had to pull hard at the handle until it opened with a shudder. She damped down her frustration.

She was one of the founding members of the Society of the Benevolent Voice in the Wilderness for the Rescue of Souls Lost in the Darkness of Heathenism, and they had been giving funds to this church in order to have permission to use it as their center of activity when they came to do their work in the Long Glades. So naturally she would notice when the church became more and more shabby. There were fewer servants, and yet there were the same number of parishioners, although that had been very small to begin with. Were those miserable wretches giving less money to the church? They should increase their giving so that the church would look less neglected and more grand.

Her bonnet had fallen askew when she yanked at the door, so she straightened it with careful tugs as she walked down the center aisle of the tiny sanctuary. She grimaced at the threadbare carpet that muffled her footsteps as she walked up to the altar. Brannon Church had no stained-glass, but even the few windows were grimy. At the front, she turned left toward the small sitting room that her organization used when they met to make charitable visits to homes in this area. However, before she reached the door, she heard voices coming from down the hallway, near the office of the curate.

Pam abhorred gossip. But she also felt it her duty to inform people of things they should be aware of. And so she felt no compulsion about tiptoeing down the hallway closer to the cracked open door of the curate's office.

"I don't know what we should do about him," the curate said.

A woman's voice answered him. Pam recognized her—a bedraggled creature who called herself an herbal woman, but she was most certainly a witch or some satanic person. She allowed people to address her by the blasphemous name of Lady Nola, even though she had not an ounce of noble blood in her. Pam detested her for everything she stood for, with her herbs and tinctures that were probably poisoning the people who came to her for relief from their injuries and sicknesses. She should at the very least not answer to the name Lady Nola. She was simply an upstart.

"He is the first one to come by in a long while," Nola said.

"Yes, it's been several months since we last had any of Willie's crew come by."

"I can understand why you would be flustered when this man showed up."

"I assumed he was like one of the others."

"He is not one of Willie's men. Neither does he belong to Mr. Dix."

"Then should we continue to treat him?"

"I have already treated him. Who will pay me for the bandages and the medicines?"

"The church hasn't had any funds since Shepherd Willie was killed. We are no longer being supported. No one told Mr. Dix about the church—perhaps no one thought to tell him, perhaps they simply didn't want him to know about it. But I don't think they realized that with Willie gone, there is no one to give the church any money, either."

"I had this arrangement with Willie. I was guaranteed payment for my medicines and service. Who's going to pay me now?"

"We can't afford to keep him for very long. There is no one to sit with him."

"You don't know who he is?"

"I had assumed he belonged to one of the gangs."

There was a pause, then Nola asked, "Can you get money from that charitable organization, that Society of Shouting in the Darkness at Sinners?"

Pam pressed her lips together. They were the Society of the Benevolent Voice in the Wilderness for the Rescue of Souls Lost in the Darkness of Heathenism, and considering they gave funds to this church, the woman ought to at least remember their name.

The curate answered, "No, they simply pay a small monthly fee to use a room in the church. Money for the organization comes from their wealthy patrons."

"Well, some of them seem quite genteel." Nola's voice was faintly contemptuous. "Mayhap they have their own money that they can donate for a sick man."

"I have spoken to one or two of them. They only give money to their own churches to minister to the needs of their own congregations, not to anyone outside."

Nola sniffed in derision. "So *Christian* of them."

"We should just toss him out."

"He is too injured," Nola said.

"Since Mr. Dix killed Shepherd Willie, if he hears what we've done for this man, it may bring trouble upon us. He is obviously not one of Mr. Dix's men who are taking that strange potion."

"Hush," Lady Nola hissed at him. "We mustn't speak of that." There was the scrape of a chair against the stone floor. "I must go back and check on him."

Pam was alarmed. Not simply because she might be

discovered. She tried to tiptoe back to the sitting room as quickly as possible then rattled the sitting room door quite loudly. The voices from the curate's office abruptly ceased. Pam opened the door, for once thankful that it squeaked, and entered the sitting room.

She paced the tiny room, too agitated to sit. They had an injured man in the church. And he was likely some criminal. If he was so terribly injured, he must have befallen some sort of violence. She must tell someone about the man, but there was no law enforcement in this area. Who could she tell?"

She must do something. She could not allow this church to continue to harbor a dangerous man, no matter how injured he might be. He might rise up and attack one of the women in her organization.

Well, she would simply have to find someone and *make* them come to take this criminal away. Pam knew that she could be very persuasive when she put her mind to it.

She straightened her shoulders, then firmly walked to the door and pulled it open to another horrible screech. The hallway outside was empty. When she glanced down toward the curate's office, his door was now closed.

She marched out into the sanctuary, but a movement at the far side of the room made her pause behind the edge of the wall. When she peeked out, she saw Nola exiting the steps from the basement. Nola then walked toward the front of the church, and with an almost effortless shove, she opened the stubborn front door, letting in a flash of weak sunlight that seemed blinding compared to the dimness within. Then she was gone.

Pam had no wish to follow Nola outside, and she suddenly had a strong curiosity about the man that the curate and the herbal woman had been speaking about. She felt almost like a criminal herself as she crossed the front of the sanctuary. She hesitated at the top of the steps leading down into the stone basement, then headed down into the depths.

The church's basement was not large, but it was built of solid stone blocks. The ceiling of the basement was rather high, and it was well lit by numerous small windows set high along the walls.

Pam followed a stone wall to her right to where she knew there was an alcove, which held a small cot. She had always wondered why there was a cot in the basement, when the curate had a comfortable couch in his office where he could sleep if he were kept at the church late at night.

She turned the corner of the alcove and stopped short. There was an injured man lying on the cot, and he turned toward her, no doubt hearing the sound of her half-boots echo against the stone floor. He tensed when he saw her, but he did not speak.

"Who are you?" The question escaped from her lips before she could check herself.

The man said nothing.

There were bruises on his face, and blood seeped through his coarse tunic at his shoulder and his side. His knuckles were bloodied, and there were cuts on his lip.

"Were you fighting?"

The man said nothing.

Pam's lips pressed together for a moment. "You mustn't fight, you know. We must strive to love one another. No good can come from fighting."

The man sighed, then turned his face away from her.

Pam huffed and headed back toward the basement stairs. The man was most definitely a criminal, and she would find someone to tell so that he could be carted away. She did not want such a man under the same roof as her organization.

She marched toward the front of the church and tried pushing against the door as she had seen Nola do, but the door barely budged. She had to ram her shoulder quite hard against the rough wood to make it open.

Once outside, she hesitated, looking around. She wasn't quite certain where she should go to find someone to tell about that man.

While she was looking around, trying to decide, a light voice suddenly sounded behind her left shoulder. "I beg your pardon, but do you belong to the Society of the Benevolent Voice in the Wilderness for the Rescue of Souls Lost in the Darkness of Heathenism?"

Pam whirled around. She had not even heard him walk up to her, and he stood quite close. She instinctively took a step back.

The man standing there had very pale eyes. He was dressed in breeches, a waistcoat, and a jacket, far finer than a common worker, but the fabric was not as rich as a nobleman's attire. He gave her a charming smile.

Pam replied in dulcet tones, "Why, yes. Are you interested in our organization?"

"I have been watching your group, and I am so impressed by the righteous light that you shine upon the stark streets. You appear to help anyone no matter how destitute or needy."

"Yes, the message we give to them surely brings them hope in their dark hours, so that they can even forget about lack of food or clothing or shelter or income," she said grandly.

Something flashed across the man's face, almost like a sneer. But it disappeared so quickly that Pam realized she must have imagined it, because he was again giving her that gentle, charming smile. "I'm sure that their worries are washed away by the light of your good words. Please tell me about whom you have helped most recently."

Pam immediately began speaking about the woman most on her mind. "Just yesterday, we visited with Mrs. Scott, who has several children, although the woman is shockingly inefficient in quieting her brood. She always seems more interested in the tea and biscuits that we bring with us." Pam sniffed. "I personally do not agree with some members of our group who bring foodstuffs with us when we visit, because the word of God is of more value than bread. But some of our members have more refined tastes, and they prefer tea and biscuits when speaking to these women, who often don't even have a scrap of toast to offer with their watery tea, much less milk and sugar to serve with it. So I can see the necessity of bringing our own tea things when we visit. The women do seem more receptive to speaking with us, but I believe they are more interested in being fed, which certainly goes against the tenants of our foundation. Now that I think about it, I really must speak with our other members quite firmly about this today."

When she paused to draw breath, the man quickly asked, "Do you also minister to the sickly? And the injured?"

Pam remembered the injured man. "I just spent … a little time sitting with a man in very poor shape."

Interest flashed across the pale-eyed man's face. "Won't you lead me to him?"

Pam hesitated. She wanted to tell someone about this injured criminal, but she knew nothing about this pale-eyed man, and he certainly did not look like law enforcement.

Seeing her hesitation, the man added, "I have some interest in medicine and I may be able to help the man feel better so that he is no longer dependent upon your group's charity."

Pam immediately said, "Of course. Won't you come with me?"

She let him back into the church, and the pale-eyed man quite politely opened the difficult front door for her. As they walked down the center aisle, she corrected the man, "My organization only pays a fee to the church to use the facilities, and it is actually the church who is burdened by this convalescing man."

"But I am sure your group does a great deal to ease his suffering," the man said.

She led him down the basement steps, and then into the alcove. As soon as the injured man saw her companion, his eyes grew wide, and he tried to sit up.

The pale-eyed man quickly strode over to him and placed a hand upon his shoulder, forcing him back down onto the cot. "Do not be alarmed," he said in a gentle voice. "Everything will be all right now." Then the man said in a quiet voice, "Silas, he is here."

Pam looked around, because it sounded as if the pale-eyed man had spoken to someone nearby, but there was no one there. "Who were you speaking to?" Pam asked.

The pale-eyed man said nothing, simply smiling down at the injured man, who began to grow more and more agitated.

Within a few minutes, Pam suddenly heard heavy booted feet coming down the basement steps. They were not the sound of the curate's footsteps.

She yelped as a huge, hulking man suddenly appeared in the alcove. But he ignored her and instead crossed over to the cot, picking up the man and pulling him out of bed.

Pam grew alarmed. While she certainly wanted this man out of the church, because she did not want him to taint the reputation of her organization by being under the same roof, she also did not wish him to be manhandled in this way. "What are you doing? You will injure him."

The large man ignored her and brushed past her as he carried the weak man out of the alcove.

"Do not ignore me!" Pam stamped her foot. "What are you doing? I demand to know."

The pale-eyed man came up to her with that same gentle smile. "We are simply taking him somewhere where he can recover more fully."

"I do not believe you. This is quite irregular. I demand you put him down this instant! I shall tell the curate—"

The pale-eyed man suddenly backhanded her across the face. Her world tilted, and suddenly she was on the cold stone floor. Her cheek began to grow hot and throb where he had hit her.

She saw two pairs of booted heels as they walked away from her. The larger man climbed the basement steps, but then the shoes of the pale-eyed man stopped and turned to face her.

In that same gentle voice, he said, "I thank you for your generosity in sharing with me this man's location." Then the shoes turned around and climbed the basement steps.

Only then did Pam suddenly feel the explosion of pain in her head where the man had hit her. She could only lay whimpering on the floor and listening to the men leave the basement.

Chapter Eight

Phoebe was not foolish enough to think that she could simply start asking questions in the Long Glades. Luckily, she had two very experienced previous residents to ask for guidance.

She bent to speak to the man sitting on the ground, with dirty bandages around his calf where the dark rust color of blood was seeping through. She pointed back up the street and said, "There is a cart there, and a young woman and a young man. They could dress your wound."

The man thanked her, although his expression was still rather suspicious and incredulous at her offer of charity, but he hobbled up the street toward the cart. As Phoebe turned away, Calvin leaned closer to her and whispered, "This one."

They were approaching a young woman who had been watching Phoebe speak to the injured man. Phoebe smiled warmly. "We have come from Shokes Apothecary Shop," she said. "We have been sent to see if anyone is in need of doctoring."

"Why would you do that?" the woman demanded. Her eyes were more suspicious than the injured man, perhaps because the man had been more desperate for relief from his pain. This woman did not appear to have any type of injury.

"We were here last night when that crazed man went rampaging through," Phoebe said, undaunted by her harsh tone. "We were with our brother, and he went off to help some people who were in danger." She hoped her mask of worry was not too melodramatic, as she added, "Our brother never returned last night, and we have been very worried about him. So we have returned to search for him and also to offer help to anyone who may need it. Were you injured last night?"

Some of the suspicion receded from the woman's eyes. She shook her head. "I stayed far away from that scrummage."

"If you know of anyone who may need bandages or a tincture, please send them to the cart." Phoebe again pointed back to the top of the street. Then she moved on.

Calvin said, "I remember her from when we used to live here. She likes to gossip, and if she had seen something, she would have told you."

Phoebe had been letting the twins decide whom she should ask about Mr. Ackett. Sometimes they would have her speak about him, other times they insisted on being the ones to ask.

At first she had thought they would ask everyone they spoke to about Mr. Ackett, but Clara had insisted that asking the right person was more important than asking many people.

On the other side of her, Clara whispered, "I think we should ask him." She subtly gestured ahead toward a man leaning against the wall to a candle shop.

Calvin added, "You'll need to ply him with some coin."

He was obviously not injured, but since Clara had pointed him out, Phoebe took a closer look at him. He had heavy-lidded eyes and a relaxed posture, making it seem as though he hadn't a care in the world. But there was a sharp, observant gleam in his eyes as they took in everyone around him. He appeared uninterested in anyone walking past him, except for once or twice when he gave a subtle hunch to his shoulder to turn his ear toward two or three men walking past, as though trying to catch some of their conversation. He might appear to be waiting for someone or killing time, but he had a definite purpose in standing there. Sometimes after catching a snatch of conversation from some passing men, he would idly follow them for a few steps before stopping to lean back against another building.

Phoebe asked Clara, "Who—no, *what* is he?"

Clara sent a strange look toward her brother on Phoebe's other side, who returned it. Then Clara said, "He looks like he might know something, doesn't he?"

"Don't know if he'll tell you, though," Calvin added.

She may as well find out. Phoebe stepped up to the man. "Were you here last night with the crazed man? We are offering bandages if you were injured."

The man had likely seen her speaking to people as she made her way down the street, and it would have been difficult not to have already heard about why she was there. But he still flinched a little when she came up and spoke to him directly, almost as if he hoped she would overlook them. She could tell that he was debating whether he would answer her or turn and walk away. But he finally grunted. "Got no injury." His voice was gravelly, as though he had not used it much today. He scratched at the stiff, straight brown hair sticking out from under his shapeless hat. His eyes drifted away from Phoebe, as if he wanted to be elsewhere.

"We are looking for our brother," Phoebe said. "He was with us last night, and he went off to help some people who were in danger. Perhaps you might have seen him?"

He gave her a strange look, as if weighing her words and her expression all at once.

At least he wasn't dismissing her. Phoebe took a step closer to him, so that she could discreetly slip him a coin, which he took from her hand with a flash of practiced ease. "What's he look like?"

"Tall and slender, dark hair. Brown shirt and trousers, brown coat. But no hat."

He shook his head. "Could describe almost anyone." He hesitated, then added, "But I didn't see any man like that without a hat."

She smiled at him. "Thank you, sir." Then they continued on.

Clara said softly, "If he didn't see Mr. Ackett, then it is likely he didn't come down this way."

Phoebe turned to Clara and asked again, "What is he?"

Calvin opened his mouth, but then seemed to change his mind and instead said, "I didn't know him."

"He, uh ... looked like he was an unobservant sort," Clara said in feeble tones.

Phoebe continued down the street, telling people about the apothecary shop, but since the twins didn't indicate for her to ask anyone else about Mr. Ackett, she did not mention him. Then they turned back toward the cart.

As they drew near, Keriah had just finished bandaging the leg of the injured man Phoebe had sent to her, and Mr. Rosmont helped the man hobble away. But then Keriah began packing up their things.

"You are finished?" Phoebe asked her.

Keriah's eyes were bright. "One of the women I treated for an injured shoulder said that she was on the next street over, and she saw an injured man who looked like Mr. Ackett heading toward Jay Street last night. Mr. Rosmont said we shall head there next."

"Excellent work," Phoebe said with a grin.

"People are more willing to open up to me when I am bandaging their wounds or giving them poultices," Keriah said.

Mr. Rosmont returned from helping the injured man. He picked up the handles of the handcart and wheeled it behind Phoebe, Keriah, and the twins. They turned the corner, and Calvin and Clara directed them toward Jay Street. Once there, they set up the cart again, and Phoebe and the twins walked down the street to tell people about Keriah's healer services.

There was more tension in the air on this street. The twins did not direct her to speak to as many people about their supposed brother. But they directed her to speak to a man lazily walking toward them. There was something about him that put her in mind of the man next to the candle shop on the other street. He carried himself as if he hadn't a care in the world, but his eyes flickered around him, and he occasionally spoke to people he knew on the street.

Phoebe asked him about Mr. Ackett, and he also had that wary look in his eyes. He answered her with only one or two words, and even when she offered him coin, he surprised her by refusing and brushing past her.

Before continuing, she stopped and turned to the twins. "He is like that other man, although this one was not is willing to give up his information. You must tell me what they are."

Calvin looked uncomfortable, and seemed to be looking at Clara to rescue him. But another look passed between the twins, and Calvin sighed. "Not many people know this, but there are some men on the streets paid to keep an eye out for anything that's happening," he said slowly, reluctantly. "They listen in on conversations between certain people."

"Certain people?"

"They're told who they should follow or who they should overhear."

"Who is it who pays them?"

"There are a few people who make it their job to know things," Clara said. "They sell that information or use it in other ways."

"They are like a gossip rag?" Phoebe asked.

Clara giggled at that, but Calvin looked offended.

"No," Clara said, "they are more like a newspaper. Except that if you know who to speak to, you can pay to read certain columns that have what you want to know."

"Why can't we ask one of them?"

The twins abruptly sobered, and there was apprehension in their faces. "Those are not good men to speak to," Calvin said.

"Not for a young lady," Clara added.

Phoebe had the feeling that if the twins were alone, they might be able to speak to people like that, but she certainly was not allowing them to roam the streets by themselves, even though they had done that for many years before coming to work for Laura. Not with men on the loose who could become crazed and destructive in the blink of an eye ... or with the swig of a potion.

She also reasoned that while the twins seemed to think it relatively safe asking the men who gathered the information, if she approached one of the men gathering and selling it, they may just as easily sell the information to Apothecary Jack.

Phoebe had been observing who the twins chose for her to speak to, and had started noticing a pattern. Some were women who looked helpful and motherly, or who enjoyed spreading gossip. Others were people who responded with suspicion, and yet the twins had her speak to them anyway. But they were all people who seemed to be aware of their surroundings, who weren't simply caught up in their own business. Some of them were not very open to Phoebe, but she thought perhaps the twins were choosing people who might have the greatest chance of knowing the information she needed.

Phoebe was feeling particularly useless. It was Keriah to whom these people were opening up, because she was providing help and charity to them. Phoebe was simply pointing them toward her friend. While what she was doing was important, she also began to feel that anyone could do what she was doing, and she was simply being indulged by the twins, who were with her to protect her. She did not want to be a foolish, spoiled young woman out on a lark to have a bit of fun. They had been walking the streets for many hours, and it was already late afternoon, yet they had had very few leads.

She remembered what she had told Aunt Laura last night. Did she really believe that God had a purpose for everything that happened to her? Did she really believe that God was guiding her? Did she really believe that this was what God wanted her to do with her life? She had said that she was aware of the danger, which may be true, but she didn't feel that what she was doing was helping Mr. Ackett in any way.

But she also realized that perhaps she was looking at it simply with her own eyes, and maybe she needed a different perspective of the situation. Last night she had been so convinced that she was a piece in all of this, that she had a place in all of this, that God had placed her in the midst of this.

Heavenly Father, I pray for Thy guidance, here in this place. I beg Thine help to find Mr. Ackett.

At that moment, she raised her eyes and happened to pick out from the crowd the figure of a man half-hidden in the entrance to a narrow alley. He had the flushed cheeks and bleary eyes of a man who had been drinking heavily, apparently for several hours. She made her way down the street toward him, speaking to other people and directing them toward Keriah's cart. Before she reached him, she asked Calvin, "How about him?"

"I don't think he'll speak to you," Calvin said.

"But I think you're right, miss," Clara said. "He looks like someone who has been up all night."

"That is also what I was thinking," Phoebe said.

He had the attitude of a man who wanted to be overlooked. He huddled in the entrance to the alley and met no one's gaze. And yet, his eyes took in everything that happened in front of him. He did not have the sharp observant look of the other two men who had been paid to keep an eye out, and in his inebriated state, she wasn't entirely sure how much he might have noticed, but he had perfected the art of not being noticed by others.

Phoebe approached him and offered medical attention, which he brusquely refused in a deep, gravelly voice. He swatted his hand through the air, as if swatting her away like a fly. "Move along, missy." He hunched his shoulders as if to make himself even smaller and somehow disappear. "You're blocking my view."

Phoebe continued down the street, and after a few yards, she turned back as if returning to the apothecary court. But as she approached the alley, she gave a swift glance around, and then ducked around the corner of the building, past his hunched figure, to disappear into the narrow, fetid darkness.

He stiffened when she ducked past him, but he did not look back at her where she stood behind him, and he said nothing to her. No one could see her from the street unless they were directly across from the alley entrance.

"I'm looking for my brother," she said. She gave the usual story and described Mr. Ackett, accompanying her words with a coin dropped behind him, where it plunked into the dirt.

His head turned slightly at the sound, but his lips pressed together.

"I assure you, no one saw me. And no one will know I spoke to you."

His eyes drifted out to the street again, and he took another swig from the jug he was holding. He remained silent for so long that Phoebe wondered if he was going to answer her. Then he slowly said in a very quiet voice, "I was on Turner Lane last night, just minding my own business." He rubbed at his mouth with his dirty sleeve. "I saw an injured man who looked like that entering Brannon Churchyard."

Her heart thudded. "Thank you," she said.

He sniffed and huffed. Then he added, "Later that night, I was in another alehouse. I heard Mr. Dix's men were looking for an injured man."

Her skin grew cold.

He continued, "So you better keep your promise not to say where you got this information from, or we'll both be in trouble."

Phoebe tossed another coin onto the ground. "Is that enough of a promise for you?" Then she slipped out of the alley and continued walking up the street.

Clara and Calvin had disappeared when she had ducked into the alley, but now they reappeared at her sides like ghosts. "Did he speak to you?" Clara asked.

Phoebe nodded. "Brannon Church. Let's tell Keriah."

It took them another hour before Keriah finished treating patients and they were able to head to Brannon Church. Calvin was tense as they walked the few blocks there. "You should let me and Clara go in first, miss," he said.

"Absolutely not," Mr. Rosmont said from behind them.

Calvin looked behind, then slowed so that they walked more closely together. "That church used to be one of Shepherd Willie's hospitals."

"Hospital?" Keriah asked.

"If one of his men were injured, they could go there and the curate would call for someone to attend to them," Clara answered. "He gave money to the church regularly in return for this service and to ensure they kept their mouth shut, but Jack killed him. I don't know what they do when they find an injured man now."

"Would they call for a healer?" Phoebe asked.

"Maybe, but if Jack is now paying the hospital," Calvin said with a dark look, "Mr. Ackett won't be there anymore."

An invisible hand squeezed Phoebe's heart, but she said, "Let's have faith." She wanted to believe that God had led her to that drunken man so that they could find Mr. Ackett before Apothecary Jack did.

The church sat in the crook of a junction where three streets met. They approached from behind the church, passing an unkempt graveyard surrounded by a rotting wooden fence.

Phoebe was surprised by the sound of a loud thud, like a shoulder slamming into a heavy wooden door, accompanied by the squeak of heavy hinges. She hesitated, because the sound had come from around the corner of the church.

Two figures suddenly appeared, having just exited the front door of the church. One was slender, and better dressed than most of the people in this area, while the other man was very tall and broad, with a mangled ear covered in knobs of pink scar tissue. A third man who had been leaning against a building across the street peeled himself away and followed the others.

The larger man had another slender figure slung over his shoulder, but was carrying him effortlessly. His passenger was dressed in dark clothing, but there were darker spots on his shoulder and his torso that looked like bloodstains.

Keriah, walking beside her, suddenly stopped and gasped. "That's Mr. Ackett!"

Behind them, there was a heavy thunk as the handcart was suddenly dropped onto the cobblestones. Then heavy footsteps, and Mr. Rosmont sprinted past them.

The man in finer clothing, walking in back, looked over his shoulder and saw Mr. Rosmont bearing down on them. He shouted something to the larger man, and all three of them took off down the street with Mr. Rosmont in hot pursuit.

Phoebe felt as if the air had been sucked from her lungs. The man who looked back had been the pale-eyed man she had seen at the Farrimond's party outside the library, the man dressed like a servant who was not a servant. Had he seen her? Had he recognized her?

But what was more important was that they had Mr. Ackett.

Keriah had begun running after Mr. Rosmont and the four men, but her shorter legs made her seem like a flea hopping after the swifter runners. Phoebe also began running after them, but she paused when she reached the corner of the church. "Calvin, get her back!" She pointed out Keriah, and Calvin took off at a run. They didn't have a hope of catching up to them, and it would be foolhardy for them to be separated in this area while attempting to chase them. She turned back to collect the handcart—she was reasonably sure she was strong enough to be able to wheel it.

But then a shocked voice suddenly froze her in her tracks.

"Miss Sauber?"

Phoebe turned and met the startled eyes of Miss Tolberton, the young woman from the last archery party she had attended.

"Miss Sauber, is it really you?" Miss Tolberton took a step toward her. "What in the world are you doing here?"

Thorne had been reluctantly impressed with the two young women.

Miss Gardinier's cheerful, positive demeanor while treating patients and her open friendliness encouraged them to speak more freely with her. Many were positively garrulous and chatted with Miss Gardinier as though she were an old friend.

He also remembered the drunken man whom Miss Sauber had spoken to. He had talked to him last night, but the man had refused to speak in anything more than grunts. And yet he told Miss Sauber about seeing an injured man enter Brannon Churchyard when all she'd done was slip into an alleyway and drop a few coins.

Also the young women didn't act like silly society misses out doing a bit of playacting. Miss Gardinier was earnest about helping her patients, and Miss Sauber's country accent was flawless as she spoke to people. She was gentle and kind and patient, she was not melodramatic. She didn't overplay her role as he had sometimes seen other more seasoned agents do.

He immediately tensed when he saw the two men exit the

church, one of them carrying a third man. He had barely needed Miss Gardinier's gasping words identifying Mr. Ackett to drop the handcart and sprint after them. Unfortunately, one of them had turned and spotted him, and they took off.

A third man had been waiting outside, and he ran with the other two, but soon it became apparent that he was not as fast. He veered off down a narrow alley, but Thorne kept after the other two, since they had Mr. Ackett.

Even though the large one was carrying an unconscious man, they were incredibly swift. The streets were not very crowded, and so they had a clear path and could run at full speed.

Thorne quickly realized that their top speed was a great deal faster than his.

He thought he had a bit of luck when they turned left down Gormby Street. He remembered that road from last night—it was a wide, relatively long street, but where the men had turned, it narrowed considerably and became a dead-end between two buildings and a high brick wall, with no way for them to escape except to double back.

But when he turned the corner after them, he was startled to find the alley empty. There were no other pedestrians, and the two men had completely disappeared. He walked down a little ways, searching the buildings on each side to see if there was perhaps a narrow passage between buildings or an open doorway, but there was nothing. The wall at the end was solid and impossibly high. There was no way for them to have escaped the alleyway, and yet they were not there.

His frustration at himself bubbled up like a pot of boiling water. He clenched his fist and slammed it into the wall, causing a dull thump. For all this talk of not wanting civilians with him, he had failed at the one thing he had been sent to do.

The enemy had Mr. Ackett.

Chapter Nine

Laura took only Aya with her on her errand, not because she didn't trust her servants, but in order to spare them from what she might find. They all knew about Mrs. Jadis.

They took a dingy hackney coach to a side street that ran parallel to Bond Street, but several streets over with shops much less affluent and much more discreet. She hadn't actually been to Gildow and Sons jewelry store, but she had heard about it often enough. Every noble-born wife in London had heard about it, and some wealthy merchants' wives as well. They all pretended it didn't exist, and yet they were destined to come across some juicy *on dit* at least once a week that featured this store.

The shop was much more modest than she had expected. But then again, they prided themselves on outward propriety as though to assert that their patrons' reputations would be equally unsullied. The store had a simple brown door in a brown wall, clean and neat. Drawn across the small windows were rich velvet drapes in a cream color as if to defy the dirt of the street from marring their brightness.

The hackney stopped and Laura hesitated before exiting. She did not want to do this. She had to do this.

"We can simply return home, my lady," Aya said quietly. She didn't touch Laura, but her voice and her presence was like a warmth covering the tightly clenched hands in her lap.

Laura swallowed, staring at the straw strewn across the floor of the carriage. After a long moment, she muttered, "It must be done." She exited the hackney as if shot out from a pistol.

Aya paid the driver and instructed him to wait as Laura walked with leaden steps toward that innocuous brown door. It had a fresh coat of that drab brown paint, and the latch was brass that shone like a star. She gripped it and pulled open the door.

It swung open easily, on well-oiled hinges, and the cool darkness inside beckoned her like a spider to the fly.

There was a gentleman at the counter who casually turned to look at her, but then started at seeing a woman enter the shop. The clerk's eyes also widened.

She knew the man, Mr. Foriest, the younger son of the Earl of Bambrough. His father had had children young and so was still hale and hearty while his children popped out grandchildren every year. Mr. Foriest had two daughters but no sons by his wife, Mrs. Maryann Foriest, the daughter of Sir James Egleby. However, Mr. Foriest's youngest girl had none of the coloring of either of her parents. Mr. Foriest was also well-known to favor the affections of a widow calling herself Mrs. Sutten, who was only a few years older than his eldest child.

Mr. Foriest turned back to the clerk, but Laura saw the reddening of his ears. Men came here because they did not expect to see or be seen by respectable women. If they didn't care about that, they went to the more popular establishment of Rundell and Bridge, a few streets over.

Normal women of the upper classes would not travel to this area, much less be seen on these streets, and certainly they would not enter any of these shops. But Laura was not a normal woman.

She stood quietly, and stared holes in Mr. Foriest's back, cloaked in dark gray superfine. She did not often see his wife at social functions, and even if she did, she would be unlikely to gossip about this incident, but Mr. Foriest did not know that.

The voices of the customer and the clerk were low in the small, richly decorated front room of the shop. They had also drawn their heads closer together, likely to prevent their conversation from being overheard.

Mr. Foriest seemed rather impatient to conclude his business. He turned and left the shop without a glance at Laura, to whom he would normally bow and briefly converse if they were at a social function.

The clerk looked sourly at her as she approached the counter. He busied himself with the paperwork of the recent transaction, with a quiet but firmly worded, "Please wait a moment." Laura felt that he probably took longer than he needed to, but she waited patiently.

When the clerk could finally shuffle his pages no longer, he turned toward Laura with a barely audible sigh. His voice was faintly surly as he asked, "How may I help you, ma'am?"

Because of the nature of the shop, Laura thought it best to attempt to ease the tension. In a quiet voice, she said, "My husband has been dead for ten years. I have no wish to stir up the ghosts of the past. His affairs mean nothing to me now."

The shoulders of the clerk relaxed a fraction. Laura wondered if she had just spoken a lie. The ghosts of the past constantly haunted her. When she had seen the pocket watch, those ghosts had come screaming out of the woodwork, even though no one else could hear them except for herself.

She continued, "However, I need to know the contents of an old order from ten years ago, just before his death. Do you keep orders for so long?"

The clerk's eyes flickered from side to side. "Yes, but ..."

"Surely an order so old can harm no one?"

The clerk was clearly torn, since the shop prized itself on its discretion. It would certainly not give out information to a woman if the man were still alive and the order were recent. Laura wondered if anyone had ever before come in and asked about an old order from a deceased client.

She studied the clerk. Young, not more than twenty-five, by her guess. He still had the pimples of youth dotting the edges of his face and jawline.

"This order was years ago. Would you have been the one to take it? Or is there someone else who would have handled the order?"

Her leading question made his eyes brighten with relief. "It would have been my father. Wait a moment, please, ma'am." He disappeared through a small door set in the wall behind the counter.

Laura caught Aya glancing around the shop in distaste, even though all there was to see were the curtains and the wooden counter. There were no display cases or any wares laid out for customers to finger.

"Did you not know about this place?" she asked her maid.

"I knew about it. I'm surprised you did, my lady."

"There are many unhappy women of my acquaintance. They hear of such places from other unhappy women. For many years, I was an unhappy woman, also."

She said the words calmly, without emotion to color them, but they made Aya's gaze soften. Her maid stepped closer to her. "Those days are far behind us."

"I think that they are about to reappear like cockroaches, just when you least expected them."

The door opened and a shorter, older man stepped through. He had his son's face—sans pimples—but his hair was fine and wavy, white with glimmers of silver. His eyes were also colder as they regarded her, although his words were perfectly polite. "I beg your pardon, ma'am, but we cannot divulge the contents of any orders. We strive to protect the privacy of our clients."

She knew that unlike his son, he could be negotiated with.

She set a sack of coins upon the counter, while holding his attention with her eyes. "Surely a dead man has no privacy."

His eyes lingered on the sack. She had filled it with a great many coins. He cleared his throat. "If the client in question is, in fact, deceased … What was his name, ma'am?"

"Lord Wynwood."

Even in the dim light of the shop, she could see his wrinkled skin pale. His gnarled fingers, calloused from the delicate work he did, nervously plucked at a velvet cloth lying upon the counter. "I do recall hearing of Lord Wynwood's death. Ten years ago, I believe?" He swallowed. His voice came out slightly higher as he said, "Unfortunately, the records of orders are not kept beyond a year."

She had met him barely a few minutes ago, but she knew in a moment that he was lying. "Surely you keep them for at least five years?"

"No, ma'am."

That was a lie, also. So they kept them at least five years. "I had heard that you kept them for at least eight years."

"I do not know from whom you may have heard that, ma'am, but that is untrue."

That, also, was a lie. At least eight years. She drew herself up and said in her haughtiest voice, "Where do you keep your records? I wish to look through them myself."

"We do not allow customers to—"

"Where are they? In back?" She peered at the closed door behind him.

"No, they are not on the premises, ma'am."

Another lie. They were likely only a few yards away from her.

She should have expected that this particular order might have been extra-special. After all, Wynwood had to have drawn the symbol for the jewelers to engrave upon the inside case of the pocket watch. Had they recognized it? Perhaps not, if they had agreed to fulfill the order. Perhaps they had realized what they had done only after the order had been delivered and paid for. Had that particular group discovered the order?

"Would you have been the one to arrange the order? Surely you could tell me that much," she chided, attempting to sound cajoling but fearing she sounded irritable.

"I am afraid I do not recall, ma'am." He said it smoothly, a line he had likely said before to an irate wife. Laura was watching his eyes, his jaw, his hands, and he was most certainly lying.

"You do not recall? Were you not the only one working here at the time?"

"It was myself and my father, ma'am."

"Well, where is he? Perhaps he might recall the order."

"He died several years ago, ma'am." The man's eyes were cold and hard, and Laura felt a twinge of guilt for attacking this man who was only trying to make a living. It was not his fault that she disliked how he did it.

"I apologize," she said quietly, and the man's tight jaw relaxed a fraction. "Then it was only yourself and your father working here at the time of Lord Wynwood's order?"

He hesitated, then nodded.

"I suppose it was your father, then, who took his order?"

"I'm afraid I can't say, ma'am."

He was too good at dodging her question. "Could you at least tell me if it was only one piece in the order, or if there was another?"

He started, just the tiniest motion. "I can't remember."

That was a lie. He knew enough about the order to know how many pieces. Her suspicions seemed to be correct—at the same time as when he ordered the pocket watch, Wynwood had ordered *something else*.

She simply didn't know how to discover what it had been. She thought she could guess, but hoped she was wrong.

Laura knew the man was only doing his job, but she couldn't

prevent the sneer of displeasure as she turned back toward the door. Aya made to follow her, but at the last minute darted back and took the sack of coins, seeing as how the man had been so singularly unhelpful.

There must be a way to discover what else had been in the order. Did the two men live above the shop? Could she possibly sneak in to look through their records? Good gracious, was she really contemplating breaking into the man's store to riffle through his orders?

She exited the shop, briefly blinded by the sunlight after the dimness of the shop, but quickly ascertained that the unreliable hackney driver had taken their money and left them. She would need for Aya to find them another hackney.

There was a figure in front of her. Probably another customer entering the shop. She made to step around him, keeping her head down. She had no desire to face the embarrassed expression of yet another philandering male.

The figure sidestepped to block her path. Startled, she looked up.

Sol stood there, so wrathful that it was as if fire were kindling behind his eyes.

In some ways, because he had known her so well, Sol hadn't wanted to believe that there was something she was concealing from him. It had seemed so out of character for her to attempt to hide what she had been doing, to lie about it.

And yet, because he knew her so well, he knew exactly when she was being evasive and secretive. He also suspected it had to do with this mysterious group, or her late husband, or both.

And he didn't understand why she would keep it from him.

But he had dealt firsthand with enough criminals to know that it was serious, no matter what she might try to tell herself or him. So in order to fool her into relaxing her guard, he had retreated, excusing himself soon after Mr. Rosmont had left her house. He'd used the abilities he'd honed over the past several years to follow her, unseen.

He knew the shop she had entered, even though he had personally never bought anything from it. It had been easy to pay off her hackney driver and wait for her to reappear.

He hadn't expected to see the pain etched into her face as she exited the shop, as if she'd had an old, severe wound reopened. He hesitated, but then moved to block her path.

Her maid, Aya, gave a little yelp and froze. Laura stared dumbly at him for nearly fifteen seconds before saying, "Sol?"

Then she embarrassed him when she stepped to the side. "I beg your pardon. We're blocking the door."

"I didn't come to shop," he ground out through his teeth.

She tilted her head at him. "It did seem odd to me that you would come here rather than go to a more reputable shop. And you haven't dallied with any opera dancers in many years, according to the rumor mill—"

"Laura," he interrupted fiercely, "what were you doing here?" She certainly couldn't tell falsehoods convincingly, but she could prattle on and redirect a conversation better than even a chatterbox like Sally Jersey.

She looked away, and her bottom lip trembled slightly before she bit it hard enough that she might have drawn blood. "A simple errand," she finally said in a small voice.

"You and I both know there's nothing simple about it."

He expected her to try to distract him with a fit of temper, tell him that it was none of his business. But she didn't, perhaps because she knew that *he* knew that it *was* his business.

"It has something to do with my investigation," he stated flatly. He had gone beyond suspicions after seeing her behavior.

She refused to look at him, but her upper back tensed.

The silence ticked by, then he said, almost shouting, "I don't understand the secrecy, Laura."

She simply shook her head. He didn't know what she meant by that, what emotions she was trying to hold back.

The maid standing next to her opened her mouth as if to say something to Sol, then changed her mind. She looked both offended at his words to her mistress and distressed at Laura's pain. It made Sol feel like *he* was the one at fault, to batter against her like an ocean wave, trying to wear her down.

"Laura." His voice was hoarse. "I thought we had come to an understanding. I thought we were friends."

This time when she bit her lip, he did see the narrow line of blood running along the seam of her mouth.

"Is this about the birthday celebration? I thought we had agreed that we would be honest with each other." He then realized that while he had said he would no longer use her, she had not mentioned anything about her own actions. "Why would you keep secrets from me?"

She remained silent.

He did too, thinking that the silence might force her to respond to him, but she did not. He thought he might have to leave without hearing her answer when she suddenly said, "I'm sorry, Sol, but I just couldn't."

"Couldn't tell me? Why not?"

She finally looked at him, and her eyes were wide, and as white as her face. The blood rimmed the inside of her lips, which clearly showed the puncture marks where she'd bitten down. When she spoke, her voice was low and awful.

"I might have killed a woman, Sol."

Chapter Ten

"Miss Tolberton! Is that really you? I had no notion I would meet a friend in an area such as this."

Phoebe didn't have to pretend shock as she spoke to Miss Tolberton. She and Keriah had discussed their story and their supposedly missing brother, but they had not thought about what they would say if they met someone they knew from society. It had not even occurred to them that it might be possible. And yet here was Miss Tolberton, her tiny figure encased in a lovely pelisse the color of pink geraniums, in the middle of the Long Glades.

Her mind raced with the possibilities. Miss Tolberton would certainly recognize Keriah from society events, but she was not entirely sure if Miss Tolberton was familiar with Mr. Rosmont. Phoebe herself had not recognized him because he apparently did not go about in society very much, and his circles did not overlap with hers. Phoebe and Miss Tolberton's social circles were similar, so she thought perhaps she might be able to hide Mr. Rosmont's identity from her.

"Miss Tolberton, do you attend this church?" Phoebe looked up at the shabby stone walls of Brannon Church, and allowed some confusion to cloud her face. She needed to stall while Calvin retrieved Keriah, so that their stories would match.

"Oh no," Miss Tolberton was saying, when the door to the

church suddenly opened. It required a stout shove from the inside, because the door apparently stuck. An older woman peeked out, her round, cheerful face framed by a rather elaborate bonnet decorated with silk flowers. "Miss Tolberton!" The woman said. "Were you able to stop them?"

"No, Mrs. Laidlaw," Miss Tolberton said. "They were too far away by the time I came outside." She turned to Phoebe. "This is my friend, Miss Sauber. This is Mrs. Laidlaw, one of the women I work with in the Society of the Benevolent Voice in the Wilderness for the Rescue of Souls Lost in the Darkness of Heathenism."

"Pleased to meet you." Phoebe was at a loss for how to ask about the society because she had already forgotten half of its name.

The corner of Miss Tolberton's mouth quirked up, as if she fully understood Phoebe's confusion. "We are a charitable organization that visits the poor in this area. The organization pays a fee to Brannon Church in order to use the facilities. We meet here, and then we go out and visit the poor families in this area, bringing to them the illuminating light of Jesus Christ." Her smile was sweet and angelic.

Phoebe was profoundly relieved to see Keriah approaching, reluctantly following Calvin. Keriah stiffened when she saw Phoebe speaking to Miss Tolberton, and her steps quickened.

Miss Tolberton's mouth formed an O as she spotted Keriah. "Is that Miss Gardinier, also?"

"Come inside, dears," said Mrs. Laidlaw, beckoning them in. "I ought not to hold the door open for so long, and yet I do not wish to close it because who knows if I shall be able to open it again."

That was probably a fair assessment, considering how hard it had been for her to open the door. Phoebe whispered for Calvin and Clara to remain with the cart, resting outside the front door, and explain the situation to Mr. Rosmont when he returned, then she and Keriah filed inside the cool church.

Phoebe was immediately struck by the smell of mold, age, and the faintest scent of mouse droppings. The church was not very old, and the furnishings had been fine when they were new, but now there was an air of neglect, as though it had not been cared for very well for several months. There was a fine layer of dust over everything.

Mrs. Laidlaw led them along the side of the sanctuary to a small hallway and opened the first door, which screeched like a wailing cat but was easier to open than the front door. Inside was a sparsely furnished room with a large table and uncomfortable-looking wooden chairs around it, but someone had brought in a pretty tea set.

Miss Tolberton introduced Keriah, and then Mrs. Laidlaw picked up the teapot. "I shall go to the kitchen to fetch some hot water. Please make your friends comfortable, Miss Tolberton." She left through the protesting door.

"Miss Tolberton," Phoebe said as she and Keriah sat down, "I had no idea you were such a good Christian."

"My father taught me to always care for those in need. When I came to London for my debut, I found myself desiring to continue the good works that I had been used to doing in the country. I heard about this organization through a friend, and desired to be able to help in the neediest of areas."

"How very generous of you." Phoebe had had no idea that Miss Tolberton had such religious fervor.

"But Miss Sauber, Miss Gardinier, you must tell me why you are in this very unsafe place. You're also dressed quite strangely." She was not so rude as to stare, but she had clearly noticed that their dresses were old and plain, more fitting for maids or servants. She herself was not dressed as fashionably as at a society function, but her dress was made of fine material that emphasized the slenderness of her form.

Under the table, Phoebe stepped on Keriah's toes to prevent

her from opening her mouth. Keriah had often gotten them into trouble because her explanations of their behavior were always more wild and fanciful than could be believed. "Keriah's aunt, Mrs. Gardinier, is a much respected herbalist, and her family is close friends with Dr. Shokes. Are you familiar with his brother's apothecary shop?"

"Oh yes," Miss Tolberton said. "Dr. Shokes is very well respected by nearly everyone in this area."

"Dr. Shokes often requests that Keriah's aunt make medicines for him from the herbs she collects in the country. Since Keriah has recently arrived in town, she was delivering some medicines to Dr. Shokes yesterday when that crazed man appeared. Did you hear about that?"

"Yes, one of the other women told me about it." Miss Tolberton's hand pressed to the lace at her throat, which peeked above the neckline of her pelisse. "It was quite shocking. And you were here when it happened?"

"Yes, it was very frightening. However, we were astonished when Mr. Ackett suddenly appeared, and he saved us from that fearsome man."

Keriah had turned toward Phoebe, her eyes widening a fraction. Phoebe could tell that she was silently asking her why she mentioned Mr. Ackett, but her question was answered by Miss Tolberton herself.

"I was ever so surprised to hear that there was an injured man in the church, but imagine my amazement to recognize Mr. Ackett! And then to suddenly have those rough men barge in and carry him out. They did not hesitate and moved directly into the basement, where he had been hidden. I'm very concerned for him, for he seemed gravely injured."

Phoebe bit her lip. "We were very troubled about him. After he saved us, we could not find him after things had quieted down." She then realized she had not thought through how they would have known Mr. Ackett was missing, but Keriah came to her aid.

"My family has known the Acketts for many years," Keriah said. "We were very concerned when we discovered he had not returned last night."

Keriah did not have the telltale twitch between her eyebrows that usually indicated she was making something up. She had never mentioned that the Gardiniers were friends with the Acketts. Was it true? It seemed to be, from Keriah's demeanor.

And then Phoebe remembered Keriah's hand gently brushing the hair away from Mr. Ackett's forehead in that alley next to the burned-out factory. Perhaps it was not a made-up story, after all.

Phoebe took up the explanation before Keriah could embellish more. "We felt responsible since he saved us from that crazed man last night. Dr. Shokes had asked us to return to the Long Glades today to offer medical aid to those who were injured from last night, so we have been asking about Mr. Ackett from the people we meet."

Miss Tolberton looked rather confused. "So Miss Gardinier's aunt ... and Dr. Shokes ... But you and Miss Gardinier were helping the injured?"

At that moment, they were interrupted by the noisy squeal of the door hinges as Mrs. Laidlaw returned with the teapot. "Here you go, my dears."

"I was simply bandaging wounds," Keriah said. "My uncle is a surgeon and he taught me. It is my aunt who is quite skilled with medicines."

"Your aunt?" Mrs. Laidlaw asked Keriah. "Is your aunt Mrs. Carmelia Gardinier?"

"Yes."

"Why, I have heard of her." Mrs. Laidlaw beamed as she poured the tea. "Dr. Shokes speaks quite highly of her. She apparently makes many of his medicines for him, since the herbs that she grows in the country are quite fresh. I should not say so," she said, leaning closer and lowering her voice, "but she is apparently a much better chemist than Dr. Shokes's poor brother." She passed tea around to all of them. "I am afraid I could not find any biscuits or cake in the kitchen."

"Oh!" Miss Tolberton jumped up and went to a basket that had been sitting in the corner. "I bought some treacle buns for a visit today."

"Now, Miss Tolberton, you know Mrs. Wright does not like it when you bring food with you when we visit these ladies." But Mrs. Laidlaw's rebuke did not have much heat in it.

"I know she does not approve," Miss Tolberton said, "but I say, what housewife will be very happy to listen to strangers who don't even bring treacle buns with them?"

Phoebe was surprised to find she quite liked the soft, sweet bun with a slightly sticky glaze. "How long have you been working with this organization, Miss Tolberton?" she asked.

Miss Tolberton tilted her head. "I don't quite remember …"

"Oh, three or four years now," Mrs. Laidlaw said. "Miss Tolberton is quite well-liked by the women we visit. Many of them have brothers or husbands or sons who belong to the gangs, but Miss Tolberton is unafraid to visit the families."

"There is no danger," Miss Tolberton said. "The men are rarely at home when we visit, and the women seem to appreciate the company." She dimpled. "And the treacle buns." A crease suddenly appeared between her brows. "Mrs. Laidlaw, have you seen Mrs. Wright? Usually she is here before us."

"I have not seen her," Mrs. Laidlaw said with a note of concern in her voice. "Perhaps she is ill and she is not coming today."

Even with the door to the room closed, they heard the sharp sound as the outside door to the church was yanked open forcefully. Phoebe and Keriah both leapt to their feet.

"That will be Keriah's sister's servant," Phoebe said. "He was the man who chased after Mr. Ackett." They exited the room, announcing their presence to Mr. Rosmont with the sound of the hinges, and quickly stepped into the sanctuary to greet him.

Adopting the haughty demeanor of a mistress to her servant, Phoebe said, "Ross, were you able to apprehend those men with Mr. Ackett?"

Mr. Rosmont blinked at the name she had given to him but he seemed to immediately understand the situation, especially when he saw Mrs. Laidlaw and Miss Tolberton exit the room behind Phoebe and Keriah. He took his hat and worked it nervously in his hands. "I'm sorry, miss," he said in a rough accent, "those men were terribly fast. I thought I had them, but they turned into an alley and then they seemed to suddenly disappear."

"Disappear?" Keriah's voice was rather high-pitched.

"An alley?" Miss Tolberton had come up on the other side of Phoebe. "Is it perhaps the left turn onto Gormby Street?"

Mr. Rosmont looked up in surprise. "Yes, miss."

"Oh." Miss Tolberton looked uncomfortable. "There is a secret—well, I suppose it is not truly a secret, but someone who was not from this area would not realize that there is a doorway on the side of the building closest to the end of the alley. It is not quite hidden, but it is difficult to see. The door leads through the building and out onto the next street."

Mr. Rosmont's mouth drew into a grim line.

"So you lost him?" Keriah's voice was very small.

Mr. Rosmont nodded. "Those men have Mr. Ackett."

Chapter Eleven

"You've brought me a dead body."

"He's not dead yet, Mr. Dix."

"Oh. You're right." A kick. "Wake up."

Sep was so engulfed by pain that the kick was like a tap against his side. The blow had hit his muscle and not his broken ribs.

They'd brought him before Jack Dix. And from the pounding of the floorboards under his cheek, Silas, the man who'd carried him, was leaving the room, which sounded like a vast space.

He had to try to turn this to his advantage. Did he have the strength to overcome his injuries?

He heard a gleeful giggle above him, and a thought swirled in his sluggish brain, that men didn't usually giggle. But Jack was definitely giggling.

Then he felt tiny pinpricks against his face, and opened bleary eyes. He stared directly into two yellow-green eyes.

No, one was slightly milky, but both were looking directly into Sep's, only a few inches away.

It was a cat, possibly one of the ugliest creatures Sep had ever seen. The pricks had been from stiff whiskers, and the fur on its face had been clawed off and then grown back in black and dirt-brown patches that didn't match the rest of the golden-brown fur.

But more than the cat's rough appearance, it was the baleful nature of its gaze that held him. He hadn't thought a cat could look so sadistic, so human-like.

Then a shoe appeared and the cat scuttled out of the way. "Two of you in two days," Jack said in high-pitched mirth.

Two of them? Jack must be referring to when he'd captured Michael last night. Sep had gone searching for his friend, and Michael had become ...

A monster.

Was that Sep's fate, too? He had always been willing to give his life on any mission, but he had never been faced with a death that could injure or kill innocents.

Jack's voice suddenly became harsh and grating. "You ruined my fun!"

And suddenly he was kicking Sep over and over. He hadn't thought he could feel more pain, but the blows were stronger than any he had felt before.

He remembered the last time he'd been kicked like this, about two years ago. They had been kicks from prison guards when he had deliberately been caught so that he could rescue one of the prisoners, but the guards had been frustrated and taken it out on Sep with their heavy boots.

And yet, this one slender man's kicks were heavier than the largest guard who had attacked him.

This should be familiar to him. This should be just like any other mission. None of them had gone perfectly smoothly. He had been captured numerous times. He had been tortured.

But despite the pain, he had always managed to keep a part of his mind clear and calm. He would imagine himself on a mountaintop, looking down into a valley of darkness. But he was above all of that, he was closer to God than he had ever been, closer even than when he was safe at home.

At those times, he had felt the powerful, almost tangible presence of God next to him. Those moments had brought him wonder and joy, despite the uncertainty, despite the pain. Sometimes during those missions, he had even felt that God had placed him in those dark places for a reason.

When he was desperate, and he could only rely on the Lord, the Lord had been right there. But when he was safe at home, God had suddenly felt far away.

He had not felt close to God since he had returned to England.

He tried to summon up the same mountaintop, but his mind was awash in scarlet. He tried to remember his passionate feelings, the same religious zeal that enabled him to pray to God, to believe in the Almighty's hand upon him.

But he could not feel it. He was in a desert, a desert of pain and loneliness.

He summoned up feeble words to pray. He tried to trust that God would rescue him somehow, or present an opportunity for him to escape. But now, his prayers felt empty.

He couldn't breathe. He was on the verge of passing out when Jack stopped.

"Let go of me," Jack hissed.

"You want him awake, don't you?" The second voice was far more cultured than Jack's, and yet with a sharp and jagged edge to the tone. Sep hadn't even known there was another man in the room, and he realized that the second man had stopped Jack from kicking him any further.

He recognized the refined voice, which had talked to Silas when he'd been carried here.

"I suppose so," Jack grumbled.

There was a soft thump against the wooden floorboards under Sep's head, and then suddenly Jack's horribly painted face was inches away from his. "So tell me, what did you do with my *berserksgangr?*"

Sep tried to keep his face perfectly still, but his confusion must have shown because Jack slapped on the floorboards, raising a cloud of dust that obscured his features. "The man last night!" Jack's spit split through the dust cloud and rained upon Sep's face. "My toy! My Berserker!"

He was referring to Michael. Sep said nothing.

Still with his head against the floor and looking directly at Sep, Jack began muttering, as if to himself. "You didn't kill him, I don't think you killed him. Not enough blood in that abandoned factory. That means you somehow managed to knock him out. But it couldn't have been simply a hit on the head. We've tried that. If you hit hard enough, they cock their toes up and die. They can't be knocked unconscious."

The dust had settled, and Sep could clearly see Jack's eyes when they riveted back to his. They were surrounded by concentric circles of gradually lightening shades, blackest around his eyes and transitioning to gray and then white at his hairline. "So how did you do it?"

He must want to know about the sedative that Miss Sauber and Miss Gardinier had been developing. It must have worked. Despite the pain, Sep felt the trickle of a cool stream of relief in his chest. They had saved Michael. The sedative had worked. He looked back at Jack and said nothing.

The refined voice came from directly above him. "It was some sort of drug."

Without moving his head, Jack's eyes slid sideways, looking at the man standing above them. "Oh?"

"Out on the street, long before they led him back to the factory, I thought I saw them throw some sort of powder into his face. It slowed him down a little."

"Did it just take a long time for him to feel its effects?" Jack's eyes slid from the man back to Sep.

"I don't think it was the powder." Sep felt the floor jar as the other man began pacing nearby. "There were spots of blood on the floor of the factory, and they shot arrows at me. They shot arrows at him, I think."

Jack's eyes brightened, and he smiled at Sep. His mouth was ringed with concentric circles of color, like his eyes, except that the color went from dark red on his lips, then to pink, then to white. "How rude of them to shoot arrows at you."

It took Sep a moment to realize Jack was talking to the man, and not to himself. Jack continued, "Maybe those arrows were like my grandfather's knives. Did they poison him, do you think?"

"Perhaps," the refined voice said. "There was an odd herbal or chemical smell in the factory."

Jack smiled more widely at Sep. "What did they use? Did they kill him? Or did they manage to knock him out?"

"Would he be likely to know?" the refined voice said. "He wasn't even there."

No, at the time, Sep was being beaten to a pulp by Silas. It was sheer luck, or perhaps the hand of God, that enabled him to blindly throw the glass dust and strike Silas squarely in the face. He then ran out and led him away. Silas was hot on his tail until Sep found a crowd surrounding two men in a fight, and the smell of their blood masked his own. He was able to stagger away behind two drunken men from the crowd, and Silas had not been able to track him.

"There are other things he might know," the other man continued. "His name, for one. Or the name of his friend, or the people who rescued him. And, more importantly ..."

A hand suddenly grabbed the hair at the back of his head and yanked upward. The man was so strong that half of Sep's torso lifted off of the floor. He stared into pale eyes.

"I am very curious to know who will come for you."

Chapter Twelve

The ride back to Laura's home was made in stony silence on Sol's part, but Laura's intense guilt and rioting emotions made it easy to ignore him. What would he be able to say to her? Nothing. This was a burden only she could bear. It had weighed her down for ten years, like a vulture perched on her shoulders and digging its claws into her skin.

Sol seemed impatient as she waited for the tea tray, but Laura knew her servants would not rest until they had proper refreshments. More importantly, they also wanted confirmation from Graham, who delivered the tray, that Laura was well. And perhaps they wanted to ascertain that she would be safe with Sol, considering the towering rage he seemed to be in.

Once Graham had closed the door behind him, Laura sighed and began pouring the tea for Sol. "When were you assigned to watch over Wynwood and myself?"

He frowned. "Laura, don't turn this back onto me—"

"I am not. I want to know how much you are aware of."

He seemed to back down. "Approximately two months before he died."

They had been awful months, when her emotions had been a furious storm. Looking back, her world had been colored by pitch-black loneliness, fiery red anger, sickening green jealousy. She had not been herself—or perhaps she had been the elemental essence of her sin, the deepest pit into which she could fall, in order to become fully aware of her need for God.

"Then you're aware of his last mistress, Mrs. Bianca Jadis."

He nodded, a bit confused. "She was Bianca Irvine before she married Carl Jadis. He died not long after they wed. She became Wynwood's mistress only a week after he broke up with his previous woman." He suddenly broke off, as if belatedly realizing he was discussing the cold facts about her husband's infidelity.

It still pricked her, small points of pain like dozens of little needles, but nothing that would make her bleed. Much. Her next words would cut her open much more, but she ground them out like glass through her teeth. "She was pregnant."

His brow contracted, but she couldn't tell if the news surprised him or not.

"Did you know, Sol?"

Grimness etched lines along the sides of his mouth. "Someone —maybe from my club—mentioned it in passing, but it was only a rumor. No one gave much credence to it."

"Aya heard it, and then she verified it was true. At least, she personally heard Mrs. Jadis claiming it to be true." Laura swallowed, but her throat was tight. She was still haunted by memories of Wynwood's kicks, his feet in those ridiculous pointed toes and soles as hard as stone. It was the pain of those horrible shoes that had taken root inside her belly instead and still bothered her with phantom pangs when she least expected it.

"Oh, Laura. I'm sorry." There was a depth to his voice that spoke of more than his words.

"Then you can understand why I went to confront her. I was out of my mind with jealousy. Not for Wynwood, but for ... everything else."

There was silence between them. He hesitated to speak in the face of her obvious pain, and she couldn't speak around the lump in her throat.

Finally he coughed and said tentatively, "I'm surprised Aya told you."

"I had already heard the rumor from a 'concerned' friend. She knew I wouldn't rest until I knew the truth, so she told me, although she did so very reluctantly. She also accompanied me to see Mrs. Jadis."

"I had no idea you were visiting Rachey Street as far back as then."

She looked up at him then, saw the tenderness in his eyes. "I suppose I shouldn't be surprised you know about Rachey Street. But no, this was before then. And Mrs. Jadis didn't live on Rachey Street. She owned a small house in Kensington."

"What?" He blinked rapidly. "I ... I had no idea."

She raised her eyebrows as she regarded him. "You didn't? Aya found the information for me."

He muttered something that may have been something like, "Useless agents" before telling her, "Please continue."

She had to settle her thoughts before she could. Remembering the past meant remembering her anger, her frustration, her burning envy that bordered on hatred. Or maybe it had crossed that line and she had fully despised her husband's lover. She honestly couldn't remember clearly because everything had been cloaked with her fear of how things would change for her when the child was born.

"I wanted to confront her." She had already said that. "I wanted to hear from her own lips about the baby. I don't know why, really. It would have been like inviting her to stab me through the heart. And when she first saw me and recognized me ... She was openly gloating. Sol, she was glad to see me so she could see my pain."

For once, her ability to tell truth from lie had only made things worse. She had thought she could force Mrs. Jadis to talk, so she could discern the lie, but in reality it had only been out of a desire to feel in control of the entire situation. If she knew the truth, she could control the story, she could control the outcome.

But she couldn't control anything at all, and certainly not her own fear. Nor the strong emotions that clouded her ability.

"And before she even spoke, I saw it on her neck. A pendant with the ancient crest used by Wynwood's family, the original Glencowe crest."

Sol stiffened and leaned forward. "The crest on the pocket watch?"

"The same. That crest is not on any piece of jewelry in Wynwood's family—just a few portraits, and in the old family Bible. So when I saw that shining new pendant, I just … I was never so angry in my life. I knew in that moment that Wynwood was intending to replace me now that his mistress was with child. The first of all his string of women to become pregnant. *Including his barren wife.*"

"Laura." The word came on a breath, like a tender touch to her cheek.

"I attacked her, Sol. I wanted to grab that pendant." Her voice was getting higher, more hysterical. She must hold herself under control. "It was not my finest moment. I wasn't in my right mind, but it still embarrasses me to think of what I did. I scratched her face and her neck, because I thought that would hurt her the most. Aya had to pull me off of her."

She looked down at her lap, and realized she had gripped the fabric of her dress so tightly that it had torn. She forced her white-knuckled fingers to relax, but the hand that smoothed out her skirt shook violently. She saw the white of her petticoat under the rip in the silk.

"I have thought a great deal about that day since we found the pocket watch." She ran a finger along the tear in her dress. "I thought I knew the truth of what was going through Mrs. Jadis's mind—the superiority, the pity, the mocking. But now I realize I didn't know the truth at all ..." She looked up and met Sol's eyes squarely. "... now that I suspect what was *inside* that pendant."

He actually jolted in surprise. "You mean ... like the pocket watch."

"Yes. The same symbol. The same group. Sol, I think *she was one of them.*"

He had grown chalky white, and his breath came in short gasps. "I didn't know about the pendant, but ... we kept watch over her. We investigated her. And yet, we didn't know any of this."

He reached to drink his cold tea, but his hand was not entirely steady. When he set down his cup, he said, "But she died, didn't she?"

"Aya found out later that she had died that very night after I visited her. She slit her wrists in her bathtub." Laura bent her head and pressed her fingers to her mouth for a moment. "Sol, I thought *I* was the reason she killed herself and her baby."

Sol jumped to his feet, as if he were too restless to remain seated, but then he quickly joined her on the sofa and took her cold hand in his. "It wasn't your fault."

"You don't know that. I have spent years trying to justify myself and failing. The guilt has eaten at me because it is entirely possible that I am partly responsible for her death."

"You were not the one who cut her wrists," Sol said firmly. "And also, if there was that symbol inside the pendant ..." His hand briefly tightened around hers. "It may not have been suicide after all."

"I realized that." In the dead of night, when the guilt and the weight of her secrets pressed down on her chest and made it hard to breathe. "And if so, then they killed both Wynwood and his lover."

"The decanter *was* poisoned, Laura."

"I didn't know that then." She ripped her hand from Sol's

and covered her face. "We argued that night, Wynwood and I. About Mrs. Jadis, whom I had just confronted. I could still smell her cloying perfume. He began beating me, so much so that Aya tried to stop him because he was going to kill me." Her neck tightened as she remembered what else had happened in the library. "And while he was falling down those stairs, his lover was bleeding in a bathtub. All these years, Sol, I was the only one left to obsessively remember that."

He reached up and pulled her hands away from her face. He had a strangely searching look in his eyes, and she glanced away quickly.

"You didn't cause any of that, Laura."

"But it all made me intensely aware of the evil I am capable of, Sol." She couldn't look at him.

He squeezed her hand. "Look at me, Laura."

It took her a while, but she did. His eyes were the same as always, warm chocolate brown, compassionate and strong. She felt that she could draw his strength into herself like a river flowing into a lake.

"I admit, I was angry at first when I discovered you were keeping secrets," he said. "But now I realize that you have had to carry this weight with you."

"Because I was ashamed."

He reached out to touch the curve of her cheek with the backs of his fingers. "I know you. After all these years, I *know* you, Laura Glencowe, Lady Wynwood. You carry these things because you don't want anyone else to have to do so, and because you know you have the strength to bear it. It may be your sins, but it is also comprised of others' sins—Wynwood's, Mrs. Jadis's." He hesitated, then added, "Mine."

"Sol, what are you—?"

"I was supposed to know these things, Laura, and I didn't." His face had grown tense, and the muscle ticked at his jawline. "I was completely unaware that Mrs. Jadis was involved in this group with Wynwood. We suspected there were others behind Wynwood's brash words against the Crown, but not that they would kill him to shut him up. Nor that they would do the same to a pregnant woman. I had always trusted my judgment before, but now ...?" He looked down at his hand, which still held hers. "I am sorry I did not see this. I am sorry I left you unprotected. It was my job to ensure the innocent were not harmed, but I failed you."

"Sol, now you are the one trying to carrying this burden all by yourself."

He said nothing.

"Let us both accept blame for this, then, and try to move on. Now we know the truth—or at least a part of it."

He glanced up at her. "Do you know what happened to Mrs. Jadis's pendant?"

She shook her head. "I assumed her next of kin took it."

"She had none, as far as we could tell." His voice grew bitter as he added, "Not that our information was so very comprehensive. You probably knew more about her than we did."

"The pendant is lost to us, but Wynwood's order to the jeweler is not." Before, thinking about that order had caused her to feel a claw-like grip on her heart, but now after confessing her actions to Sol, she felt hardly a gentle squeeze. The order represented more of Wynwood's secrets that he had kept from her, but now, learning what they were was not the frightening pit of mysteries that it had been.

She took a deep breath. "Sol, I am doing what I ought to have done earlier—asking for your help."

Chapter Thirteen

Phoebe felt disoriented. They had been so very close to finding Mr. Ackett—they had *seen* him. He had been injured but alive, but for how much longer?

There was a soft sound from Keriah, standing beside her, but when Phoebe turned her head, Keriah's face was calm and composed. Perhaps a trifle *too* composed for the situation.

Mr. Rosmont looked to be almost in pain. It must have been worse for him to have been so close behind them but fallen prey to a trick.

Phoebe noticed that Miss Tolberton was speaking in a hushed voice with Mrs. Laidlaw several yards away from them. "What can we do next?" She spoke to Mr. Rosmont in a low voice, but she doubted that Miss Tolberton and Mrs. Laidlaw would be able to hear them.

Mr. Rosmont had a grim look on his face. "We need to know more about the men who took him."

"The large man carrying him had a mutilated ear," Phoebe said. "I think perhaps it was the man called Silas. Uncle Sol told us about Mr. Coulton-Jones fighting him. And I've seen the slender man behind him once before."

Mr. Rosmont's eyebrows drew down. "When?"

"At Mr. Farrimond's party. He was dressed as a servant. Mr. Coulton-Jones said that Nick was at the party looking for him and Mr. Ackett." It had likely been the same Nick whom Mr. Rosmont had fought earlier this morning.

He nodded slowly. "Mr. Drydale mentioned that. Did the man recognize you just now?"

"He didn't seem to. I look different from the last time he saw me. As far as I know, he thought I was simply a guest at the party."

"So they were most certainly part of Jack's group," Keriah said in a low voice.

Miss Tolberton was still speaking in urgent whispers to Mrs. Laidlaw, but now they appeared to be arguing. Miss Tolberton glanced at Phoebe, concern in her blue eyes, then turned back to Mrs. Laidlaw.

"They could have taken Mr. Ackett anywhere," Mr. Rosmont said. "A man like Jack would have several places in London where he could hide him."

"What do they want with him?" Keriah's frustration bled out in her tone.

"My guess is that they want *all of us.*"

Phoebe blinked at him. "Us?"

"Mr. Coulton-Jones, who has been asking about Jack. The pair of you, who put him down last night without killing him. Mr. Drydale and Mr. Havner, who drove away with him. I, who was asking questions about Silas and the man they were searching for. They want answers. They want to know who would dare to work against them."

Phoebe bit her lip, then asked, "How will you find him?" Because Mr. Rosmont did not strike her as a man who would simply give up.

He tensed as he studied them. Phoebe immediately knew she wasn't going to like what he was about to say. "I'll have to find out where Jack might have taken him, and the kinds of men who know information like that are dangerous. I can't take two women with me."

It was already growing late, the time of day when women shouldn't be walking the streets unless they had something to sell. Phoebe was willing to be prudent in this case, but she expected Keriah to object forcefully.

However, Keriah simply nodded, almost absently. "I will need to return to the apothecary shop to return the cart. I will also need to find a better way to disperse the compound from a distance, and we may need something stronger than the powder we made today ..." She began muttering more complicated words that Phoebe didn't quite understand.

Mr. Rosmont looked almost relieved. "I will escort you and Miss Gardinier to the shop. Then, if I can discover Jack's location, it would be best if Mr. Havner and Mr. Drydale were nearby in order to act quickly, perhaps at the apothecary shop. We must get word to them."

Phoebe generously didn't mention that he'd neglected to add their names to that list, but it was so laughable that two young women and two children could possibly be of help against a raging madman, she supposed she could excuse him.

"Calvin could return to my aunt's house faster than myself," Phoebe said. "But I will have him find a hackney for me." She glanced at Miss Tolberton. "And perhaps one more passenger."

Mr. Rosmont nodded, then headed up the aisle to exit the church to tell the twins.

Phoebe stepped slowly toward Miss Tolberton and Mrs. Laidlaw. Miss Tolberton had her head bent as Mrs. Laidlaw spoke in a firm but low voice, but the two women turned to Phoebe and seemed to welcome the interruption.

"What happened to Mr. Ackett was quite disturbing," Miss Tolberton said.

"Yes, it was quite a blow. We have been searching for him nearly all day."

"Do you know why they took him?" Miss Tolberton's eyes were guileless.

Phoebe was quick to shake her head. "Keriah didn't mention any gossip about his family, but I wonder if perhaps he was involved in something … unsavory."

Miss Tolberton gave a soft gasp, and Mrs. Laidlaw frowned.

"I dearly hope that is not the case," Miss Tolberton said. "He seemed like such a nice man the few times I have danced with him. What shall you do now?"

Phoebe fluttered her hands helplessly. "What can we do? Unless you might know, from your experience in this area of London, where they could have taken him?"

"No, of course not," Mrs. Laidlaw said quickly, with a frown. Miss Tolberton looked down at her hands, which were crumpling a handkerchief.

"Then it is probably best that we should leave, as it will become dark soon. Thank you for your hospitality and your help in this matter."

"Certainly, my dear." Mrs. Laidlaw had returned to her previous motherly tone and expression.

"Miss Tolberton, as we are heading in the same direction, would you like to share a hackney coach with me? My pageboy is fetching one for me now. Or were you intending to remain here for much longer?"

"I should love to share a coach with you." Her answer was quick and forceful. "Thank you for offering. It has grown too late for us to visit the family we had planned for today."

Mrs. Laidlaw gave Miss Tolberton a sharp look, but said nothing.

Keriah looked curiously at Phoebe when she appeared with Miss Tolberton, but said only, "Miss Tolberton, I do beg your pardon, but we shall part ways here."

"Oh?"

"I must return the cart to the apothecary shop, and so Ross will attend to me." She referred casually to Mr. Rosmont, standing respectfully nearby in the attitude of a servant, then curtseyed and left the church with him.

Miss Tolberton watched her. "She is very good friends with the apothecary, I believe you said?"

"His brother, actually. Dr. Shokes attended to Keriah's family in the country for many years before moving to town to help his brother at his shop." The two young women sat in a far pew in the sanctuary to wait while the twins searched for a coach for them. "Where has Mrs. Laidlaw disappeared to?"

"She mentioned she wanted to look for Mrs. Wright. It is very unusual for her to not arrive without sending a note. I do hope she has not somehow become involved in this terrible business." Miss Tolberton shivered delicately, in a feminine way that Phoebe could never manage. "Miss Sauber, it is certainly unusual for your families to allow you and Miss Gardinier to provide aid in this area."

"No more than your own charitable works with your group. What was it called again?"

Miss Tolberton told her, and Phoebe encouraged her to speak about the women she visited regularly.

"You must know a great many people in that area," Phoebe said cautiously. "Did you perhaps ... know something about the men who took Mr. Ackett away?"

Miss Tolberton paled slightly, making her lips turn darker pink when she bit them. "I must confess ... I recognized two of them."

She hesitated, but Phoebe remained calm and silently encouraging her.

"Mrs. Laidlaw did not wish me to tell you, since you were so concerned about Mr. Ackett and she feared what you might do once you knew. It is dangerous to speak of these men."

That had likely been what they had been arguing about. "Dangerous? Who were those men?"

"The larger man is called Silas. He works for a man called Apothecary Jack."

"Is he an apothecary, then?"

"Nothing of the sort!" Miss Tolberton looked frightened at Phoebe's question. "I have heard nothing but dreadful stories about him. He is said to know all sorts of deadly poisons that may be bought for steep prices."

"Good gracious. And the large man works for him?"

"Apothecary Jack wields a great deal of influence in the Long Glades ... and in other areas, also."

"Was Apothecary Jack one of the other men who took Mr. Ackett away?"

"I don't believe so, but I have never seen Apothecary Jack. I have only heard that he always wears colorful face paint."

"How unusual. But none of the men were so painted." Phoebe paused, then asked ingenuously, "Who else did you recognize?"

"The shorter man, in the dark blue jacket. I believe it was Mr. Elliot Brimley."

That was the other man who had been waiting outside, and who had run away with the other two. "Are you acquainted with him?"

"Truthfully, I am not acquainted with him, but one of the other women in our organization pointed him out to me once. I am more familiar with his sister-in-law, Mrs. Ellen Brimley. She married Mr. Brimley's younger brother, but she was tragically widowed last year."

"How terrible," Phoebe murmured. "How did he die?"

"It was a putrid illness, fairly common in this area."

"I suppose Mr. Brimley has been aiding his brother's widow?"

Miss Tolberton gave a moue of displeasure. "Hardly. Rather, Mrs. Brimley is caring for him as if he were one of her own children."

"Oh. But why was he with those men kidnapping Mr. Ackett? Does he also work for Apothecary Jack?"

"Well ..." Miss Tolberton tilted her head as she thought a moment. "He does belong to Apothecary Jack's gang, but he's been mostly on the fringes, according to Mrs. Brimley, while I believe Silas is one of Jack's favored men."

"I wonder why he was with them. Perhaps he has become more useful to Jack recently."

"Whatever he has been doing, lately he has been working close to Mrs. Brimley's home. He has been visiting her almost every day in the late afternoon because she cooks for him. Surprisingly, he has been giving her some money, also, when he has it."

"How kind of him."

"It is nothing more than what Mrs. Brimley deserves," Miss Tolberton said with a touch of fierceness. "She is raising her children alone, and the least her ne'er-do-well brother-in-law could do is help out a little."

Phoebe murmured agreement, suddenly realizing that her own father contributed less toward their income than Mr. Elliot Brimley did for his brother's family.

But Miss Tolberton's words also raised an excitement in her chest. Here was a clue she could give to Mr. Rosmont, who had the means to watch for Elliot Brimley and follow him. "Do you think Mr. Brimley will follow his usual schedule and visit his sister-in-law today?"

"I believe so," Miss Tolberton said slowly. "But what could any of us do about it?"

"Keriah's sister's servant, Ross, had mentioned that he wished to continue searching for Mr. Ackett. If I knew where Mrs. Brimley lived, I could tell him. He might be able to speak to Mr. Brimley, if he arrives."

Miss Tolberton looked troubled. "Mr. Brimley does not seem to be a disagreeable man, according to his sister-in-law, but his work for Apothecary Jack is rather … criminal. He will not speak to anyone about his employer so easily."

"It is our only hope," Phoebe said. "There is no harm in trying, is there?"

"I suppose not. And I had been hoping to also help in some way. But there is a problem. It may be very dangerous for me to be seen showing you Mrs. Brimley's home, and for you to be seen, also."

Phoebe agreed with her, but she pretended to be naively incredulous. "Would Apothecary Jack really have so many eyes all over London?"

"I have been warned that it may be so," Miss Tolberton said ominously.

"Well, perhaps you could direct the coach to drive past Mrs. Brimley's house and point it out to my pageboy? Then he may inform Ross at the apothecary shop."

Miss Tolberton brightened. "That sounds like a good idea. We shall both be protected, but I shall feel I have done something useful."

The door opened sharply and Calvin appeared. The twins had found a coach rather quickly, a surprising feat since they were not in an area where the residents often used hackneys. Miss Tolberton went to the sitting room to gather the basket she had brought with her and to inform Mrs. Laidlaw that she was leaving, so Phoebe took a moment to explain to Calvin what she wanted him to do.

Miss Tolberton spoke to the hackney driver before climbing into the coach. Clara climbed rather grudgingly in after them. She had wanted to go with her brother to relay messages to Phoebe's aunt and Mr. Drydale, but Phoebe had told her she was needed for propriety for herself and Miss Tolberton. She had no doubt Clara would have rather had an adventure speeding through the London streets by unconventional means rather than a ride in a smelly coach.

The driver took them along side streets and finally down a narrow corridor barely large enough to fit the coach. As they passed a series of doorways, Miss Tolberton pointed to one that had once been painted blue, but now was a faded gray with strips of paint peeling. "That is Mrs. Brimley's home, at least for now. She mentioned last week that she may need to move, as the rent is too dear for her."

"Thank you, Miss Tolberton. My pageboy will tell Lady Stoude's servant."

She shook her head. "I do not think Mr. Brimley will speak to him."

Calvin opened his mouth to say something, but thankfully Clara had her wits about her and kicked him in the ankle from where she sat next to him, and he closed his mouth again.

Phoebe thumped on the roof to tell the coachman to stop, and they let Calvin off at the far street corner. He gave her a slight nod before darting away, quickly disappearing in the foot traffic.

"My, he's very quick," Miss Tolberton said. "But I had thought we would go to the apothecary shop?"

"It is out of the way, and I had assumed you would wish to return home quickly."

"I would not have minded the stop. I have heard of Mr. Shokes's apothecary shop but have never been there."

"I suppose I should not be surprised you would not mind visiting such a place, since he serves the poor in this area, just as your organization does."

Miss Tolberton was pleased to speak more about her organization, and also to gently complain about some of the more close-minded members, until they arrived in front of her father's home on Green Street.

"Won't you come in?" Miss Tolberton offered to Phoebe. "I should love to continue chatting with you."

"I am afraid I must stop at Lady Stoude's home to inform her of the whereabouts of her footman."

"Will she be upset?"

"I am sure she will not mind. Keriah mentioned that her family is very worried about Mr. Ackett."

Miss Tolberton hesitated, then asked in a timid voice, "I hope you will not mind if I call upon you tomorrow? I am most interested in hearing what might have happened."

Phoebe wasn't certain what she'd be able to tell her, but she replied, "Of course you may. I should like to give you an update, if Ross is able to speak to Mr. Brimley."

"Oh, thank you. Have a good evening, then." And Miss Tolberton left them.

They waited until she had entered her home, then Clara gave a soft sigh as the coach pulled away. "She's terribly genteel, miss."

Phoebe gave her an arch look. "And I am not?"

"Most certainly not," Clara said frankly. "But it's what makes you interesting, miss."

Phoebe laughed. "I hope you know not to say that to any other young lady of the *ton*."

Clara gave her a look that clearly said, *Do you think I have potage for brains?*

Phoebe told the driver to change their destination from Lady Stoude's home to Aunt Laura's. She was not surprised to find the house buzzing with activity, nor to find Calvin had arrived ahead of them.

Her aunt bullied her into the morning room for a spot of supper while Phoebe told her everything that had happened. She'd likely heard it from Calvin, also, but Aunt Laura listened with great interest, regardless.

"What did Calvin say about Mr. Rosmont?" Phoebe was shoving food into her mouth as fast as she could use her fork and knife. Mr. Havner had returned earlier with the young woman, Hetty, and had gotten some rest, so he had said he would drive them to the apothecary shop as soon as Uncle Sol arrived. Her aunt had dispatched a note to Uncle Sol's residence as soon as Calvin returned.

"Mr. Rosmont was apparently very anxious to follow Calvin

to Mrs. Brimley's home in order to watch for Mr. Brimley."

"It did not occur to me at the time, but isn't it dangerous for Mr. Rosmont to be alone? Perhaps we should send Calvin back to him."

"I was about to tell Calvin to do so, but he said that Mr. Rosmont sent a strange message to relay to Sol. He said, 'Tell Mr. Drydale that *le petit prince* will be helping me.'"

The piece of beef on Phoebe's fork dropped to her plate. "I beg your pardon? Was it some sort of ... cipher?"

"Your guess is as good as mine. He refused to say anything more to Calvin, who would not have had the temerity to question him. I am waiting for Sol with bated breath."

Phoebe picked up her beef again and said rudely around her chewing, "I have a feeling Uncle Sol will not say anything, either."

"I am almost certain he won't, but it will be fun to needle him, won't it?"

Chapter Fourteen

As far as torturers went, Jack was by far the worst Sep had ever encountered. He hadn't encountered many—maybe six or seven of them—but they all knew what they wanted when they laid their hands on him. They worked with ruthlessness and sometimes even pride and pleasure.

Jack certainly had the ruthlessness, and the pride, and he had the pleasure in spades, but he didn't seem to know what in the world he wanted from Sep.

At first he punched Sep in the face, as if to warm him up. Then he asked a question about Michael—referring to him interchangeably as his *berserksgangr* or Berserker—and then he'd beat at Sep again without waiting for an answer. Only when the other man finally said something would he stop, and then only grudgingly.

The other man—the pale-eyed one—was getting frustrated with his partner, but he was also surprisingly patient with him. He didn't bat an eyelash at the man's strange behavior and foibles, answering his confusing questions as seriously as if they made sense.

"Do you think he has a heart to bleed?" Jack was asking now, lightly tracing over Sep's chest with the tip of a small knife. It looked like a plain, all-use tool rather than a weapon, and there were dark brown stains like blood on the scarred wooden handle.

"If he does, it can certainly be broken," the pale-eyed man responded from where he sat on a chair behind Jack. "Provided he's still alive."

Jack frowned at the light note of censure in the man's voice. "He's *mostly* alive."

Sep didn't have to fake his light, quick breathing since Jack had likely broken a few more ribs with his kicking. His jaw also felt thick and heavy, and his right eye was partially swollen from a particularly spectacular jab that had made him see multi-colored stars. Jack was stronger than other men he'd fought—with the exception of Silas and Nick—but he didn't have much in the way of training, which was perhaps fortunate for Sep.

"Can he still speak?" the pale-eyed man drawled, leaning over to peer at him behind the bulk of Jack's body.

"It's a little hard to tell since he hasn't spoken yet," Jack answered acerbically.

"It might be a good idea to allow him to speak, if he has a mind to."

"I doubt that." Jack poked harder with the knife, and Sep felt the tip break through his rough tunic and the skin of his chest. "Well? Are you up for speaking yet?"

Sep just panted, trying to focus his mind and to visualize shoving the pain away into a small box. Sometimes it worked.

"See?" Jack said. "It's as if he doesn't have vocal cords."

"Does he?"

"He cried out when I kicked him earlier."

Their conversation seemed too normal, considering he could smell his own blood on the floor, considering this place was not the common room of a club or a gambling den, but a dusty barn that smelled like horses.

When Jack had been beating him, he'd managed to get a look around in brief glimpses and had seen that he was in what looked like an empty stable. Or perhaps not so empty, because he thought he heard a few faint nickers, but the stalls nearest to him had no occupants, only dirty straw on the floor. He heard a dog—perhaps two—who occasionally barked from the far end of the building.

The ceiling was not unusually high, and it was split by wooden beams like sparse fish bones. There were some small windows near the eaves, most of them shuttered ... except for one.

The windows were too small for most men to slide through. Perhaps for Jack, who was very slender, but certainly not for the pale-eyed man, and Silas would likely not have gotten his head through. At first glance, Sep would have looked too broad-shouldered to fit, but he had honed his ability to slip through small, tight spaces. He knew he could make it through in the space of a heartbeat or two.

He'd also deliberately been rolling around the floor as Jack kicked and punched him, and he'd knocked his back against the wooden post between two stalls. He pretended to be stuck there, but in actuality he'd felt the bite of a very tiny piece of metal or stone sticking out of the floor in front of the post. Each time he jerked from Jack's blows, he ground the rope tying his hands behind his back against that tiny sharp protrusion. The rope was starting to loosen.

"Do you really think we'll get him to say anything?" Jack suddenly grabbed the front of Sep's tunic and pulled his upper body toward him, so that Jack's sour-ale breath blasted in his face as he demanded, "What did you use on my Berserker? How did you get him to stop?"

Sep stared at the wild eyes, which he realized were watery blue. He had seemed ageless because of the face paint, but this close, it was clear he was in his late twenties at most. His hair had been dyed a frighteningly nauseating yellow, but the roots were a plain dirty blond color.

Sep considered telling them they'd killed Michael. It might stop his questions about the sedative.

Or it might not. Jack had mentioned earlier that they couldn't be knocked out with a blow to the head. And Sep knew that it took immense strength to break a man's neck, especially a man that strong with rage. They were asking him because they knew that normal men couldn't have killed him, and they had seen them throw powder at Michael's face.

It also implied that they themselves did not have a chemical means of stopping a man who had taken the Root and gone mad. But why would they want something like that if any of the other men on the Root could simply stop one of Jack's berserkers?

Unless a man on the Root *couldn't* stop one of them.

Sep looked at Jack's blue eyes, which seemed to spin slightly with his madness. No, a man like Jack wouldn't care if he created a monster he couldn't control, as long as it didn't destroy something precious. "Control" wasn't something he valued or desired. Even the pale-eyed man exuded the confidence to efficiently handle anything that came at him.

Sep could believe they'd create something they couldn't stop. Naturally they'd be interested if someone did.

So he decided on a gamble, because maybe they'd reveal some information he didn't already know. "We killed him." He slurred the words through his swollen jaw.

Could they smell lies? It wasn't impossible if Silas could smell face paint from twenty yards away.

Jack tilted his head as he regarded Sep. Except that instead of a slight tilt, he twisted his head almost horizontal. It made Sep slightly dizzy to look at him.

Suddenly the pale-eyed man stepped forward and shoved Jack's face out of Sep's vision with a firm but gentle hand. "A bloodless kill? *We* could do that. But I somehow doubt *you* could."

And yet this pale-eyed man said it as if it were nothing to kill a man with bare hands.

He had said "we." But during the hours they'd had him, he'd never referred to their men as "us," only as "them." Sep had the impression he was speaking about himself and Jack, and not the other men on the Root.

Jack and this pale-eyed man were stronger—he'd felt that when Jack beat him. Even beefy Silas hadn't had the kind of force as this thin, strange man.

They were *different.*

He didn't know why that was significant, but he somehow knew it was.

The pale-eyed man kneeled in front of him and pulled Sep's tunic from Jack's fist. The fingers of his other hand reached up to caress Sep's swollen face. "Who are these people for whom you are remaining silent? You are not like other men I've known. You are ..." His face suddenly changed, as if he'd heard something that Sep hadn't. "You are *invisible.*"

Sep had thought he was too weak with pain to react, but he knew he must have, because the pale-eyed man smiled thinly. "In fact, you enjoy it." His voice held incredulity, then a faint softness, like longing. "You are overlooked. I can relate to that. I wish ..."

Suddenly Jack planted his foot on Sep's shoulder—the bleeding one—and shoved him away from the pale-eyed man. "I don't have the patience for your philosophical babble today."

The pale one jerked as his touch on Sep's face was broken, as if he'd been reading a book and it was yanked away from him. The eyes narrowed as they turned to regard Jack. "Beating him more is not going to get your answer."

Jack pouted like a child. "But it's certainly fun."

Did he want answers from Sep or not? Jack was too strange a character for him to understand.

"Besides," Jack continued, "I can just give him some of the

Root to heal his wounds. Oh!" The black-rimmed eyes grew wide and his blood-red lips formed a little O. "It can be an experiment. We can test what amounts will heal him or not." He gave a smile that might have been winsome on a young woman, but looked unnerving on his painted face.

The pale-eyed man rose to stand next to Jack. They were about the same height, but the pale man gave the impression he was towering over his strange partner. "Which batch is it?"

The smile disappeared from Jack's face, and he looked sullen. "Which do you think?" he snapped.

"If it's the new one, we don't know how he'll react to it." The pale eyes slid to Sep for a moment.

"He'll react like normal!" Jack sounded like he was throwing a temper tantrum.

"Oh?" The word was laced with scorn. "So he'll react like the last dozen men who took it? He'll turn into a raging monster and we'll have to kill him."

So Jack's latest batch was different. It had turned men into Jack's "Berserkers" rather than simply giving them that supernatural strength.

Weren't they concerned about what Sep was hearing?

Not if they intended to kill him anyway.

Since their attention had shifted from him, he began working more furiously at the bonds on his wrists.

But then he saw movement, and that ugly cat stalked into the stall like the queen into a drawing room. The animal seemed to see and understand what Sep was doing, and it hissed.

"Wouldn't you be better off figuring out why this batch is tainted?"

"It's not tainted!" Jack screamed, startling Sep. Jack began pacing and chewing on his fingers—not at his nails, but at his appendages. There were red marks from where he'd already gnawed at them, and also pink scars from healed bite wounds. "It's because the well is too close to the stinking river," he muttered. "Even the dancing girls swear the water makes their breasts less perky."

"Then perhaps it would be best to move." The pale man was leaning against the wall of an empty stall, and he casually crossed his legs. "If the water is truly the problem."

Jack's face went through an array of emotions that flashed across his features, one after the other—guilt, frustration, irritation, indecision.

Sep wondered what would happen to Jack if the problem wasn't the water.

He finally stopped pacing and pulled his bloodied fingers from his mouth. "I'll do more experiments first," he said in a growl.

"Please do." The pale man pushed away from the wall, then headed away from Sep toward the back of the building where he couldn't see. "We're running out of time."

"I know!" Jack sounded like a petulant child. He muttered to himself, "I'm so stressed! I need more treacle buns."

There was the sound of a wooden door opening, then closing.

Sep tugged at the rope. It was almost loose enough for him to break it. His eyes wanted to flicker up toward the window, but he kept his gaze on Jack, standing in the middle of the floor, absently chewing on his thumb knuckle.

But in a sudden fit, he grabbed the chair that the pale man had been sitting on and flung it hard against the side of a stall. The chair broke into large pieces, and the wall of the empty stall shuddered. Some of the boards cracked.

But Jack wasn't done. He turned toward Sep with a wordless scream erupting from his mouth. His blackened eyes seemed to burn like unholy coals.

There had been many moments when Sep had been afraid. But until this moment, he had never been so utterly terrified.

Jack stalked to where he lay on the floor, the cat streaking away, and without another word, without another question about the sedative, he lifted his leg and brought it crashing straight down on Sep's knee.

It was the injured one. It had been swollen and stiff, with an inner ache from his frantic escape from Silas. But with Jack's downward blow, he felt tendons tear, felt a *pop* deep under the kneecap, like an orange squashed under a carriage wheel.

He hadn't spoken in response to their questions, but now he howled, an inhuman cry that clawed up from his throat and ruptured from his lips. The pain shot down to his toes and up to his hips, a stabbing brand that set his muscles on fire.

It took him a moment to realize Jack was screaming right along with him, but Jack roared in anger and rage that rivaled the bellowing Berserkers. Sep waited for another blow, maybe something strong enough to rip his leg right off, but it never came.

As suddenly as he'd started, Jack suddenly stopped screaming. He straightened and gave Sep a look that was almost haughty. Then he slowly and carefully smoothed his dirty waistcoat with his bleeding hands and walked away from him. A few moments later, there was the sound of the door opening and closing again.

Sep's hands were shaking. He realized he'd ripped open his bonds. Jack must have seen that, too, but he hadn't cared.

Because he knew Sep wasn't going anywhere.

Oh, God ... He couldn't manage more than those words.

He had never before felt so completely alone.

Chapter Fifteen

He had lost the men who kidnapped Mr. Ackett. The bitterness of that burned at the back of Thorne's throat like bad gin.

But he could tell Miss Sauber was up to something. She had a way of speaking to her unfamiliar friend that was so unlike her true personality that it immediately raised his suspicions.

Miss Gardinier also had a surprised look on her face when Miss Sauber approached with Miss Tolberton at her side. The young healer woman parted from them calmly and walked with Thorne back to the apothecary shop with the cart.

"Phoebe thinks Miss Tolberton knows something important," Miss Gardinier mentioned to him, as if talking about the weather.

"I thought her behavior was strange, also. I shall wait for a few minutes after we arrive at the shop."

They were met at the shop by that scamp Calvin, who was still out of breath. After Thorne had stowed the cart away and Miss Gardinier let them inside the closed shop, Calvin told them about accompanying the women in the hackney rather than heading back to Lady Wynwood's home as had originally been planned, and about Mrs. Brimley's house.

"He's supposed to arrive there in the late afternoon, sir," Calvin said, his breath finally returning. "We should hurry."

They exited the back door. Thorne paused outside and looked

at Miss Gardinier in the open doorway. "Will you be safe here by yourself?"

She nodded. "Dr. Shokes and his brother are here."

"Miss Phoebe will probably come back as fast as she can, after riding home with that lady," Calvin added.

"But Calvin still needs to return home. Is it wise for you to wait for Mr. Brimley alone?" Miss Gardinier asked Thorne.

"I've been alone many times." In the last year he worked for the Foreign Office, he'd preferred working alone. He'd discovered that it was safer that way, for his partners.

"Against *those* men?" she asked in a low voice.

He hesitated. He remembered Nick, and the large man carrying Mr. Ackett as if he were a cloak thrown over his shoulder.

Then there was the scrape of a shoe against gravel. He wouldn't have noticed if it hadn't been so close to them.

There was a scruffy urchin suddenly several yards away, squatting against the side of the building. The boy hadn't been there a moment ago.

He turned an insolent face toward him, and a glass-green eye met his.

Miss Gardinier didn't notice the boy at first, but Calvin saw the urchin at the same time Thorne did, and jerked in surprise. He recovered in a moment, saying in a rough voice, "Here, now —"

"Leave him be, Calvin." Thorne turned away from the dirty boy and told Miss Gardinier, "I shall be fine. And you." He laid a hand on Calvin's shoulder.

The pageboy stared intently at the street urchin, but his attention riveted back to Thorne at his touch.

He lowered his voice. "Give this message to Mr. Drydale—or to Lady Wynwood, to give to Mr. Drydale. Tell him that *le petit prince* will be helping me."

"Huh?"

Both Calvin and Miss Gardinier had identical expressions of confusion.

"Give him the message, exactly as I said it. He'll understand."

Calvin sighed and nodded, but Thorne thought he heard him mumbling something along the lines of, "Weird secret passwords."

Miss Gardinier's eyes narrowed as she regarded Thorne. "Who, pray, is *le petit prince*?"

"He's an agent who will be helping me."

"And this agent couldn't help us earlier? You might have saved Mr. Ackett—"

"This agent isn't for work like that. And that's all I'll say about him. Weren't you going to use the stillroom?"

She glared at him, aware she was being brushed off, but thanked him for accompanying her. She closed the door and locked it.

Calvin led him to Mrs. Brimley's home, which was back in the direction they had come from and close to Brannon Church. At the top of the street, Calvin switched to a casual stroll, his hands in his pockets, for all the world like an apprentice craftsman heading home with his journeyman. Thorne's gait and posture also shifted, and they strolled until about halfway down the narrow street.

Calvin had been picking up random stones and throwing them at rats that had begun to appear in dark alleyways and running along the edge of the road. But then he threw a pebble at a door on Thorne's left.

They passed the door, and at the end of the street, Thorne nodded. "Good job. How will you return to Lady Wynwood's house?"

The cheeky boy grinned. "Secret ways."

He didn't like leaving the boy to race across these streets alone, although he knew that the urchins did so all the time, and this boy had grown up in places like these. "Stay safe," he muttered.

"Aw, are you worrying about me, sir?" He smiled, and then darted down the side street. He disappeared as if he'd turned into a puff of smoke.

Thorne headed back toward the house. The same urchin had suddenly appeared at a boarding house several doors down and across from Mrs. Brimley's door, squatting near the base of the building. He stopped and leaned against the wall next to the boy.

"I never expected to see you on English soil," he said in a conversational tone.

"Did you really think I'd stay away?" Prince answered with matching equanimity.

"I suppose not. Do they know you're here?"

"Hardly. I never allow them an opportunity to tell me no."

"What did you overhear?"

"I know who you're waiting for and why."

Thorne paused, glancing at the occasional pedestrian that passed them. "I don't want you to be injured. I'd never be able to face him if—"

"I'd never be able to face him if I didn't help find his friend."

There was silence between the two for long minutes as the light grew dimmer. Darkness came early on a narrow street like this, with the two and three story buildings blocking what little sun filtered through the haze from the chimney stacks. The street smelled strongly of garlic along with a faint scent of rotting meat.

"I thought you'd 'never work with normal folk ever again.' Those were your words, weren't they?" The boy scratched at the dirt caking his cheek.

"I didn't have a choice this time," he growled.

"So they got in the way and slowed you down?" But there was the hint of a laugh in the boy's voice.

He couldn't lie. "No, and you know it."

"The coachman saved your life, I heard."

He certainly couldn't deny that. "How'd you find out?"

"The girl. Hetty."

He straightened, rubbing a spot on his upper back against the wall of the house. "I didn't know you'd be able to speak to her."

"I didn't. I overheard her talking to m'lady."

"How did you manage that?"

"Right place at the right time," was the vague answer. "How about the kids? And the girls?"

So Prince had been watching them nearly all day, and Thorne hadn't even noticed the boy. "The kids used to be street urchins."

"Hmm." The boy tilted his head to the side. "I did think they looked kind of rough 'round the edges."

When Thorne didn't say anything else, Prince grinned and tilted sideways, jostling his knee.

"Stop that." That was his injured side, and the boy knew it. "The shorter one is more skilled a physician than I expected." He avoided speaking the women's names since they were in public. "She treated cuts and burns better than any of the sawbones I've met." Some of those doctors had been on a battlefield, and so he didn't hold their bedside manner against them, but even the ones in England lacked that professional gentleness Miss Gardinier had.

"I saw that."

Of course the boy had. "People liked talking to her. One of her patients told her an injured man had been sighted on Jay Street."

"Hmm." Prince nodded his head with interest.

"The other one ..." He sighed, girded his loins, and confessed. "She spoke to an old drunk I'd seen last night who wouldn't give me the time of day, and she got him to sing for a few coins."

The boy gave a cackling belly laugh. "She's a lot like the

archangel, you know," Prince said, using their code name for Michael.

Thorne frowned. "She was convincing, I gran—" He'd almost slipped into his nobleman's speech, right here in the middle of the Long Glades. He had to be more careful. The problem was that subterfuge and disguise like this were not his strong suits. "I was afraid she'd be like an excited child in a play and say something melodramatic. But she was believable. She didn't sound anything like her normal self. Almost as good as you and the archangel."

"Coming from you, that's pretty high praise. But I wasn't talking about her ability to playact or fool others." The boy glanced at Thorne, and he saw the gleam of glass-green. "She has that same sense of calm in tense situations, just like the archangel does."

That was an aspect of Michael that had always frustrated Thorne but which also garnered his deepest respect. When situations became dangerous, when Thorne was so tightly drawn that he was afraid his emotions would fire off like a pistol with a hair-trigger, Michael would instead be relaxed and cool. He could think more clearly and quickly than any other agent Thorne had worked with.

"She does?"

"You didn't see her when you ran off after the ... parcel." After Mr. Ackett. "The shorter one tends to react more emotionally, but not her. Calm. Logical."

"A man's true nature comes out in crisis."

"Didn't hers, last night?"

He'd heard about it from Mr. Drydale. She'd followed orders, and she'd fired a weapon at a man. He didn't know many gently born young women who would do that, but ... "I've yet to see it for myself."

"You wouldn't believe the things I've heard about her. If I were the captain, I'd recruit her in an instant."

Thorne tried to hide his surprise, and instead ducked his head and kicked at some pebbles. He had never worked with Mr. Drydale—the captain—and neither had the boy, but they had both heard many incredible things about his judgment and leadership. So it was unusual for Prince to think Miss Sauber would be worthy of working with the captain. And Prince was not so easily won over by agents. "What did you hear about her?"

"Things I shouldn't repeat, even to you."

He scowled, but the boy laughed and said, "There's a lot you can learn from servants. They like gossiping about the upper class, but they especially like it if the person they're gossiping about is unusual."

A man was walking along the opposite side of the street who looked similar to Elliot Brimley, although it was difficult to tell in the dim light and with the man's hat pulled low over his head. Thorne watched him without appearing to do so, but the man walked past Mrs. Brimley's house. "That meddlesome woman—" Not the best description of Lady Wynwood, but Prince would know immediately who he was talking about, "—is deeply involved in all of this. Mayhap the captain has already recruited the young lady."

"I doubt it, from all I've heard about him." Prince glanced up and down the street idly. "But I think in this case, he should take his help wherever he can find it."

"Because there are so few people he can trust?" Mr. Drydale had mentioned about the mole in the department, and his superior's secretive directive to find out more about this treasonous group.

"Because in this case, I think he needs unusual people."

"That's an odd way of putting it."

Instead of answering him, Prince said, "You've been pulling yourself away from people lately."

"What does that have to do with anything?"

"I understand. After all, there was a time when I pulled away from people, too." The boy's voice was distant, and Thorne knew why.

"Don't spend any time thinking about that rotten bucket of pond scum."

A grin flashed across the urchin's face, but it was too fleeting, because the pain went too deep.

He knew he needed to tell someone his shameful sin, or there would be more instances like Hetty's arm. Out of all the people he knew, wouldn't Prince understand Thorne's anguish? But he couldn't bear to tell Prince and then see the friend he'd known for so long shy away in horror.

Thorne didn't notice the silence between them until the boy broke it to say, "My point was that you've forgotten how to work with a team."

He was probably right, but Thorne didn't answer.

"You should trust them more."

"Who?"

The boy gave him a baleful side glance. "You know who."

The civilians. "They don't belong here."

"I think you're wrong. I think they do." The boy tilted his dirty head. "M'lady said that the girl *sparkles*."

"If she had been *sparkling* and drawing attention to herself, I'd have sent her home."

"Not that kind of sparkle. Never mind." Prince sighed. "Weren't you the one who told me that trust ensures a mission's success?"

Had he really said something that motivational? "Doesn't sound like me."

The boy laughed. "True. But you did say it. So now do it."

"They're not my team."

"They could be."

Of all the people in Thorne's life, only Prince could be this candid with him, because the boy was fearless. "You know, not even the archangel is this blunt with me."

"I know. Good thing you have at least one person being straightforward with you, isn't it?"

It was true. "I'm glad you're my friend." The words slipped out before he could think, and his face felt like a furnace as he realized what he'd said.

But the boy simply looked down at his shoes and didn't respond.

It was just as well. He'd known Prince a long time, before the boy became an agent for the Crown. But there were some secrets they were forced to keep from each other, and that created a distance between them that couldn't be crossed by friendship.

Without even looking in the direction of Mrs. Brimley's house, the boy suddenly said, "There he is."

A man had just left the house, dark hair a bit long, a tense way of walking, with clothes that matched the shorter man who'd been running alongside the other two. He must have arrived before Thorne and Prince did. He turned away from them and headed up the street.

The two loungers remained there for several heartbeats, then the boy said loudly, "I'm hungry."

"You just et," Thorne replied just as loudly.

"I'm still hungry."

He sighed. "Well, come on, then." Thorne walked after Elliot Brimley, trailed by the boy.

They hadn't far to go. A few blocks over was what had once been a thriving coaching inn. The inn's dilapidated stable had too few horses for its size, long and narrow, with a pitted dirt lane running along the long side opposite the inn. With the backs of several buildings on the other side of the lane, the area was fairly dark and would be pitch black when the sun set completely.

Dogs barked as Brimley approached the stable, and suddenly

two men appeared from the shadows.

"What're *you* doing here?" The smaller of the two had his face in shadow despite the tiny lamp on the ground behind him, but his voice clearly dripped with disdain.

"Mr. Dix asked me to come."

"Did he now? I don't see him here waiting for you." The smaller man laughed, but when his partner didn't, his amusement died down and he coughed.

"I led him to the man he caught," Brimley said, anger sharpening his voice. He added with a sneer, "Oh, but I'm sure it's not as important as guarding a door to make sure the horses don't escape."

The smaller man jerked forward, but the larger one laid a beefy hand on the slight shoulder. However, he said in a gruff voice, "Mind what you say about men doing their jobs, Brimley."

Brimley backed down quickly. "Yessir."

The stable door was barred from the outside, and the large man let Brimley in, then barred it behind him. While the stable looked shabby, the door's hinges didn't squeak and it looked to have been recently repaired with fresh wood, although it was difficult to be sure in the light from the lone lamp.

They overheard all this from their hiding place in the shadows, but then Prince abruptly stepped out and began walking along the lane that ran beside the stable. Thorne didn't know what the urchin was up to, but he remained hidden and watching.

Prince hadn't gotten within twenty yards of the building when the dogs barked again. They were apparently inside the stable, but near the door being guarded.

The urchin had his hands in his pockets and his head down, the picture of a boy not wanting any trouble. He walked quickly, keeping his eyes averted from the pair near the door as if he didn't even see them. Thorne couldn't see them clearly either, but he caught the tiny gleam of light reflecting off their eyes as they followed the boy's figure until he was out of their sight. The dogs continued to bark for several minutes, far beyond when the boy would have reached the end of the street, until one of the men knocked a fist against the closed door and sharply ordered the dogs to be quiet.

Thorne slowly backed away from his hiding place so that the men couldn't hear him, then left and made his way to a parallel street where he thought the boy would end up. He loitered next to an open doorway, but was chased away by an irate woman wielding a broom. He found another corner that gave him a good view of two streets and waited.

He didn't have to wait long. The boy seemed to appear from a doorway nearby and ambled up to Thorne, taking a casual stance next to him.

"There's another door on the other side of the stable. Also guarded."

"How many?"

"I could see three, but there may be more nearby. That dirt lane ends at a larger street with lots of homes, lots of windows facing that end of the stable."

"Dogs, too?"

"No dogs on that side of the building, but the men are less lazy. Their boss might be near that side, but I couldn't get close enough to see. One of them called out to me."

He tensed. "What did you do?"

The boy repeated the curse word he'd used. While Thorne sighed at the way he insulted the stranger's manhood, it would have been unusual for him not to curse the guard right back.

"They're more nervous at that door," the boy added.

"I saw windows near the eaves, but they looked closed," Thorne said.

"Most of the ones I saw were shuttered, too. One was slightly opened, but the windows are too small. Only a skinny man or a child could get through."

"The dogs would probably hear anyone who tried that."

The boy had dropped his head, but Thorne could see him give a curt nod.

"There's no way to approach from the other side?"

"I tried getting a good look, but I don't think so." The boy peered up at him, and instead of the dirty, squinty eyes of an urchin, they were the clear, serious eyes of *le petit prince*. They were Michael's eyes, and Richard's eyes. It always struck him at odd moments, when he saw those eyes, as if it were the three siblings' bond with each other.

"You're going to need a clever way inside," Isabella said to him. "Let me know later if you need me. I'll be watching over you." Then she turned and disappeared into the night.

Chapter Sixteen

When Jack returned, he went back to beating Sep, not asking any questions, just using his fits and his feet. The blows weren't as hard as before, and it was almost as if Jack were doing it half-heartedly. The cat crouched nearby, watching with what seemed like fascination and pleasure.

Finally he stopped, perhaps because he was tired, but more likely because he was bored. If it were any other man, Sep knew that the constant punching and kicking would tire his captor quickly, but this was Apothecary Jack. He had the Root, and he had his own method of madness that kept his body fueled in mysterious ways.

Sep was a mass of agony. Some of that pain was a dark feeling, like a murky pool in a deep cave, a feeling of being shut out from the world, of being shut away from God.

But even his emotional turmoil couldn't distract his mind from the damage that had been done to his body. His ribs were on fire. He didn't know how he could still breathe. They had retied his wrists with thicker rope, and more of it, and it rubbed into his skin even as the blows made him jerk his wrists apart. With each of Jack's kicks, a fiery hot spear stabbed at his knee, made worse because he would involuntarily pull against the ropes that had been ringed around his ankles. The blows had stopped but not the throbbing and the sizzling he felt along his skin.

He tried to concentrate, to shove the feeling away, to pretend he didn't feel anything. But his brain was too sluggish, the sensations too sharp. They were stabbing at his mind to try to eradicate his memories, his reason.

And then suddenly he remembered that angelic face hovering above him. Gray eyes, honey blonde hair. She hadn't been a real angel, but she had made him feel that God had sent a protector to watch over him.

She wasn't here now, when he was at his lowest, and yet he still felt like she was watching over him. And the thought of her drew his emotions up from the cold, dark pool it had fallen into. He still felt the pain, but she was with him.

The next thing he knew, he was slowly waking from a light doze. He heard voices, but his mind and heartbeat were not quite back to normal, and so the sounds drifted into his ears and only formed words slowly and gently. There was warmth and yet something heavy lying on top of his knee, paining him, but he couldn't yet move to do anything about it.

"I think you're too focused on whatever they used on him." That was the pale-eyed man, with his smooth and yet sharp voice. "You can't even say if it will be of use to us or not."

Us. He was talking to Jack and yet he'd used the word, "us." The pale man was perhaps part of that mysterious group.

Jack's higher pitched, harsher voice grated as if he was losing his temper. "I *told* you, if I knew what they used, it might be helpful, but I won't know until I know what they used."

The pale-eyed man seemed to be walking away from Sep, because he heard the soft thump of footsteps, and the man's voice was softer. He couldn't hear everything he said, just a few words—"won't be happy," and "waste of time."

"I don't care if he thinks it's a waste of time." Jack sounded petulant, his voice much louder than the other man. "He isn't here in London, making the Root and making us money, is he?"

They were talking about someone else besides the two of them. There were perhaps more of them in the group.

The pale-eyed man sighed, a long enough breath that Sep could hear him even though he was farther away. But he didn't refute what Jack was saying.

"Whatever they used to put my Berserker to sleep, it could stabilize the Root. No matter where I grow it, no matter the differences between generations."

The pale-eyed man said something else, and Jack responded impatiently, "It's not strong enough."

The man shook his head and turned to walk back toward Jack. "This is still a bad idea."

"Anything I can try to solve our problem will take time we don't have." Jack sounded almost sane as he said it.

"It isn't really *our* problem—it's *yours*, isn't it?" The man's voice was flat. Sep somehow knew he was incredibly angry. It was as if the waves of fury were softly rolling off of him, the way the mist rolled off the river.

Jack gave a wordless sound of exasperation. "Whatever you say, it doesn't solve anything! Whether it's my problem or yours or our crazy Farmer George's problem, it still needs to be solved. I would think you'd be happy to do this."

"I don't like wasting resources. We don't know if they'll come."

"But if they do, you'll get to see their faces, won't you?"

The pale man said nothing. Then he sighed and said, "He's awake."

Sep himself hadn't been aware he was fully awake, and yet the man had known despite standing several feet away from him. He didn't want to open his eyes, but he also didn't want to be caught unaware by whatever Jack wanted to do next to him.

The warmth suddenly removed itself from his knee, causing it to stab with pain. The cat had been draped over his swollen limb, almost as if it knew it would torture him.

Jack scurried over to him, dropping to his knees on the dirty wooden floor and sticking his face close to Sep's again. At some point he'd changed his facepaint. Around his eyes was a small circle of orange, and then around that were slightly larger circles of white. His lips were also traced in orange, and then rimmed with white. And around the white, coloring the entire rest of his face, were various shades of green in splotches, dotted with narrow thorns of yellow and brown, like leaves on a bush.

"I have such a delicious plan for you." The excitement on his face was obvious, from this close up. "I can't wait for them to show up." And then the smile slowly faded, and the eyes became hard and glittering. His voice deepened as he growled, "*I want you to feel my pain.*"

Men's voices drifted toward them from the other side of the stable, annoyed, curious, unsure. Jack frowned, irritated to be interrupted, and leaped to his feet with a speed that made Sep blink.

He couldn't see clearly because he'd been dragged into a stall at some point, so his only view was out the open doorway where Jack disappeared. He heard sets of feet walking ... three? No, two men. One in heavy boots and the other in softer shoes. They stopped several stalls down from him, so he couldn't hear clearly what was said. Then one set of feet—the ones in boots—walked away.

The next voice he heard made him freeze.

"I came willingly." The man stuttered, and higher pitched than the last time Sep had heard him—speaking to his wife and his brother at his apothecary shop.

"Yes, but it does make me wonder why," Jack drawled.

"I can help you make the sedative. The one they used to stop —"

"*What did they use?*" Jack roared. Sep flinched in surprise.

"Who were they?" The pale-eyed man's voice was softer, but no less intense.

"Ah ... ah ..."

"One at a time, *me first*." Jack spoke through gritted teeth. "What did they use?"

"Ah ..." Mr. Farley Shokes's voice became even higher, with the level of his fear. Sep wondered if Jack were threatening him, but then his next words explained his fright. "I don't know exactly what they used ..." There was an awful silence, then Mr. Shokes continued, "... but I can tell you what instruments they took out—I think—and what herbs they seemed to have used."

"Calm down," the pale man said, and it was clear he was talking to Jack. "He won't be able to give you any information if you look at him that way. Now, tell me." He sounded gentle and soothing. "Who exactly made this sedative?"

The edges of his vision began to blacken, and Sep realized he had stopped breathing. Surely Mr. Shokes knew what would happen to Miss Gardinier and Miss Sauber if he told the pale-eyed man their names? There would be nowhere they would be safe. He would be essentially handing them over to Jack.

Sep's hands had been retied behind his back, but he began furiously working at them again. He had to stop him. He couldn't lie here and let him speak those names. He'd die first.

"Hmm, our other guest is upset," the pale man said. He must have heard Sep's struggles, even from so far away. "I know one of them was a woman. I saw as much last night."

"I ... I didn't know their names," Mr. Shokes finally said. "They just ... used my stillroom."

He was a terrible liar. Sep expected to hear the sound of a fist striking the apothecary in the face or the stomach, but instead came a much more terrible sound—Jack's dulcet tones, like a duchess inviting the man for tea. "Come now, don't be like that. You'll make my friend upset, and if you think I'm strange, he's even worse when he's angry."

"You're going to make him—ugh, there, he did it."

The sharp smell of urine assailed him only seconds later.

"Oh, you poor thing." Jack was still attempting to placate Mr. Shokes. "What was your name again?"

"F-F-Farley Shokes."

"Mr. Shokes, I think we have another pair of trousers for you. Then let's talk more about that sedative. That's an easier topic of conversation, isn't it?"

They moved away, and then suddenly the pale man was standing in the open doorway to the stall. Sep hadn't even heard him move.

The man looked down at him with an inscrutable expression for a moment, then he suddenly bent down, tugging his glove from his hand. His eyes were heavy and lifeless lumps of lead.

"I'm going to kill your friends." The voice was just as heavy and lifeless. "The ones who took Jack's Berserker last night. The ones who have left you here to die. Why do you remain silent? Don't you know they've abandoned you?"

The words he used struck all the harder because of how Sep's prayers had seemed so empty.

"I do not make empty threats." The man leaned closer. "Think about them one last time before I kill them."

And then his fingers were on Sep's face.

There was a slight pain in his forehead, then a buzzing in his ears. But the pale man looked like he was in even more pain, with the skin tightening around his eyes and his teeth clenched together. His breathing came fast and light.

The touch was only for a minute. Finally, words exploded from the pale man's bloodless lips even as his fingers trembled against Sep's temple.

"The archer! The coachman!" It sounded as though he were demanding it from Sep.

Sep didn't know who the man was talking about. Lady Wynwood's coachman? He'd barely spoken to the man.

"The man giving orders to you!"

He had been trained to do everything he could to protect

them. He kept them locked away in the depths of his mind, the safest place to keep them when being tortured like this. Something he'd discovered by experience, unfortunately.

"Why aren't you thinking about them?!"

Sep didn't think he could hide his confusion, not with the amount of pain he felt, and not with the strangeness of the man's words. Jack had often said things that seemed unrelated to reality, but this ... it was almost as if ...

"Why are you only thinking about that girl?!"

She was still watching over him, her gray eyes that seemed to keep his mind afloat when it only wanted to drift down into the cold and dark. How had the pale man known that he'd been holding onto her for his lifeline?

Then the man drew his hand back. He was panting, and his eyes had become bloodshot. He also looked incredibly frustrated. Sep somehow knew that was a good thing.

The man regained his composure quickly, standing and tugging his glove back on. It was fine leather, to match his finer clothes, which were of more somber colors than Jack's, but still expensive material. Practical clothing, rather than at the forefront of high fashion. But at the same time they were the cut and color that would enable him to blend into any crowd, whether poor men or rich men.

There were sudden steps rapidly returning, and the pale man seemed slightly embarrassed as he turned to face Jack.

"What were you doing?" Jack drawled, and yet there was an edge to his question that seemed to ask something else entirely.

"Nothing," the pale man answered curtly.

Sep knew he'd discovered something significant. The pale man's behavior was something he desperately wanted to keep from Jack for some reason.

He couldn't quite believe what it appeared the man had been doing when he touched him. He didn't think such a thing was possible. It also made him feel vulnerable, a stain on the one place of safety he had, his own mind. It had been invasive, as if the man had forced his way into Sep's home and peed in his bed.

Was it possible because of the Root?

Jack leaned against the doorway to the stall and gave Sep a smile that felt like a blade drawn down his spine. But when he spoke, it was to the pale man. "You feel it, don't you? The need to give him the Root."

There was a struggle on the man's face at Jack's words, as if he wanted to deny it but couldn't. And Sep realized that he really did feel something powerful, something he couldn't understand.

The pale man finally replied, "It doesn't need to be done right away. We could try to find out more about what he knows."

"He's not going to tell us. Even you can see that." Jack spared Sep another creepy smile, then turned that upon the pale man. "Why, do you have some other little tricks up your sleeve to *pry open his mind*?"

His last words were as pointed as a wooden stake, but the pale man's eyes and face remained as cool as white marble. "It would be less messy if we had something like that."

Jack scoffed. "Messy is fun."

"I only worry because I don't want you to kill him too soon."

"If it looks like he's going to die, I can just give him the Root."

"And if it turns him into a Berserker?"

"Well then … we'll both win, won't we?"

The pale man didn't answer, but looked over at Sep, then back to Jack.

Jack continued, "From what Maner said, there are people searching for an injured man from last night. That means they're close, they're breathing down our necks." Jack sounded more and more excited. "And they'll hear when he becomes deranged and come to *rescue* him rather than killing him. Won't that be wonderful?"

The man frowned. "It'll completely destroy the stable."

Jack waved a careless hand. "I don't care. It isn't as if I'm still using it. So what do you think? We turn him into a Berserker, and then let him loose!" Jack's voice was exultant with victory and he spun in a pirouette on the balls of his pointed leather shoes. "I'll have whatever they use to save him, and ..." He stopped in front the pale man and pointed a finger at his chest. "... you'll have *them.*"

The pale man sighed. "Yes, I suppose that's true. But we wait until they're close."

"Of course, of course. I stationed my men close by but out of sight."

The pale man began walking away. "I must leave. I'm meeting with a seller."

"Does he need more blood already?" Jack asked, as if discussing flour or sugar. "That was quick."

The pale man left the stable, and Jack headed back toward where he'd led Mr. Shokes, leaving Sep alone.

Sep's mind whirled with everything he'd heard and seen. A part of him wanted Mr. Drydale to come for him, but who else would help in the rescue? Who was the archer the man had mentioned?

But if they came, Jack would only turn Sep into that ... Berserker. It was entirely likely that Miss Gardinier and perhaps Miss Sauber would accompany them, since they had been the ones working on the sedative.

If his rescuers weren't killed, they'd fall into Jack's hands. If they succeeded in sedating him, Jack would discover what they'd used to do it.

And all the while, Mr. Shokes was only a fear-soaked minute away from cracking under the pressure and telling them about Miss Gardinier and Miss Sauber. And maybe even the sedative, if he was able to discover enough from searching in his stillroom.

He couldn't allow Jack to turn him into a raging monster, to harm Mr. Drydale and whoever else came with him. He also couldn't allow Jack to get a sample of the sedative, which he seemed to need for his tainted batch of the Root.

The cold, hard, logical course of action would be to kill himself. While Sep had been willing to die on any of his missions, his superiors had known he was unwilling to commit murder or suicide. After feeling so close to God so many times, he couldn't take a life that the Almighty had created. Only God had that right. And that included Sep's own life.

But what could he do? The panic began welling up inside of him, an acidic bubbling in his gut.

God, help me.

No sooner had he silently prayed that simple prayer when someone entered the stable, from the door where the pale man had left. The door's hinges were silent, but it rattled in the ill-fitting frame as it opened.

Jack must have also heard it, because his footsteps approached. But he remained outside of Sep's field of view, which was bounded by the doorway to the stall.

A minute later, a man appeared. He was shorter than Jack and Maxham, with long dark hair, but he carried himself quite tightly, as if his muscles had forgotten how to relax. He had a gray hat, a mass of fabric that was somehow larger than his narrow head. His eyes darted everywhere before bouncing to Jack and giving him a subservient bob of the head.

"Brimley," Jack hissed at him, "what are you doing here and not where you were supposed to be—out of sight?"

"Silas sent me to tell you that he was forced to move locations." Brimley's voice was pitched a little high, and his Adam's apple bobbed. His eyes slid toward Sep, and a toothy smile spread across his face, with the edges of his mouth nearly touching his ears. "How nice to see you here." He laughed at his own joke until Jack's hand whipped out and smacked him in the head. His hat flew off.

"You gave your message. Now get out of my sight." Jack had stepped forward and now Sep clearly saw the irritation in his face.

Brimley's mouth worked side to side. "Do you need me to stay here to help? You don't have anyone here on the Root—"

"Shut up, you dolt!" Jack hissed at him, with a glance at Sep. But then his mood once again shifted faster than a clock pendulum. He gave Brimley an almost fatherly smile. "Actually, I have a very important task for you."

"Yes, Mr. Dix?"

"Go get me some treacle buns."

Brimley blinked at him. "Treacle buns?"

"Treacle buns."

His face became sullen. "At this hour?"

"Be quick about it." Jack's voice had lost the fatherly tone and now held the crack of a whip. "I'm going to talk to my s-s-s-stuttering little apothecary or doctor or whatever he's calling himself." Jack left Brimley standing there. With Sep.

Brimley at first seemed to have forgotten Sep's presence. He ground his teeth, his hands clenching and unclenching. Sep hadn't thought he could look even more tightly wound, but he did now.

Then he turned toward Sep, and a cruel light came into his eyes.

He approached the open doorway to the stall, and suddenly a knife had appeared in his hand. Gloating, he crouched down. "It's too bad Mr. Dix has plans for you. I'd have liked a crack at—"

Sep took advantage of his exaltation to snap out with his bound feet and kick the knife from Brimley's hands. He had considered trying to knock it down in the stall so he could attempt to grab it, but he decided it was more important for Brimley to be denied its use. The metal flew through the air and ricocheted off the stall opposite, flinging in an odd angle even further away from its owner.

"You!" Brimley bounded to his feet.

Sep attempted to kick at his knees, just as he'd been crippled, but his swollen joint slowed his movements, and he missed. He twisted around to try to keep his feet aimed at Brimley's body as the short man kicked out at him, but then he landed a glancing blow to his knee that sent his head spinning.

Brimley kicked at Sep, but his blows were wild. Some landed on his thigh, some on his ankle, several to his bound hands at his back.

But Sep realized Brimley wasn't on the Root. His blows were like pillows compared to Jack's.

"What are you doing?"

The harsh voice came from a tall man who had suddenly appeared. He had a handsome face, with a wide jaw and a strong, dimpled chin, and curly black hair.

Brimley immediately stopped, although he had a sullen look on his face. "I was just talking to my friend, here."

"Mr. Dix gave you a job. I suggest you do it before he finds out you're still here." The man's deep voice was even, not sneering or sarcastic, but stern and critical.

Brimley shuffled out, followed by the dark-haired man, who not only appeared to have some authority over him, but appeared to intimidate the other man. He might be on the Root to be able to cow Brimley so thoroughly. Brimley had said that there weren't any men on the Root in the stable, but perhaps he'd rectified that situation.

It was even more urgent for Sep to escape, even if he had drag his knee after him.

His hands hurt from where Brimley had kicked him, but as his thumb throbbed, it suddenly reminded him of something

Michael had told him once.

It was when they'd been escaping from the botched mission. They'd hitched a ride on a smuggler's boat that was unfortunately carrying gunpowder, and a careless flame from one of the smugglers had caused it to explode when out at sea.

They'd grabbed onto pieces of wood from the wrecked boat and started swimming. But while Sep's family estate was near the sea and he swam even when the waters were too cold for a sane man to brave, Michael wasn't as strong a swimmer. They'd stopped often for him to catch his breath. During those breaks, he told amusing stories, perhaps to keep his mind off the desolate surroundings of the open waters of the Channel.

One story had been about when he'd been chained to a wall in a different prison, a year or two before Sep had met him. The way he'd escaped had made Sep cringe, but it was his throbbing hands now that triggered that tiny, insignificant memory.

He could escape. He knew exactly how, if he could steel himself. But what was more pain compared to what he'd already endured for the past night and day?

He waited a few minutes, until the pain from Brimley's blows had begun to fade, especially the sharp accidental blow to his knee. Then took several deep breaths.

This was going to hurt.

It was more difficult than he had anticipated to dislocate this thumb. He tried several times, but only managed to sprain it.

Then Brimley returned from his errand, much faster than expected. He was munching on a treacle bun while holding some in a none-too-clean napkin against his chest.

Sep froze when he heard the back door to the stables open and then the sound of footsteps approaching, but Brimley only passed the open doorway to the stall and continued toward a room along the side of the stable, set in between the stalls. He could clearly hear Jack's voice, "Wouldn't you like a nice treacle bun?" He must have been speaking to Mr. Shokes. Then in a sharper tone, "You were quick."

"The innkeeper's wife next door had bought some earlier today," Brimley replied.

"I suppose I'm not really complaining, but we barely had time for our chat, did we?"

Mr. Shokes didn't answer Jack, whose tone sounded menacing even though the words were sweet.

Then the dogs started barking.

Unlike before, they didn't stop, perhaps because whatever set them off hadn't left the vicinity and the guards were too lazy to silence them.

Sep belatedly realized he could use the sound to mask his grunting efforts. It was as he rolled onto his back to try to find the right leverage that he looked up at the dark ceiling of the building.

And what he saw made him smile.

Chapter Seventeen

Durbin Street was well-lit by a series of brothels, some looking more clean than others, some loud and raucous, others quiet and more discreet. Thorne tried to pretend to smile at the women who approached him, but something in his face made them veer toward his companion instead.

Mr. Drydale was much smoother in his regretful refusal of their services for the evening. There were a few girls who were painfully young, and Mr. Drydale slipped some coins into their thin hands.

"It would help if you would look less like a man about to start a fight," Mr. Drydale murmured to him.

"I *am* about to start a fight."

"But not with these women." He smiled and put off another prostitute, this one a bit older and full-blown like a faded rose.

He huffed. "It's too difficult for me to switch mindset. I'm either a gentleman on the street or I'm a brawler. And I can't do what we need done if I'm a gentleman." It had been easier for him to pose as a servant earlier this afternoon after chasing after Mr. Ackett's captors. It might have been a disaster if he'd had to pose as himself, a gentleman of the *ton*, in front of Miss Tolberton and Mrs. Laidlaw.

"I suppose I can understand that. We haven't passed it, have we?"

"It's here." They turned left at the corner onto Kirkhouse Road, a narrow street lined with a mix of alehouses and miscellaneous shops, and walked only a block before pausing at the entrance of an even narrower dirt lane on their left. Along one side was only a long stable, while along the other side stood the backs of the brothels they'd just passed on Durbin Street.

Sol frowned. "Are you certain about this?"

"This is what I was trained for." He flexed his hands. Finally, he'd be able to unleash this thing inside of him that was clawing at his stomach. He could unleash it upon men who had harmed others, who would try to stop them from rescuing Mr. Ackett.

That's what he told himself. It was like a leash made of thread, roped around the neck of a rabid dog.

Mr. Drydale gave him a level look that Thorne couldn't read, then he nodded and walked down the nameless dirt lane.

Thorne continued on Kirkhouse Road for another block, turning left at the corner at a darkened shop whose sign was so faded he couldn't read it. After another block, he turned left again onto Fuller Lane. He had his hands in the pockets of his disreputable trousers, wearing the old boots he took from his steward in exchange for a new pair for the hard-working man. The steward's hat also sat on his head, a wide-brimmed style typically favored by a man from the countryside, and smelling faintly of cow dung. As the women had on the other street, the men on this one avoided looking him in the eye and often veered a few steps away from him than absolutely necessary.

He slowed his steps as he approached an inn. There was laughter and loud talk as well as the sour smell of old ale and the sharper smell of urine from a drunk standing on the side of the road and relieving himself. Beyond the inn stood a separate building that was the stable, and alongside that lay the narrow dirt lane.

Across the cobblestone street in front of the inn were a series of boarding houses and brothels. One brothel in particular had small open windows facing the street, shaded with curtains that were edged with gentle lamplight. However, no shadows moved in that front room, and there were no lights on the floor above. Other brothels had women moving in and out of the front doors, but this one had its door firmly shut.

Thorne stopped just shy of the inn, near a darkened forge, then crossed the street. He leaned back against the wall of a boarding house, the wood unusually warm from a roaring fireplace or stove inside. And he waited.

He didn't wait long. Within minutes, dogs began barking from within the stable, but no raised voice hushed them. Soon a figure in the distance tottered along the dirt lane, stumbling on potholes. He must have wandered close to the stable wall for support and woken the dogs. He paused at the corner, swaying on his feet, then turned the corner. He meandered toward the center of Fuller Lane, his steps slow and shuffling.

Suddenly an empty post chaise came down the street at a good clip, but when the driver saw the unsteady drunken man, he sharply reined in the horses until the vehicle came to a stop about halfway between the open inn door and the barred front door of the stable.

"Oy! Get out of the way!" the coachman yelled at the drunk.

The inebriated man simply looked up at the coachman and doffed a rather fine hat. "My good man, you're blocking the road."

"You're the one blocking the road!"

"I am not. I'm having a nice stroll and searching for a certain esh-establishment." He said the last word with the precise pronunciation of a man trying not to sound as pickled as he really was.

"There's plenty of those around here. Pick one."

"It must be a particular one. A particular lady is awaiting my call. But I do believe I am lost—"

"I don't care if you're searching for China, get out of the way," the coachman said.

The drunken gentleman drew himself up. "You're very rude. Why should I do as you say?"

The coachman jumped down. "I'll make you move."

"Oy!"

At first, Thorne didn't see the source of the voice, since the post chaise was in the way, but then a tall, heavy man appeared next to the drunk and the coachman. "What are you doing?"

"About to have a brawl," the drunk said haughtily, although the way he limply put up his fists made him look like he was trying to pet a dog. "Stay out of the way."

The heavy man grabbed the drunk's arm. "Not here, you're no—"

The gentleman suddenly stopped weaving like he was three sheets to the wind and responded with a jab to the nose that knocked the man's head back. He was about to follow up when the coachman stepped in and swung a roundhouse that connected solidly with the heavy man's jaw directly to the side of his chin. He fell to the dirt, unconscious.

"I could have done that." The gentleman sighed. "You're undermining my masculinity."

"I was too wound up," the coachman replied.

Despite this strange conversation, Thorne still waited, leaning against the wall and cloaking himself with the deepening evening shadows. The carriage had hidden the blow from view, and there was no outcry from anyone on the street or from the inn.

The coachman and the gentleman disappeared from sight behind the carriage. There was the faint, uneven sound of dragging something large and heavy. The coachman returned to lead the hired post chaise around toward the stable doors, and the unconscious guard was nowhere to be found.

The barking continued to ring in the chilled air, and irritated voices from the inn called to the stable to shut the dogs up. Thorne continued to wait, but now a buzzing vibrated through his gut. This was wrong. Something was wrong.

As the post chaise drew closer to the front of the stable, the dogs' barking frenzy increased. The gentleman and coachman seemed oblivious to anyone else who might be on the street, even if they had seen Thorne, hidden by the corner of a building and by darkness.

And no one responded. And the dogs continued to bark.

The clock was ticking. Thorne shifted uneasily.

Finally the gentleman made a strange sweeping motion with his hand above his head. Thorne left his partially-hidden space, glancing up and down the deserted street before joining them before the stable.

In his earlier reconnaissance, Thorne had only seen one guard at each door, and he had suspected this one wasn't on the Root because his hearing had not seemed bothered by the loud barking of the dogs. Mr. Drydale had agreed with him that there were likely more guards hidden in the buildings nearby.

So they had expected a trap of some sort once they took out the guard. Thorne had been ready with a surprise ambush on anyone who responded from the surrounding buildings, and Miss Sauber had been in hiding nearby with an arrow laced with sedative paste strong enough to take out a man on the Root.

But no one had arrived, and that made him nervous.

"Hurry," Mr. Drydale said. Thorne couldn't see to whom he was speaking until a small pair of street urchins appeared as if from out of the evening shadows at his elbow. They were accompanied by a tall, lanky young man and a slight, shorter boy, but a closer look showed that the boy, at least, was a woman in men's breeches. In contrast, Miss Sauber's slender figure and the masculine way in which she had changed her gait would have made it difficult for Thorne to guess her gender if he hadn't known who she was.

Miss Sauber immediately headed around toward the long side of the stable, followed by one of the street urchins. Halfway down, one of the high windows was partially unshuttered, and Miss Sauber lifted Calvin effortlessly above her head. He climbed onto her shoulders, and then she grabbed his ankles and hoisted him up a few more inches until he could pull himself in through the window. Thorne had to admit some surprise at the young woman's strength.

This was the reason Mr. Drydale had eventually called them in. Any man on the Root—and most certainly Jack, if he was inside—would have heard if they tried to sneak inside, but the barking dogs masked sound effectively.

However, they'd waited in vain for someone to respond to their false accident. They couldn't allow the dogs to bark for too long, and yet they needed that to mask the sound of Calvin climbing into the stable. So Mr. Drydale had made the decision to bring his team out of hiding.

Thorne unbarred the front door and cracked it open slowly, so it barely creaked. Inside, two dogs caught sight of him and jerked toward him, their barking becoming more ferocious. They were held back by rope tied around their necks and anchored to a hook on the wall, but the rope was long and the dogs could have run a few feet outside if the door were opened wider.

"Shaddup," came a deep voice out of view, and a bone flew at a dog's head. Both creatures' attentions were caught by the bone, and there was a short growling struggle before one retreated with the prize. The other dog returned to barking at the crack in the door.

Otherwise, there was no reaction from the man who'd thrown the bone. Bored and not watching the door? Or not in a position to see that it was cracked open? Obviously not on the Root, or he'd have heard the door being unbarred from outside, and the dogs' barking would have irritated his sensitive hearing.

Thorne had been expecting another guard not on the Root, but the fact they didn't see the door right away was pure luck.

"The good Lord was watching over us."

He shoved the memory away and yielded his place to Miss Sauber.

She lifted her bow and aimed an arrow through that tiny crack in the door. Thorne stood behind her and could see inside the stable, up where Calvin crouched on the rafters, holding a fully-packed bag by a rope so that it dangled above the center of the large space.

She loosed. And missed.

"Amos? That you?" It was a second voice from inside. There were at least two guards, then.

To her credit, she wasted no time and grabbed another arrow, notching it and aiming again. Thorne moved behind the door, waiting for the guard to react further.

She missed again. Over the sound of the dogs, Thorne heard the sound of raised voices from deeper inside the building. Within a few seconds of the second arrow, the guard on the other side of the door tried to push it open more, but Thorne braced himself. It cracked open only a few inches.

"Hurry!" he hissed.

Miss Gardinier, standing beside her and holding her quiver, stretched out her leg and gave him a swift kick in the shins. The shock surprised him more than the small blow.

Miss Gardinier blasted him with a glare that clearly said, *You're not helping matters.*

"Oy!" The guard shoved hard against the door, but Thorne threw his weight into it.

"What's going on?" the second guard demanded. Mr. Havner joined Thorne behind the door to help him.

Miss Sauber exhaled slowly, the arrow steady in her drawn bow, and loosed a third time, just as both guards threw their weight against the door.

As the door jerked open another few inches, Thorne saw a brief glimpse inside. He didn't see the arrow hit, but he heard a strange popping sound, then saw a sudden explosion of fine white powder, spreading out in a much more violent reaction than he would have expected from a mere arrow's shot at a bag.

Earlier, when discussing the plan, he had asked Miss Gardinier, "What is that?"

"A special powder I concocted, encased in an innovative detonation system—"

"She created an exploding bag," Miss Sauber interrupted, "so that the extra-fine powder will fill the room like a fog. To obscure our faces."

Thorne was astonished. On previous missions, he had tried fighting with a cloth over his nose and mouth to mask his features, and it was both uncomfortable and difficult to keep in place.

Immediately after she hit the bag, the coachman knelt and tossed some pieces of meat inside the stable, toward the dogs. When planning their attack, they had been at a loss as to how to handle the dogs as well as the guards inside, and Mr. Havner had mentioned that stable masters often kept their dogs hungry so they'd be more ferocious and alert. So Miss Gardinier measured out sedative to rub into some pieces of meat that Calvin procured for her.

"What's—?" one of the guards exclaimed.

The dogs' barking stopped after only a few seconds, and Thorne didn't hesitate to pull open the door. The powder swirled thickly in the air, obscuring his vision, but he was close enough to the guard to see his widening eyes as he caught sight of them.

He didn't hesitate and gave a fast, sharp jab to the man's nose. The guard was quicker than he expected and jerked his head to try to dodge it, but it caught the side of his cheek.

The second guard stood next to him, and Thorne quickly

lashed out with his other fist. He didn't intend to connect, and the man reacted as he had wanted, stumbling back a few steps. Only Thorne stood in plain view, and so the guard was surprised when the door opened wider and the coachman appeared, advancing into the stable to throw a punch at the second guard.

The first guard recovered quickly with a blow aimed at Thorne's torso, but he managed to block most of the force with his elbows and jabbed again. This time, the guard stepped back to dodge.

Behind him, the rest of the stable was a field of white, but because the dogs had stopped barking, he could hear the distant sound of scuffling feet. But there wasn't the sound of boots running to aid the guards.

Good.

Thorne stepped forward.

Sep wouldn't have seen the boy if he hadn't been on his back, trying to dislocate his thumb. Without the sound of the dogs barking, Jack or one of his men on the Root would surely have heard even the soft sounds Calvin made as he crept along the rafters high above Sep's head. He wasn't directly above him but rather several yards closer to the middle of the building, but Sep could see him since the walls of the stalls were not very high.

But the sight of the boy made him grit his teeth and twist his hands. In a sharp motion, he dislocated his left thumb.

The pain was somehow sharper than any of Jack's kicks and punches, maybe because his body knew this injury was self-inflicted and was trying to warn him that he may not be in his right mind to be doing this. The pain traveled up his wrist as he managed to slide his hand through the tight ropes binding them, and then he was free.

He was about to sit up when he saw Calvin raise a wicked-looking knife, take aim, and loose it directly at him.

The boy's aim was true. The knife landed with a heavy *thunk* in the floorboards only a foot from Sep's loosely bound hands.

"What was that?" Jack asked sharply.

Sep nodded his thanks to the boy high above, but Calvin was already untying a long rope wrapped around his waist, at the end of which hung a large, overstuffed bag. He dangled it down from his perch and then seemed to wait.

Sep struggled to slip his hands completely from the ropes but was startled by a faint sound whizzing above him, which he could hear above the dogs since it was so close. It reminded him uncomfortably of a bullet's passing, although he hadn't heard a gun report. He looked up in time to see an arrow shoot past, making that same noise again. It had just barely missed the bag Calvin was dangling.

"There's someone here! You! Get Silas!" Jack yelled. Soon Brimley ran past the opening to Sep's stall, heading toward the back door.

Sep didn't have much time. If Mr. Drydale had sent a rescue party—and Calvin's appearance suggested that—then Jack would hurry to implement his plan.

But Sep refused to be turned into a monster.

There was an abrupt popping sound above him and suddenly the air filled with fine mist. No, it was powder, so fine that it was a little choking, with a faint chemical smell, but it obscured visibility for about ten yards in all directions. That must have been what was in the bag.

His hands were free, but rising to his feet after being beaten on the floor for hours was difficult. Every joint felt like hinges rusted nearly completely shut, and every movement jabbed as if there were tacks embedded in his muscles. His knee had swollen so much that he would have to cut his breeches off.

Assuming he escaped.

The dogs had suddenly stopped, so he clearly heard Jack yelling at Mr. Shokes. "So eager to lend a hand to ol' Jack Dix! Did you lead them here?"

"N-n-no, Mr. Dix, I swear—"

"Oh, so you sweaaaaaaaar ..." Jack drew out the last word in a long, wordless growl that took twenty syllables. When he next spoke, it sounded as if he was gritting his teeth. "I should be delighted they're here, but they're unfashionably early. Come with me."

Stamping feet, accompanied by stumbling feet. Sep struggled to balance on his injured leg, plucking Calvin's knife from the floor.

Jack actually said, "Gack!" when he saw Sep on his feet, freed and armed. Because of the powder, he'd had to come quite close, and Sep could see that Mr. Shokes was with him, his collar caught in Jack's fist. Although Mr. Shokes didn't understand the situation, he still paled at seeing Sep unbound.

Jack shoved Mr. Shokes away from him, then straightened and tugged at his flamboyant purple waistcoat. "Why do I have to do everything myself?" he muttered. Perhaps because of the powder, his eyes had become bloodshot, emphasizing the orange circles around it. He was hatless now and had been tugging at his nauseatingly yellow hair, and combined with the splotchy green face paint dotting the edges of his face, he looked like a wildman who had emerged from a thicket.

"This is ridiculous," Jack said. "You don't stand a chance against me, you know."

"Then kill me. I'll give you a good fight."

Jack's eyes narrowed, obscuring the whites, until it looked like he stared at Sep with the orange circles for eyes. "You'd rather die than drink it, wouldn't you?"

Sep didn't bother to answer him.

Jack's head whipped toward the front of the stable and stared at something in the misty powder. He began pumping his hands in tiny, agitated motions. It reminded Sep of a chef he'd seen once beating a slab of meat to tenderize it. "I don't have time, I don't have time!" Jack dug inside his jacket pockets and unearthed a glass vial. "Drink this."

It took Sep a moment to realize Jack wasn't talking to him, but to Mr. Shokes. When he didn't respond immediately, Jack reached out and pulled the apothecary toward him with an arm around his neck.

"Drink this and defeat them, and I'll tell you how I make it," he purred into Mr. Shokes's ear.

"Don't," Sep croaked.

Mr. Shokes's eyes darted between him, Jack, and the vial held under his nose. It must not have smelled very pleasant, because he was straining his face away from it. "W-what were you talking about before, making him drink this?"

"No, that would have made him into a *berserksgangr*. This is the Root."

At the word, Mr. Shokes's eyes focused on the dark red liquid and he stopped straining against Jack's arms. "This is it?"

Sep heard footsteps from the front of the stables. Someone was approaching cautiously. "Don't do it," he said.

Jack interrupted him. "Shut up or drink it yourself." His orange-ringed lips pulled into a wide, grotesque smile. Then without even looking at Mr. Shokes, he used one hand to pry open the man's mouth while popping the cork with the hand holding the vial. He poured the contents down Mr. Shokes's throat.

He gagged at first, then drank the small dram of liquid.

"Well, *he'll* be upset," Jack murmured to himself, "but I think we're done with you."

Mr. Shokes froze at the words and began coughing.

Jack only laughed. "Too late! Toolatetoolatetoolate!"

But the coughing became deep and harsh, as if Mr. Shokes was going to vomit out his lungs. He grabbed his stomach, his face turning purple. Pink-tinged saliva dripped from his mouth and from his nose. And then suddenly he stopped coughing. His eyes rolled up, his limbs began shaking, and he collapsed onto the floor in convulsions.

"What did you do?" Sep demanded.

Jack turned to him with a ferocious snarl. "This is *your* fault for not drinking it!"

Except that would have happened to *him*, instead.

Mr. Shokes suddenly arched his back, every muscle taut, the veins pulsing at his elongated throat and his teeth grinding with loud screeching notes. A howl of pain erupted from his throat, as if forced through a thick tongue.

And then he abruptly became limp, eyes half open, more of that pink-tinged saliva drooling from his cracked mouth and running across his face from his nostrils.

Both Jack and Sep stared at him for a long moment. Finally Jack reached one foot out and nudged the still form. Mr. Shokes didn't stir.

Jack let out a sudden shriek that sounded more like an eight-year-old girl than a man. "Nothing is going right today!"

Sep didn't relax his fighting stance with the knife, nor did he move from his defensive position inside the stall, but he felt a surge of hope. Jack had no more men in the stable or he would have sent them to the front. If he waited long enough, his team would come for him. He wasn't certain how they'd fare against Jack, now that he knew that Jack and the pale-eyed man were stronger than the others on the Root, but if there were enough of them, perhaps ...?

As soon as he thought that, the back door opened and slammed shut, and booted feet came running toward them. Sep recognized one of the men right away—an almost skeletal frame, narrow shoulders, ears sticking out from his head. Nick. His companion was even larger than he was, with curly dark hair and a stern expression, the same man who had chastised

Brimley earlier. They were followed by Brimley himself.

"It took you long enough!" Jack stabbed his finger toward the front of the stable. "Stop them! And you!" The finger jabbed at Brimley. "Your job is to recapture *him*!"

The finger now directly pointed at Sep.

Jack turned and raced away, not toward where he sent his two bruisers on the Root, nor escaping out the back door, but across from Sep's stall and down a little ways. There was the creak of another, smaller door.

Brimley stepped into Sep's view, his lips pulled back from blackened teeth, a vicious look in his eyes.

Chapter Eighteen

It took only a few minutes for Mr. Rosmont and Mr. Havner to defeat the two guards at the door. Phoebe could feel Keriah's body thrumming with tension as she stood beside her, but they did not interfere.

The dogs had eaten the sedative and while it did not affect them immediately, within a few minutes they were wobbling on their feet like drunken men. Keriah had measured the sedative carefully so it would not be a lethal dose and they would only sleep for a few hours.

Mr. Rosmont gave one of the guards a sharp hit to his jaw, and he fell back onto his back, the whites of his eyes showing from half-open lids. Clara darted forward with lengths of rope, and she deftly tied complicated knots around his hands and feet.

Mr. Havner was not so quick and strong as Mr. Rosmont, but he also incapacitated the other guard and helped Clara with the ropes. By now the dogs were asleep.

"C … John says he's about halfway down." Clara stumbled over the false name Mr. Rosmont had insisted they use and pointed toward the figure of her brother, still on the rafters. The powder had risen but was not thick near the roof of the building, and they could hazily see his figure even from where they were at the front of the stable. He was pointing down at an area slightly past him, near the midpoint of the building.

This affirmation that Mr. Ackett was indeed here caused a small knot to loosen in her chest. There had been no way to know with certainty before they enacted this bold attack.

"Stay behind me," Mr. Rosmont ordered. He drew a long knife from its sheath on his belt and cautiously strode into the powder-fog. As they followed him, Phoebe glanced behind at Uncle Sol, who gave her a nod and then closed the door, remaining outside.

The powder swirled around them as they swam through it, the chemical smell and the smoke-like feeling in her lungs reminding her of the frantic hour in the stillroom when Keriah had been making it. The powder was steadily drifting toward the ground, and it would not blur their faces for much longer. Uncle Sol had been concerned about the possibility of Jack escaping after getting a good look at each of their features. Phoebe and Keriah were again dressed as boys, but Keriah's delicate steps fairly shouted her gender and wouldn't fool anyone who got close enough.

She had slung her bow and quiver over her shoulder, and now she and Keriah were both armed with knives. Uncle Sol and Mr. Rosmont had looked concerned when they had strapped the knife sheaths at their belts, but the alternative was sending them in only armed with Phoebe's bow. (Keriah had been in the middle of suggesting pistols if Phoebe hadn't deliberately kicked her ankle, because the suggestion of giving the inexperienced women firearms would have sent Aunt Laura and Uncle Sol into apoplexies.)

She and Keriah had broken their silence about their unorthodox training with their Gypsy friend, Vadoma, but Uncle Sol and Mr. Rosmont had clearly been skeptical. After all, who had heard of genteel young women having knife-fighting training from a Gypsy, of all people? So Phoebe had given up trying to convince them that they knew how to use the knives and had simply requested some sort of weapon to protect themselves, which they had reluctantly agreed to.

Voices reached them from deeper inside the building. Keriah gave a gasp. "That's M ... er, Paul." She managed to remember his code name. Paul the prisoner, which was rather grim, but Mr. Rosmont had come up with the names. "He's alive."

"He sounds like he's in trouble." Mr. Rosmont increased his pace despite the increasingly low visibility in the powder.

She felt the thudding of the booted feet through the floorboards before she heard them, and that before she saw the shadows moving toward them through the mist. She pulled Keriah back with her before Mr. Rosmont could tell them to do so.

The two guards who appeared seemed to radiate power in every movement, whether it was walking or standing. The slender one sneered at Mr. Rosmont and Mr. Havner, while the taller one reminded her of a bull just before it charged.

"We have to get to him," Keriah whispered to her.

The eyes of the taller man flickered toward them, and Phoebe knew with certainty that these men were on the Root, if she hadn't already suspected it. But then Mr. Rosmont attacked him, and his attention was drawn away from the women.

Best to take advantage of it. She turned to Clara. "James, stay and help them. Use your black-coated knives." Keriah had made up two paste sedatives, a strong dark green-colored one that was for a man raging on the Root, and another black-colored one for men on the Root who had not been overcome. They had coated some of the twins' throwing knives with each.

Phoebe pulled Keriah into the stall next to them, but she tried to resist. "I'm not hiding here."

"We're not hiding, blockhead." Phoebe raced to the divider of the stall and grabbed Keriah by the waist.

"Wait, what—?!"

She wasn't quite strong enough to toss her friend over the

wall like a sack of potatoes, but Keriah cleared most of the wall with only her legs kicking at the air for a few seconds before she slid down on the other side. Phoebe took a running leap and planted a foot against the wall to help lift her higher while grabbing at the top of the wall. She used her momentum to hoist herself up and then kicked her legs sideways over the top so that she could drop down and land on her feet.

The wall had rattled under their weights, but she hoped the two men were too busy with Mr. Rosmont, Mr. Havner and Clara to pay attention. Keriah had landed on her rump and was picking herself up. Phoebe shoved her toward the far wall. "Go."

They cleared that wall the same way, and then peeked out of the stall opening. The fighting was happening in the aisle behind them, with the men's backs to them for the moment. "Run!"

They sprinted down the stable until the powder mist obscured the men's figures from view. She looked up but couldn't see clearly enough to find Calvin on the rafters. Where was Mr. Ackett?

Phoebe nearly stumbled over the body on the floor, then had to stifle a scream when she recognized Mr. Shokes, Dr. Shokes's younger brother.

Earlier that afternoon, when they'd returned to the apothecary shop to prepare, she and Keriah had been mixing the powder mist when Mrs. Shokes knocked on the stillroom door, coughed, then asked, "Have either of you seen Mr. Shokes?"

As usual, Keriah was focused on her work and only partially aware of anything else, but her eyes flickered up toward Mrs. Shokes and then to Phoebe before returning to the mortar and pestle she was working with vigor.

Phoebe was almost glad to leave the smelly room—almost. Outside the stillroom, she asked, "Mr. Shokes is not with Dr. Shokes? I believe he left to call upon a patient."

"No, Farley was still here when Augustus left, but I haven't seen him for several hours. I was with the children, and then in the kitchen, and I went looking for him but can't find him."

Phoebe felt an iciness in her veins, although she couldn't explain why. She remembered Dr. Shokes's concern about his brother discovering what they had been doing in the stillroom. If Mr. Shokes was not with his brother, where could he possibly be?

Maybe the reason Phoebe became alarmed was because there was a strange tightness around Mrs. Shokes's eyes, as if she almost knew where Mr. Shokes was, but didn't want to admit it to herself.

"I'm afraid we've been here ..."

Mrs. Shokes smiled. "Of course you have. He's been so interested in your work, I suppose I half expected him to be here, pestering you. Would you like me to make some snacks for you?"

Phoebe hastily refused.

And now she saw Mrs. Shokes's smile again as she stared at the still body of her husband.

Keriah had knelt to look at him, but seemed to be taking a long time to examine him. Phoebe became aware of the sounds of a struggle ahead of them.

The powder was thick here, so she could not see clearly, but the shadows moved in a way she recognized from their times in the Gypsy camp. They moved like fighters. And there was no one else here who would fight Jack's men except ...

"Luke, I think it's Paul!"

Keriah was on her feet in a moment, and she also saw the shadows. She darted forward.

They had to get dangerously close before they could recognize Mr. Ackett, who moved stiffly as if he were in great pain. He wielded the knife Calvin had thrown to him against the man who had been with Silas and the pale-eyed man at the church,

Mr. Brimley.

This was not a knife fight like she had seen between Gypsies, who managed to still move fluidly in dance-like rhythms even when in a serious bout. Mr. Brimley also had a blade and jabbed with jerking motions, his feet shuffling and stamping. Mr. Ackett's movements were more practiced and experienced, but slow, and he held the fingers of his left hand in a strange way.

What could they do? How could they help? It suddenly dawned on her that while she and Keriah had had many mock fights with wooden blades, this would be real, with steel edges that could kill.

Suddenly Mr. Brimley landed a punch with his left fist that landed on Mr. Ackett's torso. He must have already been badly injured because the single blow made him drop to the ground. Mr. Brimley moved in with knife held high.

Keriah didn't hesitate. She rushed forward and threw herself upon Mr. Brimley's back.

Phoebe dropped her bow and quiver and followed, knife held ready. She had fashioned temporary leather sheaths that kept the blades coated with the black paste Keriah had made, and the paste made the weapon look like a shadow in the powdery mist.

Mr. Brimley had swung around but Keriah held on, her legs flying out as he whirled. He finally spun quickly and twisted his shoulder, and she went flying into the wall of the stall opposite. He still held his knife and turned back to Mr. Ackett, but Phoebe was there.

Her heart pounded and her hands shook, but she couldn't let fear drive away everything she'd learned. She deliberately recalled the beginnings of previous mock battles with Keriah, guided by the calls of Vadoma on the sidelines. She thought of the rare battles with another Gypsy, always with black eyes gleaming and smile wide to test the little girls pretending to be fighters.

Mr. Brimley did not smile, but her fear began to trickle away. He was not as skilled as other fighters they had fought.

His mouth set in a wide, ugly line, he bore down on her, knife coming in from a wide angle. He was slow. She deflected it easily and swiped at him.

Her cut was not strong enough—her Gypsy instructor would say she had not cut with intention. She barely tore his shirt, much less skin. She was not like Keriah, who had helped her surgeon uncle so often that cutting flesh and making blood fly was nothing to her.

But she only had to hold out for a few moments longer.

More wary of her, Mr. Brimley jabbed with his knife. She swiveled even as she brought her blade up backhanded, but he jerked out of the way. He swung at her a bit wildly, and she dodged the tip of the blade.

And then suddenly Keriah was next to her with her own blade.

Now the fight had truly begun.

Sep struggled to get to his feet, but the pain felt as if his broken ribs were puncturing his lungs. He had to help Miss Sauber and Miss Gardinier against Brimley. They didn't stand a chance ...

And then he saw them fighting. And he stopped trying to get to his feet because he was too shocked.

The two women fought Brimley in perfect synchronization, knives clinking almost casually as they parried his attacks. Miss Sauber was faster and more mobile, dodging and deflecting, engaging more of his strikes. Miss Gardinier deflected the occasional onrush, but seemed to be waiting for an opening. When Brimley overshot his swing at Miss Sauber and exposed his left side, Miss Gardinier swiped in with a deep cut across his ribcage that made him cry out.

It was as if they'd done this before.

Miss Gardinier's limp was more noticeable as she evaded Brimley's thrusts, but Miss Sauber was quick to reclaim his attention with the faster arcs of her blade. At first he thought she was protecting her smaller partner, but then he realized she was distracting their opponent, drawing his aggression upon her, all so that Miss Gardinier could reach in at the right moment to attack him again with her blade, this time a deep wound to his thigh.

Then Miss Gardinier said a curious thing. "Two cuts should be enough."

Their fighting style changed. Miss Sauber guarded against Brimley rather than assailing him, only using occasional swipes to drive him back. Miss Gardinier also defended against him, but no longer took advantage of openings to injure him.

After a few minutes, Brimley's movements became sluggish, his eyes unfocused. Sweat trickled down his face and his knife arm dropped. The two women remained wary, but did not attack.

Within a few minutes, Brimley had fallen to his knees, then slumped to the ground.

Miss Sauber stood warily over Brimley, but Miss Gardinier rushed to Sep. Her gray eyes were wide as she dropped to the floor in front of him. She reached out to him, her hand touching the side of his face, the fingers trembling against his skin. Her hands were warm and soft, but even more than her touch, he could feel the depth of her eyes as he drowned in them. There was concern for him, almost hidden by the scar of a past pain, and the flicker of something fervent that thrilled him.

Then she blinked, and he was back in the stable, a mass of pain and lightheadedness. She began checking him in a way that should have embarrassed him, but he had to concentrate too hard to not vomit all over her from Brimley's last blow to his stomach.

"I'm so glad ..." Her voice broke, and she swallowed. In a more even voice, she said, "I'm so glad we found you."

"I'm happy to see you." Such inane words, and yet they carried the weight of all his feelings over the past several hours.

Miss Sauber had left Brimley's unconscious form. She now leaned closer and whispered, "Where's Jack?"

He shook his head. He had expected Jack to reappear once the two women were fighting with Brimley. He didn't know where he'd gone. He hadn't seemed the sort of person to flee, especially when he had men on the Root like Nick and the other large man.

"We must take you out of the building." Miss Sauber knelt on his left side and slung his arm over her broad shoulders.

Miss Gardinier did the same on his right, but as they lifted, her leg suddenly wobbled and folded. He hadn't been expecting it, but since Miss Sauber supported him quite solidly, it only caused a small hot stab in his knee.

Miss Gardinier's head was bowed, and she bit her lip, but it did not seem she was in pain from her injury. It looked more like frustration. He recalled her limp whenever he saw her in a ballroom, and the fact she did not dance. He wanted to say something to her, but his brain emptied, and his tongue was thick in his mouth.

A swirl in the mist was all the warning they had before a small figure came running up. It was Calvin's sister, Clara, and she was in the process of slinging a bow and quiver over her shoulder. He realized Miss Sauber had likely dropped it in order to engage with Brimley.

Miss Gardinier eased herself back under his right arm. "Let's go." She was shorter than Miss Sauber, who took the brunt of his weight and eased the strain on his knee. They turned toward the other end of the stable from the door that Jack's men had used.

They passed near Mr. Shokes's body, and he felt a shudder go through Miss Sauber's frame. "Should we check him?"

But Miss Gardinier shook her head. "We must get Paul out first."

Unease joined the nausea in his stomach. Where was Jack? Would they escape before he returned?

Maybe because he was thinking about his captor, he heard the barest brush of a boot sole against the floorboards and immediately jerked sideways into a stall, dragging the two women with him. Clara was quick to dart in after them.

Keriah opened her mouth but he closed his hand over it just as louder footsteps sounded. He recognized the cadence.

It was Jack.

Chapter Nineteen

Two of Jack's men appeared out of the powder mist, but Thorne had been able to sense the violent intent in their gazes long before they came into view. One was Nick, while the other stood taller with a square jaw and hard eyes. Those eyes flickered away for a moment, and that's when Thorne attacked.

The man blocked the punch with ease, and his return was faster than Thorne could track with his eyes. But something in his body responded to the man's muscles bunching, the angle of his shoulders and torso, and he somehow knew to twist his body to deflect some of the pain of the blow.

But only some. The rest was like a sledgehammer to his side. If he'd taken that punch full-on, he might not have been able to get back up again.

Thorne threw another punch to get some distance from the large man, who suddenly flinched and hopped back, reaching behind his thigh. The guard's hand reappeared holding a throwing knife with streaks of blood. Clara's, which had been coated with some special medicinal paste concocted by Miss Gardinier for the men on the Root. The man tossed the knife aside angrily.

Michael Coulton-Jones had told Mr. Drydale about fighting Silas and Nick at the church. They were strong and fast, but they were not as well trained as a soldier. Both Thorne and

Michael had not only been soldiers, they'd also gone through the rigorous hand-to-hand fight training, and they'd both had deadly bouts while on missions.

It was possible to defeat a man on the Root. He simply had to be smarter about it.

This man was impossibly fast, faster than any man he'd ever fought, but he realized from his instinctual reaction to the body blow that he could predict his opponent's moves by reading his body language. Perhaps the man didn't bother to try to disguise or prevent his opponent from reading his moves simply because he would be faster and stronger than anyone else he fought, or perhaps it was simply because he lacked training.

Either way, Thorne would use it to his advantage. If he could read the man's movements, he could dodge the attacks. He wouldn't be able to dodge all of them, but he could at least evade him enough to not take a fist directly.

But since he could read what stroke was coming, he also knew how he could use it against the man.

The man's muscles bunched and Thorne knew he was pulling back for a roundhouse. He moved almost automatically, stepping closer and inside the man's long reach, then using his bent left arm to deflect the attack. It still felt like being hit with a metal pipe. At the same time, Thorne jabbed him in the eye with stiff fingers.

The man jerked back, blinded for a moment. Thorne followed as fast and accurately as he could with a left uppercut that hit him exactly on the chin, then a right cross that connected on his jaw. The man remained on his feet but dazed, blinking his teary eye. A normal man would have already been stumbling and falling to the ground.

They circled each other, staying light on their feet and wary, but another knife from Clara found home in the back of the man's shoulder. He wrenched it out and hurled it in her direction, but it only clattered to the floor.

Thorne read the left punch a fraction of a second before it flew, and he leaned left to try to avoid most of it while at the same time throwing his own left. The man clipped Thorne's head, dazing him, but his own clout still managed to connect solidly with the man's right jaw.

He seemed dizzy from either the blow, or else the sedative from Clara's knives was starting to take effect.

Despite stars in his vision, Thorne immediately followed with a right to the other jaw and another left cross to the temple.

The man finally stumbled backward and fell to the ground.

Thorne rushed in and followed him down, pounding continuous punches at the man's face until he was unconscious.

His side ached with every rapid breath, but with some help from Clara's accurate aim, he'd managed to take the man down.

He looked up in time to see Nick dodge Clara's thrown knife. He was far faster and more nimble than Thorne's opponent, and the coachman had obviously taken a beating. Unable to use his whip in the enclosed space, he faced the smaller man with a sturdy wooden cudgel, but he was moving more slowly than before, his shoulders more hunched, and he bent over his stomach a little more.

"Go help the others," Thorne told Clara. She darted away as he moved in to help Mr. Havner.

Nick gave Thorne a wicked smile. "I've been wanting to play with you."

"The old man warmed you up for me."

"Respect your elders," Mr. Havner ground out.

Like Thorne's opponent, he could read what sort of hit Nick was going to throw, but since he was so incredibly fast, it was harder to react in time. And he easily attacked both Thorne and the coachman one after the other, so quickly that they had a difficult time defending against him.

He laughed as he danced away from the coachman's hook and even evaded Thorne's simultaneous jab that should have caught him on the ear. He pummeled them again, hooks and crosses that were a blur in front of Thorne's eyes. He managed to partially deflect all but one blow to the side of the head that made his ear ring and his neck snap sideways.

His body wouldn't respond to him. He was barely keeping on his feet. He was wide open for an attack …

That never came.

Nick had suddenly stopped his assault and gripped both arms around his middle, bending his body in half with a pain that contorted his entire face. He turned red to the tips of his ears, and the veins popped from his vulture-like neck.

Michael had told Mr. Drydale about this, a lucky instance that saved their lives in the church. And here it was happening again. They could beat him.

Suddenly the front door of the stable opened, which shocked him. Mr. Drydale had been outside with Isabella guarding those doors.

The floorboards bounced with the weight of heavy running feet, and Thorne spontaneously leaped aside as a huge form crashed through the space where his body had been only a moment before.

"Silas …" Nick's voice was weak with pain.

"Go," Silas told him as he turned to face Thorne and Mr. Havner. His pale short hair atop a square head towered above them, and his shoulders were the width of the Atlantic.

"But—"

"Go, Nick."

The slender man scuttled away.

Silas faced them, eyes calm as he took in their labored breathing and stiff movements. Unlike Nick, he didn't seem to revel in the violence, but he faced it with a proficiency that sent a shiver down Thorne's back.

Thorne put up his hands.

Sep kept his hand clapped over Miss Gardinier's mouth as the footsteps drew closer. She and Miss Sauber, both still supporting his arms, had become blocks of ice. Clara, standing in front of them, was barely breathing.

The steps stopped. He walked inside the stall where Sep had been bound. He returned to the central aisle of the stable, and then suddenly there was a loud banging and stomping that echoed through the space.

The old wooden slats of the horse stall were warped, so he removed his hand from Miss Gardinier's mouth and leaned closer to peer between two boards.

Jack was pummeling the wood of the other stall, his feet kicking and banging on the floor, his painted face a hideous mask of rage. Splinters flew in the air while dust billowed up from beneath his feet. But he was only hitting with his right hand. In his left glimmered glass the color of blood.

Just as suddenly as he had started his tantrum, he stopped and straightened. He took a deep breath and a long exhale.

He had stopped next to Brimley's unconscious body, and he gave it a swift kick. Sep thought he might engage in another outburst, but he only kicked the man once. Brimley didn't wake.

Jack suddenly knelt next to him and began sniffing like a dog, in short snuffles. Then he took one long sniff, filling his lungs, and exhaled with a guttural, "Ah."

Jack poked at the body with the finger of his empty right hand, and Sep realized he was poking at the knife wounds. He swirled the tip of his forefinger in the blood on Brimley's shoulder, then brought it to his mouth and tasted.

"Did they use the same ...?" he muttered. "No way to know, no way to guess. They might use something different for a Berserker."

Beneath his arm, Miss Gardinier's shoulders stiffened. She had realized what Jack wanted.

In the distance, a door opened and slammed shut again. That was the front of the stable, the direction Miss Gardinier and Miss Sauber had come from.

Jack straightened and looked into the powder mist for several long seconds, then a shadow grew darker as it approached. The figure lurched from side to side as it moved, and it appeared to be hunched over.

Nick walked forward in a swirl of white powder. He clutched his stomach with both hands, a posture Sep recognized when he'd first fought Nick at the church with Michael.

"Mr. Dix ..." Nick's voice was a thin thread, and he was sweating heavily. He didn't look up at Jack, but stared at the floor while doing his utmost to remain upright. "I'm sorry, Mr. Dix. I ... I can keep fighting if I get another dose of the Root. I burned through that last dose ... I almost had them ..."

Considering Jack's frustration a moment before, Sep wouldn't have been surprised if he backhanded Nick in the face. But there was a sudden gleam of white surrounded by orange, and along with the smile was a voice as sugary as March-pain. "Of course, my boy. Here you go." Jack held out the vial he'd had in his hand when he arrived at Sep's stall to find it empty.

Nick grabbed the vial and bobbed several times. "Thank you, Mr. Dix. I won't disappoint you, Mr. Dix."

"I know you won't. Drink it down, now."

Nick tossed back the contents, and although his face was still tight with pain, there seemed relief in his eyes. Jack held out a hand and after hesitating in surprise, he handed the empty vial back to him. Jack pocketed the vial and then stood regarding Nick with eyes that seemed to shine with excitement in their orange rings.

At seeing Jack's face, Nick's relieved smile faltered. In the next moment, a bolt of pain shot across his features and he clutched even harder at his stomach than before. He fell hard on his knees, making the floor shudder and dust puff up to obscure his expression. He began to gag.

In a flash, Jack was behind Nick with one arm around his chest and the other holding his jaw tightly closed. "Don't want that to come up, do we?" Another gleam of white teeth in that orange ring of face paint.

Nick floundered, twisting left and right, his hands grabbing at Jack's arms, reaching up to tangle in his wild hair, but Jack held him effortlessly, still smiling all the while. Nick had been weakened by whatever caused his stomach pains, but to Jack, he was no stronger than a crying infant.

Sep had already suspected it before, but this proved that Jack and probably the pale-eyed man, too, were taking something *different from the Root.*

Nick was clearly in agony. His legs kicked out in spasms, his fingers became rigid claws, and his back arched. He no longer fought Jack, but his torso twisted left and right. It looked as if every muscle was rock-hard with tension.

Then from the depths of his throat came a growl.

Jack immediately released him and backed far away. Wariness now shone alongside the glee in his eyes. There was also a trace of tenderness in his gentle smile, like a mother regarding her beloved child.

And then abruptly, he whirled and sprinted toward the back door. "Silas!" he shrieked. "Leave them!"

For a few seconds, Nick remained alone, his body still stiffly contorted, swaying slightly on his feet. His eyes were wide but unfocused, and his mouth had grown so slack that spittle dribbled down from a corner.

Sep was about to urge the women to leave when running steps preceded the huge figure of Silas as he came hurtling down the center of the building, following Jack's bolt toward the back door. But his pace slowed when he saw Nick.

His face registered shock, pain, grief. He came to a stop and stood next to Nick's unresponsive figure. Silas's hand reached out toward him as if to grab his shoulder, but then dropped limply at his side. His mouth grew into an agonized grimace, his jaw tight and pale. His eyes flickered toward the back of the stable, toward where Jack had disappeared. Sep didn't think Silas could see Jack's figure, but that gaze burned with betrayal and anger.

Nick suddenly twitched and his unfocused eyes began to dart around him. His mouth drew into a snarl, and his face flushed bright red with rage. He had not yet focused on Silas, and he drew his head back and howled, the grating sound of fury rising up to the rafters above.

The scream shocked Silas from his anguish. With a last, sad glance at Nick, he also took off running toward the back door.

As soon as he passed, Sep tightened his grip on the women's shoulders. "We have to leave now." It had been too long since Nick drank the tainted Root. Michael had become a Berserker quickly. Nick would start raging soon.

Miss Gardinier looked troubled, but Miss Sauber nodded and began guiding them out of the stall, toward the back doors, after Jack and Silas. There was no help for it, because Nick stood between them and the doors they had entered.

Miss Sauber turned her head and shouted, "Peter! Jude! Run!"

They hurried as best they could while supporting him. Miss Sauber was stronger than expected for a woman and she was also closer to his height, so she carried the brunt of his weight. But it still seemed achingly slow, like running through treacle. Behind them, he listened for the sound of Nick's cries of ferocity. Hopefully the powder was still thick enough to hide their figures from his sight so he wouldn't come running after them.

Closer to the doors, the powder was thinner and they saw the outline of the door. It was closing.

Panic jolted through the nausea in his gut.

The door slammed shut, and then there was the sound of the bar dropping down outside.

They ran up against the door, but it wouldn't budge.

In the distance echoed another slammed door, and the faint *thud* of the bar falling into place.

They were trapped with the Berserker.

Chapter Twenty

Sol leaned against the wall under the unshuttered window of the stable, trying not to act as edgy as he felt. He was too exposed here, with the long empty expanse of the stable wall running on either side of him. He tried not to look at the bright outlines of windows on the other side of the lane facing the stable, hoping no one would casually glance out of one and see him. He certainly didn't want Calvin to slip and fall, but he wished the boy would hurry up.

A soft scrape above his head made him turn and see two spindly legs sticking out of the window. They flailed for a moment, then the boy's entire body dropped out of the window —making Sol's heart jump in his throat—but he abruptly stopped his descent, hanging only by his hands.

Biting back a rebuke for the daredevil child, he gave a soft whistle between his teeth, holding his hands up, and the boy dropped into his arms.

"Did you see him?" Sol asked.

Calvin nodded, his eyes gleaming in the faint candlelight straying toward them from the nearby shuttered windows.

They scuttled through the darkness back to the front of the stable, sneaking behind the post chaise, which still stood in front of the stable door. The huge bulk hid them from view of the street. Earlier, Sol had unhitched the horse and tied it to a spindly bush growing from the base of the inn next door to keep the animal out of the way.

He needed to guard the door now that they'd removed Jack's man, but it would be the height of folly to wait in plain view and beg to be ambushed. He'd found a small strip of dirt running between the inn and the stable, barely big enough for a man to walk, although anyone would be hard-pressed to squeeze past the piles of refuse that nearly choked the passageway.

They crouched down near the entrance of the alley, cloaked by the shadows. The dirt was hard-packed here, and he guessed the guard they had removed had also been hiding here as he kept an eye on the door. They had tied up the guard and laid him out behind them in the passageway, although it was a tight fit. He was still unconscious from the light dose of sedative that Miss Gardinier had given to him.

Sol was on edge for a multitude of reasons, not least of which was that he'd been anticipating a trap of some sort, and yet no one had tried to stop them or capture them when they knocked out the guard. What were Jack's intentions? The man wasn't stupid, and he probably had a plan. Sol simply didn't know what it was, and that worried him. He'd always prided himself on being able to analyze and predict men's plans and movements, but with Jack he was confounded no matter what scenarios he tried to envision.

It seemed to take too long. Yet how long was it supposed to take to invade an enemy's stronghold and rescue a prisoner, likely injured and guarded by men with supernatural strength? Sol sighed. He'd like to see his superiors debate an answer to that question.

The dirty street urchin suddenly appeared at Sol's elbow like a ghost, making him jump. He grabbed habitually at his pockets, but then remembered he was wearing an old jacket and was carrying nothing of value.

"Something's happening," the urchin said.

He was completely at *point nonplus* until he got a better look at the urchin's face. It was only the shape of the eyes that made him realize who had just appeared. And then he tensed even further, for several other reasons. "What is it that's happening?" he demanded.

Calvin had started in surprise at seeing the newcomer, but now the boy's eyes narrowed. "Is that …?"

"A man ran out the back door." The street urchin had even disguised her voice.

"You're Lady Aymer," Calvin burst out before she could continue. "You were outside the apothecary shop."

To Sol's surprise, she nodded to the boy. "'Evening."

Sol frowned and glanced quickly between the two of them. "Are you certain about this?" he asked her. For some reason he was not privy to, she was at the highest level of security within the Ramparts. He had only found out about her by accident when he had been mistakenly given the report of her unusual first mission with her brother.

"Yes. It is acceptable." She smiled at Calvin. "He and his friends helped to save my brother, after all."

The boy grinned back at her, accepting her presence with barely a note of surprise.

Sol bit back a groan. Having her identity revealed to Laura's household, and probably to Phoebe and Miss Gardinier, was going to cause him no end of trouble at the department, but the fact she was here did make him relax a fraction. He needed the help. "I wasn't certain you'd join us."

"I was having a look around." Prince shook her head. "I could find no one watching the stable from the buildings around the entrance. But I had difficulty checking the buildings around the stable's back door. A man exited the back door and entered one of those buildings."

He didn't ask how she would have peered into those rooms in order to check.

"I came as fast as I could to warn you," she added. "There is still a guard by the back door, but he appears unalarmed."

Sol nodded. They hadn't had enough capable agents to be able to disengage the guards from both the front and back doors, especially when he needed Mr. Rosmont and Phoebe to be able to ambush anyone in hiding who might respond to their attacks, so he'd settled for focusing on the front door alone and leaving the back door guard unaware.

He and Calvin straightened. They all fell into a taut silence as they waited, keeping watch over the door, straining their ears to hear what was happening inside, alert for anyone who might approach. Sol could tell Calvin's body was rigid with anxiety even though he pretended a casual pose leaning against the wall next to him.

It had seemed too long, but he hadn't the means to check his pocket watch. Then he recalled he didn't have it.

He was feeling unusually vulnerable, perhaps even useless. He was too used to being the one in his home or office, waiting for the results of an operation, not out in the field, with his own objectives that he had to accomplish.

It also made him feel vulnerable that he was able to see and hear and envision everything that could go wrong. He had sent civilians into that stable—not a detached, written order, but with his own mouth, seeing them with his own eyes.

What had Laura said to him? *"People are not your chess pieces that you move around on a flat board. They interact with each other, and they bleed."*

He had understood her words logically, but he hadn't truly understood the full scope of his responsibility. It had slammed him in the face when he'd made the decision to use Phoebe as bait to lead a crazed Mr. Coulton-Jones into their trap.

Just like that situation last night, the one at this moment reminded him that he had to personally face the consequences of his actions and orders, that he must witness them firsthand.

He owed that to these people, who had all wanted to be a part of this and who looked to him for commands.

And because he was seeing these events with his own eyes, because his own hands had shut the stable door behind Phoebe, he'd become aware that there was a caution blanketing his vision, whereas before, he would view a mission with ruthless efficiency. He wasn't certain if that caution would save lives, or if his prudence would cause this entire mission to go awry.

His eyes barely registered the moving shadows before two men ran from around the side of the stable. The shorter one immediately pushed the post chaise further out of the way, and his movements made it seem as if the heavy coach weighed the same as a dinner plate.

He was on the Root.

Sol had been prepared to defend the door against a man on the Root, but he knew his limitations. He had no chance against two of them, and yet he couldn't allow them to attack the people inside, who were not expecting an enemy to approach from their rear. His indecision made him hesitate.

The taller man murmured a command as he pulled open the door and ran inside. From the dim light from inside the building, Sol caught a glimpse of a tall, broad figure with pale hair cut short. And a disfigured ear.

The one outside barred the door behind him, and he handled the heavy wood with ease.

Well, that decided things for him. And yet, the lone guard was undoubtedly several times stronger than Sol.

And the only partners he had were an eleven-year-old boy and a young woman.

Calvin had pushed away from the wall, his hands already reaching for the throwing knives hidden under his clothes. Earlier that evening, Miss Gardinier had coated them with something sticky and black-colored. She had done the same with the knife Sol had sheathed at the small of his back.

Before he could speak, Prince said, "I'll distract him." And then she was gone like a wisp of smoke.

Sol's options would have been even more limited if the guard had headed to this spot to wait, but luckily he stood at attention in front of the door. Sol removed the two sedatives Miss Gardinier had left with him, a bag of some type of heavy grit and an oiled cloth packet. He stared at them for a second, then pulled out his knife. He had run through the scenarios in his head. There was only one in which he had a chance at success.

While he'd been fiddling with sedatives, Calvin had disappeared from his side. He spared a trace sliver of worry in his mind for the boy, but from what he'd seen, he knew the former street rat could handle himself and, more importantly, work with a team. Sol would need his teamwork now.

He tied a comforter around his nose and mouth while he waited for Prince to make her move, but he did not need to wait long. He heard her long before she came into view, a high-pitched childish wailing that seemed to pierce the night. Soon a young boy came running blindly around the corner of the stable, his head hidden in his hands. The boy attempted to slip past the guard, a hand reaching toward the door, but the man grabbed the child so quickly that his arm was a blur.

"What are you up to?" The guard's voice was harsh, unmoved by the tears and wailing.

"I … I need … inside." Prince interspersed her broken words with hiccoughs and loud sniffles.

"No, you're not. What do you need to go inside for?"

Instead of answering, she cried louder and buried her face in her dirty hands.

Sol used the noise to creep toward the man, whose back faced him. One hand cupped the large sedative bag while the other held it tightly shut so that the man wouldn't happen to smell the contents.

The unsympathetic guard shoved Prince a few steps back. "Get out of here."

"But ... Brimley ..."

The man's name made him pause, but he answered her by pushing her even more roughly, making her stumble and fall. "You're mistaken."

Still crying, Prince groveled on the ground. "Please help me ..."

Her plea earned her a half-hearted kick, which she avoided. She crawled away a few feet then stopped, wails dying instantly as she scrabbled at something on the ground. She got up, staring at it in her hand, and took a few tentative steps toward the guard. "You dropped this."

Sol almost missed her cue. She had gotten close to the man, and he frowned and bent over her outstretched hand. And then her foot lashed out and she kicked him in the groin.

Sol reflexively curled his body as the guard howled in pain. Barely a second later, there was a strange, fast-moving shadow and a faint swish of air that passed right next to Sol. Even in the darkness he could see a small knife protruding from the back of the man's thigh.

After kicking him, Prince darted away. But despite his pain, and even the distraction of the knife in his leg, the guard whipped an arm out and grabbed at her. Fortunately he caught her sleeve rather than her arm, or he likely would have broken it.

Prince twisted to get away, throwing her full weight around. Her struggles made him jerk around in a circle, but he held her fast.

Sol didn't even see when she pulled out a knife and slashed at him, cutting through the fabric of his own sleeve, making him jerk. She yanked herself away, but her sleeve tore with an audible rip where he still hung on. He grabbed at her again, but only clawed at empty air.

Sol had moved toward him after Calvin's thrown knife, but had stopped when he'd captured Prince. As soon as she was clear of him, he darted forward and flung the powder inside the bag full into his face, immediately bouncing backward.

But the guard, even with his privates aching and a sedative-laced knife in his back, swung a beefy arm toward Sol faster than he could blink. The blow caught him in the stomach. It would have been a full blow if he'd been only a few inches closer, but even so, he doubled over and was knocked several feet away. He wasn't aware of falling until the hard stones slammed into his back.

That didn't go quite as he'd planned.

He curled himself on the ground even as he reached inside his pockets.

He expected the man to follow up on him quickly, but he was still surprised to see the boot in his vision almost instantly. He instinctively rolled and heard the harsh clank of metal on stone from the guard's knife, stabbing the stones rather than Sol's head.

Sol had always intended to draw the man in to attack, although not necessarily from a position on the ground. But the missed knife caused him to bend over, slightly off-balance, pulling his head near to Sol.

He whipped his hand out and pushed the oiled cloth packet into the man's mouth, then shoved as hard as he could against his jaw, clamping his mouth closed.

The man had stiffened in surprise at the mode of his attack, which allowed Sol precious moments to cause the paste sedative in the packet to ooze out into his mouth through the slit he'd cut in the packet a few minutes earlier. The guard shook his head back and forth like a dog while Sol held onto his chin as long as he could.

The man grunted and his lips pulled back from his teeth, causing spit and sedative to shake out. Sol turned his head, and only then did he realize the comforter he'd wrapped around his mouth had slipped. He prayed the sedative wouldn't fly into his nose and mouth.

"What's going on?" a man's distant voice sounded.

He couldn't let a bystander become involved. "Stay back!" he yelled.

He knew he wouldn't hold the man long, but he lasted longer than he'd expected. His hand slipped from his chin even as the man exerted his superior strength on his jaw and forced it open enough to spit out the packet. In his struggles, man's boots had come to straddle Sol's legs, so he tried to scuttle backwards, but he knew he was too slow.

Then two shadows came racing toward them. Calvin slashed at the man's hamstring, although from the movement of his knife Sol could tell the cut wasn't deep. At the same time, Prince darted in and stabbed a knife into the meaty part of the man's other thigh. Calvin's attack barely made the man flinch, but Prince's stab wound caused him to emit a grunting cry and kick out at her. She wasn't as quick as Calvin in retreating, and the foot caught her in the chest. She rolled backwards several times before lying unmoving on the ground.

While the man's leg was still raised from kicking at Prince, Sol aimed his foot sharply at an exact spot on the man's other knee, the leg supporting his weight. His knee jerked outward at an unnatural angle and the man cried out as he fell. Sol rolled away in the opposite direction.

But then an iron hand grabbed at his ankle and pulled. Sol's felt his ankle pop at the movement. He kicked at the man's hand with his other leg.

Another whirling sound in the air, and the man's shoulder jerked from Calvin's thrown knife.

"How long does it take for that slop to work?!" he demanded from no one in particular.

As soon as he said it, he felt the man's fingers loosen from his ankle. The guard began spitting on the ground, as if belatedly realizing that the paste was causing his slower actions. Sol realized that when the man had first been dosed, he'd been so focused on fighting him that he hadn't spent any time in trying to remove the paste from his mouth. The combination of that, the powder, and Calvin's sedative-smeared knives was finally having an effect.

The man released Sol's ankle and tried to get to his feet, but he was unsteady and dizzy. He gave a roar of frustration, then promptly passed out.

Sol's breathing was harsh, his heart beating hard and fast from his exertions.

The bystander who had called out earlier came up with tentative steps. "You hurt?"

Just his luck to attract the attention of the one Good Samaritan in all of the Long Glades. "I am well," he growled. "Ye'd best not get involved in this."

Maybe it was the intense look he gave him, but the Good Samaritan gulped and walked swiftly away.

Sol hastened away from the unconscious guard, rising shakily to his feet as he made his way to Prince's still form. She groaned and moved her hands against the ground, raising herself a few inches by the time he reached her. He helped her to sit up.

She grabbed her sternum where the man had kicked her and winced. "What kind of cur kicks at a child?"

"But you're not a child."

"But I look like one!" She groaned again and rubbed her breastbone.

"I hear noises inside," Calvin said urgently at Sol's side.

They helped her to her feet and ran to the closed door. But just before Sol opened it, he heard it.

Roaring. Screaming. A primal sound no sane man would make.

His hand froze.

Calvin's eyes were wide.

"What's wrong?" Prince demanded.

"There's a crazed man on the Root inside."

They stood in silence for an anguished moment.

"We can't leave them inside," Calvin implored him.

"We can't let it out onto the streets to harm innocent people."

None of them voiced the second concern that had come to mind—*who* was the madman on the Root?

That guard had been told to bar the door and wait out here for a reason, which made it likely Jack had purposefully made a monster. It was probably the same method he'd used on Mr. Coulton-Jones. Had the guard been instructed to hold the door and ensure the madman killed the people who arrived to rescue Sep?

No, Jack surely knew they had stopped Mr. Coulton-Jones, and he may even know they didn't kill him. He could assume they would come prepared to do the same thing to any other man he made to drink the Root.

Was that what Jack was after? Their means to put down a Root-fueled madman? The barred door would trap the team inside, but it also trapped the monster, possibly making it easier for them to stop it.

And the guard at the door who had been on the Root could rush in and ... capture them all? By himself? Except that Sol was reasonably sure it had been Silas who entered the stable, before the monster had been made.

Sol finally felt as if he had a tenuous grasp on Jack's plan. He'd wanted the people who would come for Sep, which was why he took him alive. He also wanted the means they used to put Mr. Coulton-Jones to sleep. Silas inside and the guard outside would help him accomplish both of those.

But knowing what Jack wanted didn't help him now with the

decision about what to do. Calvin's sister was inside. Mr. Rosmont. Mr. Havner. Miss Gardinier. And he recalled the determined expression on Phoebe's face just before he'd closed the door behind her.

Laura would never forgive him if anything happened to her. And yet, a crazed man on the Root would harm or even kill innocent people on these streets who were completely unprepared for the attack.

He had been staring at the closed door for long minutes before Prince touched his arm. Even in the dark and through the grime she'd smeared on her skin for her disguise, she was deathly pale, and her eyes had a haunted look about him.

But her words and her voice were firm and calm. "They went inside prepared to encounter men on the Root, even those who have gone mad. You must trust your team, and trust God."

As he did with Laura, a part of him wormed with discomfort at the mention of God in any context other than a church service. It seemed ludicrous to even think about the Almighty in this kind of situation, with team members—*his* team members who were captive and trapped, dealing with gang leaders and a supernatural alchemy ...

Exactly. Supernatural. Who else to deal with the supernatural, but the supernatural? Distant Sunday messages which he thought he'd forgotten suddenly appeared in flashes in his memory, of a God who parted the waters and then walked on them.

He nodded. "We leave the door barred."

Calvin bit his lip, but didn't object. He stared at the door intently, as if willing himself to see through the wood.

"Prince, run to check the back door," Sol told her. "We must know if the guard is still there and if the door is barred. If it's safe, bar the door."

She had vanished before he could add, *Be as quick as you can and don't be seen,* but it would have been redundant. She knew her job better than he did.

And he knew *his* job. He looked around at the buildings, some windows lighted and some not, some noisy and some quiet. Occasional shadows flitted, some of them pedestrians and some not. Potential victims of the man on the Root if he should escape.

Sol knew he must not allow that to happen.

The closest thing at hand was the post chaise. "John, come with me."

Calvin hesitated a split second, unfamiliar with the name he'd been given before the start of the mission, then followed Sol to the vehicle. He was glad he'd thought to unhitch the horse earlier and tie it out of the way. Sol grabbed the shafts to back the heavy coach toward the double-doors.

It was awkward since Sol couldn't rely much on Calvin, who though strong, was still a child. He couldn't get proper leverage between the wide shafts to put his full weight into his pushing, and his entire torso ached from the fight with the guard. The first few inches had him straining the hardest, with Calvin pulling from the boot.

It took agonizing minutes, but he managed to position the coach before the closed doors with enough room for the doors to open. He took a moment to catch his breath.

"You going to open the doors and ram him?" Calvin asked.

"Maybe." He didn't want to have to open the stable doors. Now that he'd gone through the effort to move the coach, he realized it would take too long to get the coach going fast enough to be a threat to a crazed man on the Root. He might need to use the coach to simply block this entrance as best he could, and then find some way to block the other doors, also.

And that was assuming the crazed man didn't decide to plow straight through a wall.

Suddenly Sol realized the sounds inside the stable had died down. Should he be glad or alarmed? How long had it been that way? He'd been so focused on the post chaise that he hadn't noticed. Did it mean his team were all dead? Or did it mean the monster was defeated?

The minutes ticked by, long and tormenting. A dozen times, Sol decided to open the door, and a dozen times he convinced himself not to.

"You must trust your team, and trust God."

If he couldn't do either of them, he was useless as a leader.

The sudden rattling of the doors made both him and Calvin jump. The door fell silent, and they stared at it dumbly.

Then a muffled voice at the door said, "Matthew?"

It was Phoebe. With a gusty sigh, he ran to lift up the heavy bar and swing open the doors.

The first face he saw was Phoebe's, tired but drawn. Then they stepped forward and he could see that slung between herself and Mr. Rosmont was Sep.

Sol rushed to take her place and help Sep stagger out. The man felt like a bag of bones, and one leg hung completely limp. Even in the darkness he could see the splotches of bruises that covered his face.

But he was alive.

"Must leave quickly," Sep rasped. "He's after the sedative."

Sol nodded. His suspicions were correct. "We have to hitch the horse quickly." Where was Prince? She should have returned by now.

"Mr. Shokes is inside," Keriah said.

"What?" Sol turned his head to look at her.

"Took tainted Root," Sep whispered. "Then collapsed."

Tainted Root? Sol hadn't even considered such a thing, but now he wondered if it had to do with the increased numbers of crazed men in the Long Glades. "Is he alive?" Sol demanded.

"I didn't feel a pulse when I first saw him, but I didn't check very carefully because we wanted to save Paul," Keriah said as she gestured toward Sep. "We can't leave Mr. Shokes there."

They didn't have time. If Jack had intended to capture them, he'd be entering the stable soon, now that the sounds of the monster had died down.

But Jack also thought the front door was barred and they were trapped. Keriah was right. "Peter," he snapped at Mr. Rosmont, who immediately turned to re-enter the stable.

The distant sound of the back doors opening made everyone freeze.

The powder mist had mostly fallen to coat the floor now, and Sol was able to see all the way to the end of the long building. He couldn't see clearly, but visible was the huge hulk of a man next to a smaller figure with colorful face paint. Even from that distance, he could tell Jack was livid upon seeing the clear evidence that the front door guard had failed at his job.

"Get them!" he snapped, and Silas rushed forward.

"Hurry!" Sol moved quickly to get Sep into the post chaise while Mr. Havner ran to re-hitch the horse.

With their faces set and determined, the rest of them moved forward to intercept Silas, to buy time to get Sep away. Not one of them even flinched at the goliath bearing down on them. Phoebe moved to the front, arm drawn back to loose an arrow.

And then he heard the roar.

An inhuman sound, tearing out from a throat unused to making it. A bit higher pitched than the madman from before.

"Matthew!" Phoebe shouted.

Sol turned to look.

Silas had passed the halfway point of the long building, but he'd stopped, one leg trapped on the ground.

No, trapped in the grip of Mr. Shokes. Or the monster that had *been* Mr. Shokes.

His face was contorted with a wild rage, focused intently upon Silas's leg. He'd reached out with one hand apparently as Silas was moving past him and had nabbed his ankle. Now his other hand clamped around it, even as Silas was struggling to free himself.

Silas was *struggling*. A man already large and powerful, made even more so by the Root. But he couldn't break free from Mr. Shokes.

Beyond them, framed by the open back door, Jack's eyes were wide, his mouth set in a grim line, and Sol clearly saw him swallow.

Mr. Shokes roared again, and Silas roared also as he kicked back and forth to try to escape his grasp. Then he fell to the floor with a great *thud* that raised a temporary fog of powder from the floor.

Sol turned away, hurrying even faster to get Sep inside the post chaise.

At that moment, Prince came running up to them.

Sol huffed out a breath of relief that he needn't have feared for her, and she was safe. Before she could speak, he ordered her, "Hitch up the horse!"

She ran to help Mr. Havner.

He deposited Sep rather unceremoniously on the floor of the carriage, leaving his legs dangling. He would have to pull them in himself. Sol raced back to the door in time to see that Silas had escaped Mr. Shokes and was even closer to where they stood, but bending down.

He picked up Nick's inert form, slinging the man over his shoulder as if he were a string of onions. He looked up at them, and Sol could see indecision in his eyes. Facing them, or facing Mr. Shokes?

He turned and sprinted toward the back door.

Mr. Shokes had risen to his feet, but he wobbled unsteadily, like a newborn foal. His attention was on the ground, and he didn't seem to notice Silas bearing down on him until he was almost upon him.

Silas slowed his stride only enough to kick at Mr. Shokes. It made the man stumble backwards a few steps, but then Silas was past him, focusing more on escape than subduing him.

Mr. Shokes roared again and chased after him, but his legs were shaking in a strange way, as if the muscles didn't work properly or his joints were injured. Silas easily outdistanced him and darted out the back door just after Jack's disappearing form. Then the doors slammed shut, and Sol heard the sound of the wooden bar being dropped into place.

Sol was actually relieved to see the other door being barred. It made his decision easier.

He raced to remove a small bundle from the post chaise, then went to swing one of the two double doors closed. Mr. Havner hadn't yet hitched the horse to the vehicle, and he called, "Jude!" He gestured for the coachman to head inside. When Prince made to follow, he stopped her with a hard grip on her shoulder, and pushed her away.

"Bar the doors!" he ordered her, then entered the building and grabbed the other door. The last thing he saw was her white face before the doors closed behind him.

Chapter Twenty-One

As Sol shut the door, behind him, Mr. Rosmont shouted, "Everyone, get back!"

Mr. Shokes was pounding on the locked back doors and had not yet turned to notice them. Sol motioned for all of them to duck into an empty stall nearest to the doors.

"He seems erratic," Sol said in a whisper. He hoped Mr. Shokes either didn't have the superior hearing of other men on the Root, or couldn't hear them over the sound of his own banging against the doors.

"Paul mentioned he drank tainted Root," Keriah said. "There's no way to know what was wrong with it and how it will affect him."

"He's obviously still stronger than a normal man," Mr. Rosmont said.

"This stable won't hold him, and he'll rampage through the town," Sol said. "We must stop him before he can escape."

"We don't have any more of the sedative." Keriah's voice had grown higher in pitch.

"What?" He turned to her.

"When we stopped the first raging man, it took more sedative than with … the other man." Her hands were shaking. "It also took longer for the sedatives to affect him."

"Nick was already on the Root," Mr. Rosmont said. "That

may be why."

The pounding on the doors stopped. They could clearly hear the frightened whinnying, the stamping feet of the horses in the stalls nearby where they stood. There weren't many horses, but they were all close to this side of the building.

Sol peeked around the edge of the stall. Mr. Shokes had noticed the sounds and was heading toward them, but as before, his legs moved disjointedly and it was as if he were careening down an uneven slope with an injured leg. He listed side to side, bouncing against the wooden stalls on either side of the open central aisle, occasionally falling to the floor and only slowly picking himself up.

"Think of something," Mr. Rosmont hissed, then stepped out of the stall and ran to meet Mr. Shokes in the more open area in the center of building. Mr. Havner followed with his cudgel in one hand and his whip in the other, although Sol wasn't certain there would be space for him to use it.

Upon seeing them, Mr. Shokes screamed again, spittle and blood flying from his wide open mouth. Mr. Rosmont came in aggressively with a downward blow of a knife smeared with black-paste sedative, but Mr. Shokes grabbed his arm like plucking a branch from a tree. With a sharp swing, he tossed Mr. Rosmont against the wall.

"You two!" Sol said to the twins, who immediately nodded. He grabbed Calvin and raised him high above his head until the boy could plant his feet on Sol's shoulders. Phoebe did the same for Clara, and the two clambered up onto the rafters above their heads. They carefully made their way along the beams so they could get a little closer to the fighting and use their sedative knives to help whenever they saw an opening.

After throwing Mr. Rosmont, Mr. Shokes lumbered toward where he lay, but instead of attacking him again, he seemed to lose interest in him. His attention was captured by something on the stall wall next to Mr. Rosmont, and he began pounding the wall, breaking wood. After a shocked moment, Mr. Rosmont scrambled away. It was as if Mr. Shokes had forgotten he was there.

"Options!" Sol barked to Phoebe and Miss Gardinier.

"We don't have any more green-paste sedative for arrows or knives." Keriah was breathing hard and fast. "We had to use too much on the first man."

"I said options, not limitations!"

Mr. Shokes stopped abusing the stall and turned, his head down as if confused or dizzy. He saw Mr. Rosmont and stumbled toward him, but the twins aimed knives that hit both his shoulders. He shrieked, but instead of pulling the knives from his body, he swatted at them like flies. One flew to the ground, but the other bent at an angle in his muscle, causing him to bat at it even more, spinning his body.

His movements brought him close to Mr. Havner, who had backed away but now was trapped next to the wall. Mr. Shokes spotted him.

He attacked with flailing fists, swinging and punching with no target other than Mr. Havner's body. But despite his unschooled movements, he was strong and fast, and a fist clipped Mr. Havner's head. He jerked away, but his legs gave out under him, and he dropped his cudgel and whip. Mr. Shokes moved in and pounded the coachman's body a few times.

Mr. Rosmont yelled and stabbed Mr. Shokes's back. The crazed apothecary whirled on him, swinging his fists again. Mr. Rosmont skillfully batted each unsteady roundhouse aside to avoid a direct blow against his superior strength. Mr. Shokes lurched forward off-balance, and Mr. Rosmont ducked under his swinging arms to move behind him.

Mr. Shokes whirled on him, but the twins threw more knives at his chest, and he curled in on himself and roared. He again batted at the small knives, and his head swiveled around as if looking for the invisible attacker. Then abruptly he crouched and began beating against the floor for no reason they could discern, over and over until white powder almost obscured his figure.

Mr. Rosmont had fallen back so that he was within only a few yards of their stall for a moment, and they could see him through the open doorway. He yelled to Sol, "You have to find a way to kill him! A bullet through the head or the heart." His eyes flickered to Sol with a glint of steel. "I can do it."

Sol involuntarily glanced at the bundle he'd dropped at his feet—a wooden case with his personal pistol, unloaded. He'd brought it, but hoped he wouldn't need to use it.

Phoebe's entire body was drawn like a bowstring about to snap, her eyes wide and frightened.

"Dr. Shokes would be devastated," Miss Gardinier protested. "We must try to save his brother."

"That's not the way we do things!" Mr. Rosmont snapped.

Sol would normally agree with Mr. Rosmont. Killing Mr. Shokes would be the fastest and most efficient way to ensure the residents of the Long Glades remained safe from this monster.

But he saw Phoebe's face, and in it, he also saw Laura's.

"People are not your chess pieces that you move around on a flat board. They interact with each other, and they bleed."

He felt the weight of responsibility again, a weight he had never fully felt when sitting behind a desk and dispatching agents. He was too used to only thinking about the greater good and not the innocents who would be caught in the midst of the conflict.

He had put Laura's family members in danger at the birthday celebration. One of the young girls had become injured.

The most efficient decision would also be the most ruthless. It would completely sever their relationship with Dr. Shokes, including Miss Gardinier's longstanding family friendship with him. In a colder light, Dr. Shokes would never trust them again, and he already knew too much about their work against Jack, about the Root.

But even more than the cold pros and cons, he would have to stand before the man and explain that he had ordered the shot that killed his brother.

It was something he was not actually obligated to do. Instead, he could keep Dr. Shokes in ignorance and order everyone to do the same.

But if he did that, he would be ashamed of himself. He didn't want to become a man like that, who hid behind his merciless decisions with a veneer of self-righteous secrecy, concealment for the good of the country. He felt he had to answer to the consequences of his choices.

And he couldn't give the order and then face Dr. Shokes. He realized he wasn't that kind of man.

They had to try to save him. It was the honorable thing to do.

"That's the way *I* do things!" he shouted back at Mr. Rosmont. "Give me options!"

"We don't have any!" Miss Gardinier wailed.

Without warning, Mr. Shokes bounded to his feet and barreled toward Mr. Havner like a battering ram. His hunched shoulder caught the larger man high up along his ribs, carrying him to smash against the wall.

The twins sent two knives flying but only one hit Mr. Shokes in the shoulder blade. Barely a second later, Mr. Rosmont had dashed forward and slashed the exposed back.

Mr. Shokes gave a screaming gurgle deep in his throat as he twisted and flung his arms out at Mr. Rosmont, but he had already danced away. Then Mr. Havner struck at his leg just before rolling away under a wild backhanded fist.

Phoebe's eyes were solid as stone as she turned to Miss Gardinier and put her hands on her shoulders. "Calm down. Think. What do we *have*?"

Miss Gardinier's eyes were darting everywhere, but Phoebe

grasped the sides of her face and forced her to look into her eyes. After a moment, Miss Gardinier exhaled deeply, and her agitation relaxed.

"We have three bags of sedative," she said slowly, "but it's the powdered one."

The one that Sol had thrown into the guard's face. He wasn't even certain if it had helped, since he'd also needed Calvin's sedative knives and the paste he shoved into the man's mouth.

"It was meant for a larger area. It might take down a man on the Root, but it would make a normal man unconscious almost immediately, and I don't know if it will work on ..." Her eyes darted toward where they could hear Mr. Shokes's animal-like snuffles and growls.

"So if we used it in here, it would fill the building?" Phoebe's voice was low and slow. He realized she was using it to keep her friend calm and methodical in her thoughts.

Miss Gardinier spoke slowly as she considered. "It's heavier, like damp, loose dirt or sand. Once it falls to the ground, it won't rise into the air the same way as the white powder we used, and once it dries it will lose its potency. But it wasn't meant for enclosed quarters like this, with the walls and no wind."

"Would we be affected if we stayed far enough away?" Sol took his cue from Phoebe and pitched his voice low and gentle, unlike the way he'd spoken to any of his agents before.

"We would be safe for a little while if we covered our noses and mouths."

"If we could capture him and hold him in one place, and then dose him with the powder, maybe ...?" Phoebe looked to Sol.

"We would need to do more than hold him. We need to trap him, to isolate him away from us and keep him from moving in order to limit the area we needed to dose him."

"And you'd need to find a way to get someone close enough to dose him." Miss Gardinier's voice was growing stronger, less quavery.

"I threw a bag of powder into a guard's face outside, but Mr. Shokes is much faster than that man. I don't think even Mr. Rosmont could get away fast enough."

Miss Gardinier shook her head. "Inside here, the powder would be too strong. You wouldn't want to fling it in his face in a wide arc, for it would fill the building."

"And we might need to use all three bags," Phoebe added.

"We only need him to be weak enough to restrain him," Sol said. "Then we could lock him away while you make more sedative, however long that will take."

Miss Gardinier frowned. "That's possible but ..." She shook her head. "I don't think his heart will be able to withstand this kind of exertion for more than an hour or two."

Sol pulled his mouth in a grave line. There was a tightness in his chest as he said, "If the sedative doesn't work, we must kill him to protect innocents in the Long Glades from being harmed or killed by him."

Miss Gardinier bit her lip, and her throat spasmed.

Sol met Phoebe's panicked eyes. He said, "I will do it. I don't want any of you to have Mr. Shokes's blood on your hands."

Phoebe's gaze grew even more upset, but she also quietly accepted his decision.

"Come on." He ran out of the protective stall while shouting to Mr. Rosmont and Mr. Havner, "Hold him!"

"What'd do you think we've been doing?" Mr. Rosmont darted in to slice at Mr. Shokes before he could lift a beefy hand at Mr. Havner.

Sol ran to the front door again and pounded. "Prince! Open!"

He worried for a long moment that Jack had sent reinforcements to the front door to capture whoever had closed it, but he also knew that Prince was skilled enough to hide before they could even realize she was there.

Then there was the scrape of wood against wood. Sol

removed a knife and held it ready in the event it was not Prince who appeared. Now he wondered if he ought to have taken a few minutes to load his pistol.

He was surprised, and yet also somehow saddened when Phoebe stepped up next to him, an arrow notched and ready. Her face was white, but determined.

But when the doors opened, all they saw was the small, dirty urchin's face that seemed to float in the darkness beyond. He hurried to the post chaise, relieved she had not hitched the horse back up to it, and found Sep still sitting on the floor.

Just as well. "Up you go, old chap." He lifted his arm over his shoulder to help him to his feet. Phoebe came around to his other side, and they moved him quickly.

"I can help you inside," he insisted as they walked him.

Sol shook his head, but it was Prince who responded with a scoffing sound as they laid him gently on a space on the ground. She told him in a voice that tolerated no protest, "You'll stay right there."

Sol took one of the coach shafts while Phoebe and Miss Gardinier took the other. With a grunt, they got the heavy coach moving, and Prince swung the doors wider as they rolled the coach inside as quickly as possible. More than once tonight he'd been grateful for Phoebe's remarkable strength.

"Bar the door behind us," he called to Prince in a strained voice.

As the doors thudded closed, they set the shafts down and stood with hands on knees, breathing heavily.

"It's heavier than I expected," Phoebe panted. "Can we do this? Will it work?"

Sol sucked air into his lungs for a moment before glancing up at her.

"It has to."

Chapter Twenty-Two

Thorne's lungs were on fire. His old shoulder injury felt like iron spikes in his bones, and his old knee injury ached like a ball of flame. And although he'd done his best to dodge and deflect the madman's inexperienced attacks, he'd still taken several blows that left his torso throbbing as if he'd been stepped upon by a raging bull.

An unexpected fist sent him flying backward into a wall, and not only his shoulder but also his back exploded in pain. He'd been knocked around too many times for him to count by now. He lay on the floor, feeling like his lungs were ten sizes smaller as he fought to breathe.

Get up! Havner can't take Shokes alone!

He moved slower than he wanted, his muscles shaking in spasms as he tried to climb to his feet. Mr. Havner leapt back to dodge Mr. Shokes, and as Thorne's gaze followed them, he noticed movement behind them, near the front of the stable. It took him a moment to realize he was staring at the backend of the post chaise, with the tiny boot facing them.

He suddenly knew what Mr. Drydale intended to do.

He clung to the wall as he forced his legs to straighten. "Don't retreat!" he yelled to Mr. Havner. "Push him in this direction!"

"Easy for you to say!"

Another set of knives came flying down from the rafters, and while one missed and embedded into the wood of the floor, the other struck Mr. Shokes low on his back. His clothes were ripped with small holes that had become larger as he fought them, smeared with blood. But not much—the Root he'd taken made his wounds heal unnaturally quickly, and each small wound hardly seemed to slow him down.

No, he was slightly slower. Thorne didn't know if he was tiring or if the sedative on the knives was finally starting to affect him.

Mr. Shokes shrieked as the blade sliced into side muscles, and yet despite the obvious pain he barely stopped his attack on Mr. Havner.

Thorne grabbed a chunk of wood on the ground and tossed it at Mr. Shokes, clipping his shoulder. "Over here!" Thorne bellowed as loud as he could.

Mr. Shokes turned toward him almost negligently, but Thorne waved his arms and shouted again, then tossed more wood chunks at him. His aim was off and some hit Mr. Havner or bounced off the floor, but he kept throwing them. He needed the monster to focus on him instead.

Mr. Shokes looked at him for what felt like a full minute before turning from Mr. Havner and lumbering toward him. Thorne waved his arms more and began backing up slowly rather than running away from him. He threw more wood, although there was less of it where he was standing.

Perhaps he shouldn't have thrown the wood. Mr. Shokes was distracted by a flying piece and tracked it to the wall along the side. He rushed the wall like a bull, slamming his head into it, then he pounded with heavy fists. It had previously taken some damage when he kicked at it, so it began to cave in on itself, splinters flying everywhere.

Thorne darted forward with his knife and slashed at him. The attack finally got his attention. His next punch, intended for the wall, swerved and arced toward Thorne's head. He ducked and rolled sideways away from him.

The coachman appeared behind him with a blow from the cudgel, but Thorne was quick to jump forward and slice into his leg, then bounce backward to again claim his attention.

Behind them, the coach lumbered forward, boxing them in. But it was difficult to back the coach in a straight line and it scraped against the stalls on one side.

The strange noise distracted Mr. Shokes from his two annoying attackers. Spotting the post chaise behind Mr. Havner, he ran past the coachman and pushed at the back of the coach. It bounded backward, rising slightly off its back wheels, and the people pushing it stumbled. Then Mr. Shokes began kicking at the boot at the base of the cab.

Thorne and Mr. Havner both attacked his back to draw him again down the aisle, but they had lost the advantage of having a man on either side of him. The aisle was not wide enough and they had to switch places in front of Mr. Shokes. It was not impossible to do, but they occasionally bumped as they moved past each other.

They attacked him faster now than before and moved away from him with quick steps, drawing him down to the last few stalls at the end of the stable just before the wide open space in front of the back doors. There was only a dogcart in a corner, but the rest of the space was clear. He motioned Mr. Havner to the opposite side so that the two of them stood diagonally on either side of Mr. Shokes.

"Now!" Thorne yelled.

The post chaise seemed not to move for a long moment, then he realized it was inching forward slowly as they started up from the stopped position. It gained speed, and then it was rattling down the aisle toward them.

Mr. Shokes turned his head toward the sound, but Thorne yelled and brought himself dangerously close to slash at his side while the coachman did the same with a blow to his thigh. Mr. Shokes lunged toward Mr. Havner, but Thorne came forward with two sharp slices at his back to prevent him from moving too far from the center of the space.

He was too close, and Mr. Shokes twisted his torso and clipped Thorne's cheek as he tried to jerk away. It felt like a cast-iron skillet had smashed into his head.

Through the stars in his vision, he saw Mr. Shokes's hazy figure. He slashed again, desperate to keep him where he stood. He couldn't see Mr. Shokes's movement very well, but he instinctively ducked and escaped a swinging claw.

"Watch out!" Mr. Havner shouted, and Thorne rolled backward.

The dark bulk of the coach flashed past him, so close he felt the whir of air against his face and saw the spokes of the wheels flying in front of his eyes.

Then the coach came to a jerking stop as it collided and Mr. Shokes stumbled a few steps.

"We don't want him to fall!" Mr. Drydale roared from the front of the coach.

Yes, otherwise the coach would simply roll over him. They had to trap him instead.

Thorne forced himself to his feet. There was still several yards of space between the coach and the back door, with Mr. Shokes in between. He had to keep him there.

He lunged forward with his knife, stabbing instead of slicing, and cut a forearm. On the other side, Mr. Havner swung the cudgel in a downward motion and the wood connected with Mr. Shokes's ear.

"Hurry!" Thorne yelled at the same time Mr. Drydale roared, "Push!"

The coach eased forward but gained speed faster this time, and Thorne darted toward the shaft closest to him to add his strength to Miss Gardinier and Miss Sauber. On the other side,

Mr. Havner had done the same with Mr. Drydale.

With the added force, the coach jerked forward and slammed Mr. Shokes against the back door. The wheels caged him in, and the boot stuck out enough to pin his legs to the door.

"Be quick," Mr. Drydale shouted. "He might break the back doors and allow him outside."

"Quick to do what?" Thorne asked.

Miss Sauber raced back to the center of the long building. She was in time to catch first Calvin, then Clara as they dropped from the rafters. They raced around the space, retrieving the knives they had thrown which had missed or which Mr. Shokes had pulled free and thrown away.

As they ran back toward the wriggling coach, they wrapped their scarves around their faces, tying them tightly. Then Miss Gardinier gave Clara her satchel as Miss Sauber hoisted Calvin up in her arms in an astounding feat of strength. He stood on her shoulders to reach the rafters almost directly over Mr. Shokes but still a few feet away and to the side. He pulled himself up. She did the same with Clara, but on the other side of Mr. Shokes.

Miss Gardinier passed Thorne a cloth she'd torn from a cloak. "Tie this around your face." He did so while Mr. Havner and Mr. Drydale held the coach against Mr. Shokes, then took one of their places while they did the same.

"What are you doing?" The words came out in jerking puffs as he held the coach against Mr. Shokes's wildly struggling form. "I thought we used up the last of the sedative arrows."

"We have to give him the largest possible dose of powdered sedative in the smallest possible area," Miss Gardinier told him. "Clara's going to throw a bag and Calvin will pin it to the wall above his head."

"It'll just be stuck to the wall."

"She'll cut a hole in the bag before she throws it. When it's on the wall, it'll trickle down on top of his head."

He remembered what she'd told him about the sedative before they started for the stable. "She's too small. It's too strong for her to be so close to the powder."

"That's why I wanted to throw it, but Clara's aim is better and Calvin might have an easier time if she did it."

Calvin took aim and a knife thunked into the wall directly above Mr. Shokes's head, a target for Clara to direct the bag when she threw it. It was just out of reach of his hands so that he couldn't grab the bag and toss it aside.

The back doors creaked. "Hurry!" Mr. Drydale said.

Clara made eye contact with her brother, and he nodded. She cut a hole in the bag in her hands, then threw it in a slow arc. A little sedative fell in softish clumps like wet snow, and the bag's trajectory passed directly where he'd thrown the knife into the wood.

Calvin's knife flashed, but it missed, landing in the wood to the side of the initial knife target marker, and the bag passed on, dropping to the ground beside Mr. Shokes. Thorne saw it land, and some of the sedative puffed up, but then it sank to the floor in heavy drifts. It was far different from the light, airy powder that they'd used earlier to obscure Jack's vision.

Calvin's face had turned white, and he looked down toward Miss Sauber, who was helping to push against the coach with Mr. Drydale. "Relax, Calvin. Breathe."

He nodded, his eyes glittering with determination, and did as she instructed. He nodded to his sister, and she threw.

The arc of the bag this time was a little off, but Calvin threw confidently. The knife nicked the bag and some sedative dropped directly onto Mr. Shokes's head, but the majority remained in the bag and it joined the other on the floor.

Calvin suddenly called down with panic in his voice, "The knife I have left is bent." He held it up. It had probably been one that hit Mr. Shokes, but that he'd removed, and it had dented when it had flown aside.

"I have a knife," Clara called, "but I can't throw the bag and knife at the same time."

There was a beat as everyone looked to Mr. Drydale, but then Miss Sauber said firmly, "I can do it."

Thorne frowned at her, although with his face covered she probably only saw his lowered brows. "With a bow and arrow? That's a difficult shot."

"It's exactly like hunting birds. And Clara's throw is easier to hit than a bird in flight."

"Do it!" Mr. Drydale said.

She already had her bow and quiver strung across her body, so she clambered on top of the post chaise hood in order to reach the rafters. Mr. Shokes saw her and screamed at her, clawing desperately with his extended arms. She paled but didn't so much as glance at him. Thorne and the others pushed harder against the coach to keep him in place.

She pulled herself up next to Calvin on the wooden rafter, which looked as thin as a twig next to her tall figure. However, her height worked against her because the rafters were too close to the roof for her to be able to sit upright.

She gave Calvin her quiver, then clasped her bow and loosely nocked an arrow. She leaned to the side to try to aim at Mr. Shokes, but her entire body wobbled so alarmingly that Calvin grabbed at her to steady her. The beam was too narrow for her to lie down sideways to aim.

The doors creaked again. "We have to shoot him." Mr. Drydale's voice was pitched low, with a gravelly tone that spoke of how difficult it was for him to say the words.

Thorne knew he had a pistol. "I'll do it."

"No," he said firmly. "I will."

Thorne had never seen a superior with that resolute look on his face. He knew exactly what he was doing, and he was choosing this job for himself while understanding all the implications it would bring.

Thorne knew now why Michael had trusted this man. And he was willing to trust him, too.

"Come down!" Mr. Drydale called to Miss Sauber.

But rather than the frustration he expected to see in her eyes, she glanced at him with a look of ... calculation. Her gaze returned to the knife in the wall that served as their target, her eyes intense. "I can do it."

She straddled the beam, facing away from Calvin and toward Mr. Shokes. She exhaled a long breath, then turned to look at Calvin and said, "Be sure to grab my legs."

Then she shoved the arrow in her mouth, held the bow in one hand and grabbed the beam in the other, and then swung herself *upside down.*

Miss Gardinier gave a muffled shriek. Mr. Drydale shouted, "What are you doing?!" as Calvin scrambled to grab her legs, now crossed over the beam in front of him. His eyes were wide and horrified.

She swung in place a little, her stocking cap bobbing in midair, but her face was as calm as if she were serving tea. When her swaying had minimized, she pulled the arrow from her mouth and nocked it.

"It's impossible," Thorne said.

"I believe in her," Mr. Drydale answered him.

She took aim slowly, carefully. And then Thorne heard her murmur, "'Some trust in chariots, and some in horses: but we will remember the name of the Lord our God.'"

The words resounded in his head, striking a deeper chord within him that he didn't understand. He knew those words. It was a verse from the Bible, although he couldn't say from which book. But he was left with the indelible impression that that verse had once been very important to him, except that the memory was clouded.

"Throw!" Miss Sauber shouted to Clara.

The bag sailed, trailing soft clumps of sedative. Miss Sauber loosed her arrow.

It thumped solidly into the wood, but he could only barely see over the top of the post chaise. Then around the body of the cab, he saw clouds of sedative pouring down from the wall onto the floor, falling in waves like a waterfall.

Mr. Shokes screamed, but it was stopped by choking as he breathed in the sedative. He continued to scream even between coughs, and the resistance against the coach didn't abate. The back doors creaked again, louder this time.

It wasn't going to work. "We have to shoot him," Thorne said to Mr. Drydale.

"Wait a few more minutes," Miss Gardinier pleaded.

But even as she said it, the struggles began to weaken. His resistance became sluggish. The flood of sedative now poured down in thin streams. Mr. Shokes's screams grew softer, less frequent. Thorne could hear his choking gasps and harsh breaths, fast and heavy from his exertions. Thorne leaned sideways for a brief moment to look at him, and he was shaking his head and rubbing at his eyes.

Mr. Shokes pushed half-heartedly at the post chaise, and the shaking of his head slowed down. His eyes became unfocused, and then they rolled back in his head just as his legs collapsed under him. The pressure from the post chaise was keeping him upright, so Mr. Drydale gave the order and they tentatively eased back on their pushing. Mr. Shokes slumped to the floor.

Miss Gardinier moved as if to go to him, but Mr. Drydale told her to stop in a sharp voice. She did, but she shook her head. "He shouldn't have been so strongly affected by only one bag of sedative."

Mr. Drydale caught Thorne's eye, and then the two of them eased around the post chaise to warily approach Mr. Shokes. He didn't move. As they drew closer, they could see that he was very pale, even under the layer of sedative coating his face.

Just before Thorne bent down to shake him, Miss Gardenier

said, "Stop! The sedative ..."

He'd forgotten. He prodded him gently with his foot, then rolled him onto his stomach, but he didn't respond. A little more relieved, Thorne took some rope that Mr. Havner passed to him and tied Mr. Shokes's hands, then his feet. If he suddenly came awake, the ropes wouldn't stop his overwhelming strength, but it would give them enough time to get away from him before he broke his bonds.

As he finished tying him up, he saw Miss Sauber swinging down from the rafters. She had given Calvin her bow and hung down from a beam, then dropped several feet to the ground.

Miss Gardinier ran and hugged her fiercely before she'd fully straightened. Mr. Drydale's eyes blazed as he approached, but none of them had removed their scarves yet so the full expression of his wrath was hidden.

"You could have missed," he snapped.

"I knew I could do it," she replied calmly. "I've done it before."

That startled him. "You have?"

She gestured toward Miss Gardinier. "We had a dare that I couldn't hang upside down from a tree branch and hit the target. And from there, the dare became more and more difficult."

Miss Gardinier's face had turned purple, and she thumped Miss Sauber hard on her arm with a white-knuckled fist. "When you were hanging from the tree branch, your head was only a foot off the ground!"

Miss Sauber rubbed her arm and the parts of her face visible above the scarf looked sheepish as she turned to Mr. Drydale. "Could you please not tell ... Martha?"

Even with the unfamiliar name, Thorne knew immediately she was referring to Lady Wynwood.

He glanced at the arrow, still stuck in the wall with the empty, ragged bag that had held the sedative. The words she'd spoken just before she'd loosed the arrow had seemed to awaken something inside of him that nagged him like a scar. And it bothered him even more that he couldn't remember, but he felt as if he ought to. The memory was just out of reach and he couldn't quite grasp it. He didn't understand why it was important to him, and the unremittant feeling frustrated him because he didn't know how to uncover what it was about.

Then came a choking sound from the ground.

Thorne rushed back to the area behind the post chaise, where Mr. Shokes lay tied up. Miss Gardinier had said that he shouldn't have been put to sleep with only one dose. Was he awake? Would he break his bonds immediately?

Mr. Shokes's body was still on the ground, but bending back and forth at the waist. Thorne was about to warn everyone to get back when he realized the man was convulsing. His half-open eyes only showed the whites, and spit foamed at his mouth.

"Move!"

He'd never heard such a loud shout from Miss Gardinier, and he obeyed out of reflex. She squeezed past him and knelt next to Mr. Shokes before he could stop her.

But just as suddenly as he'd started convulsing, he stopped. His entire body visibly relaxed, his mouth falling open, and his head slowly dropped to the ground as if laying his head on a pillow.

Miss Gardinier examined him with frantic hands, touching his mouth and nose, his throat, his hands. Her own hands were shaking, but when she had stopped, her voice was clear as she said, "He's dead."

"From the sedative?" Mr. Drydale asked.

"It shouldn't have killed a man on the Root. I wasn't even certain it would slow him down."

Mr. Drydale shut his eyes and leaned against the side of the post chaise. Thorne could feel the regret pouring out of him. He had tried so hard to save Mr. Shokes, despite what Thorne had said.

He was used to ruthless decisions in battle or on a mission, and when he'd first heard Mr. Drydale's decision, he'd thought it foolish. It was indeed risky, even foolhardy, but he had to respect the man. Thorne wouldn't have had the courage to try it. He'd have chosen the easier way.

Only now did his mind realize the consequences, and why Mr. Drydale had been adamant about being the one to shoot him if it became necessary. He was willing to take responsibility, but he also wanted to try everything he could first.

Miss Gardinier rose to her feet. She was pale, and her hands still shook, but her face appeared calm. He could tell she had seen death before. Knowing her medical experience, he wasn't surprised.

He hadn't known Mr. Shokes at all, and had barely met his brother, Dr. Shokes. And yet he felt he ought to say something to her, but he didn't know what he could say that would make her feel any better.

He stared at Mr. Shokes's still form. "I think he would have preferred death over being a monster." He only belatedly realized the low, gravelly voice was his.

No one answered him for a long while. Then Miss Gardinier said in a soft tone, "I think so, too."

Chapter Twenty-Three

The night seemed colder than it had been only an hour before as Phoebe stood in front of the dark apothecary shop. Beside her was Keriah, and in front of them, as if shielding them and forming a stalwart rampart, was Uncle Sol.

Except when he was like this, she couldn't call him Uncle Sol. He was Mr. Drydale, an agent for the Crown, the man in charge of a confidential operation to uncover the activities of a clandestine group. He was there to take responsibility for a tragedy that was not his fault.

She had never quite seen him like this, even last night when they were trying to save Mr. Coulton-Jones. Seeing him like this now, she felt the deepest respect for him.

The rooms above the shop were dark, but when Mr. Drydale knocked on the door, there was the sound of movement inside almost immediately. Within moments, the door was unlatched and Mrs. Shokes's white face appeared.

Phoebe had been hoping for Dr. Shokes to respond to the summons, although perhaps that was cowardly of her. Mr. Drydale had not shied away from his duty, so she should not, either.

She could feel the tension thrumming in Keriah's entire body. The agitated shaking of her hands increased at the sight of Mrs. Shokes.

The apothecary's wife ... no, his widow saw the expressions on their faces, and her eyes became large, dark hollows. Her bottom lip began to quiver as Mr. Drydale cleared his throat, gathering his courage.

Mrs. Shokes reached out a hand and touched his arm in a comforting gesture, although Phoebe could see that she was trembling. "Come inside first," she said in a low voice. "You mustn't stand out in the dark and cold."

She led them to the small sitting room at the back of the shop, which she had painstakingly decorated with carefully chosen pieces of furniture designed to bring comfort and peace to the patients who met her husband and brother-in-law there. She lit the candles as if merely preparing for a routine consultation, her face focused on her task.

Phoebe and Keriah sank into the worn sofa, and Mr. Drydale and Mrs. Shokes sat in the two chairs. There was a tense moment of silence, and then she said, "It's not good news, is it?"

Mr. Drydale shook his head. His face was drawn and lined, as if his entire body was in pain. Perhaps it was. Phoebe's limbs felt on fire and yet ice-cold at the same time.

She was shocked. She was sad. Quite honestly, her emotions were a terrible messy jumble that couldn't be separated and dealt with. It was the sticky slop of guilt and tragedy over all her feelings that kept her from making sense of anything.

After Mr. Shokes had suddenly died, they had had to hurry out of the stable in the event that Jack returned. So they couldn't treat his body with proper respect and had been forced to settle it in the rented post chaise. Mr. Havner retrieved Aunt Laura's nondescript coach from the safe place he had miraculously found in which to stash it, and Keriah treated Mr. Ackett's injuries as best she could while bouncing around in the vehicle. Right now, both carriages were a short distance away while Mr. Drydale informed the Shokes family.

Mr. Drydale's jaw was tight, but his eyes were tender and anguished. "Tonight, we found your husband's body in a stable used by Apothecary Jack."

Tears welled in her eyes even as her hand flew to her mouth that he had dared to speak the name. She couldn't seem to form the words she wanted to say, but Mr. Drydale reached over to touch her hand, which made her close her eyes and swallow hard.

"I told him not to get involved with that man and his business, that nothing good would come of it," she said. And then she broke down into bitter tears.

Phoebe felt ashamed at herself as she witnessed the woman's grief. She was too wrapped up in her own emotions to realize that there were others in pain and in need around her.

Finally Mrs. Shokes asked, "Do you know ... what happened to him?"

Mr. Drydale hesitated, then said, "It's unclear what Jack might have done to him. We thought Dr. Shokes might want to examine him."

"Where is he?"

"In a post chaise nearby. We did not want Jack to have him."

She nodded gratefully, her face crumpling as more tears flowed. In between sniffles, she asked, "How is it that you found him?"

Mr. Drydale glanced at Keriah for a moment before answering. "We were searching for a friend of Miss Gardinier's family who had disappeared last night in the commotion. Our search led us to the stable, where we found our friend and your husband."

"Was your friend also—?"

"No, he was badly injured but alive."

In spite of the misery she must have been feeling, she spared a small smile. "I am glad."

"Miss Gardinier immediately tried to save your husband, but

there was nothing that could be done."

"I know she would have." Mrs. Shokes gave a larger smile to Keriah. "I know you would have done everything possible."

Keriah nodded, but looked down at her hands. Tears dripped down her nose, but she made no sound, and she couldn't meet Mrs. Shokes's eyes.

After a minute or two, Mrs. Shokes's soft weeping started to abate. Mr. Drydale asked gently, "I assume Dr. Shokes is out with a patient?" Mrs. Shokes nodded. "If you'll tell me where he might have gone, I will go to fetch him."

She told him, and after he left, Keriah moved to his seat next to Mrs. Shokes and grasped her hand. They sat in silence, and Phoebe rose with a feeble murmur about tea.

Mrs. Shokes's kitchen was small, with only a tiny hearth since the ground floor was taken up by the shop. She built up the fire, but the kettle hanging above it was still warm and full, so it should boil quickly.

A movement outside the kitchen drew her attention, and one of the children had appeared in a long white nightgown. She froze at the sight of Phoebe, but then recognized her and relaxed. "Miss Sauber?"

"Couldn't sleep, Hannah? Would you like some water?"

"Where's Mama?"

"Downstairs with Keriah. Would you like me to tuck you into bed?"

She thought gravely a moment, then nodded. Phoebe had to press her lips together so she wouldn't laugh, but then she sobered as she remembered the news Hannah would wake up to.

She walked the young girl to the room and the large pallet she shared with her sister and youngest brother. Hannah didn't ask any questions about what was happening, perhaps because she was accustomed to her father and uncle being out at all hours.

Phoebe sat next to the bed stuffed with children and stroked the girl's face. She stared at Phoebe with large dark eyes, then closed them and was almost immediately asleep.

Back in the kitchen, she stared at the flames in the hearth. In this quiet moment, she had the time and space to dig deep into the pit of her soul and try to understand what had happened.

While Keriah was treating his injuries, Mr. Ackett had told them in halting sentences about how Mr. Shokes had come to Jack on his own, in order to inform him of their experiments. As far as Mr. Ackett knew, Mr. Shokes hadn't exposed their names, or even their gender, but something about the way Mr. Ackett told the story made Phoebe suspect that it would have been possible to scare it out of him eventually.

When she'd heard that Mr. Shokes had gone willingly to Jack in order to tell him about them, the betrayal and anger had become burning coals inside of her. It reminded her of how she felt when her father betrayed her.

She tried to tell herself that her feelings were ridiculous because she hadn't known Mr. Shokes very well. Keriah knew him better, although she was closer to his brother.

Dr. Shokes had said that men would be tempted by the Root and the kind of power and prestige it would give. He himself would not have trusted his own brother with the Root sample Phoebe had found.

Perhaps they shouldn't have used his stillroom. But where else could they have done their research? And despite figuring out what they were doing, Mr. Shokes had tried to protect their identities.

But after watching his widow in tears, Phoebe's anger was mostly doused by her shame. However, her emotions were still a mix of various things. She was glad they were all still safe. She was sad Mr. Shokes was dead. She had been dreading telling Mrs. Shokes, but Mr. Drydale had taken on the responsibility. She felt empathy for how Dr. Shokes would feel once he learned what had happened to his brother.

But those embers of betrayal still smoldered inside her. She didn't like it, and yet she kept feeding it. She didn't understand why she was like this. But she was also reaching the point where she no longer cared to understand.

She and Keriah would have been powerless if Mr. Shokes had told Jack their identities, and she didn't like that feeling of helplessness. It reminded her of how vulnerable a woman was in the world she lived in, where she was subject to father and husband.

Phoebe was once again reminded that she was not truly in control of her life, despite how she left her home to live with Aunt Laura. In the end, her father controlled her, the father she couldn't forgive for abusing his responsibilities toward her.

She did not want to be vulnerable and helpless, subject to the whims of a selfish father or a weak, greedy apothecary.

Mr. Shokes had been tricked by Jack, and she grieved for him even as she felt betrayed by him. But she also did not want his death to mean nothing. She wanted to find a way to stop Jack after what he had done to Mr. Shokes and Mr. Ackett.

But what could she do? She had just been realizing the extent of her impotence.

But she was not a prisoner. She would not stand and allow her father to shackle her and lead her where he wanted her to go.

It was ironic that because of Jack's dark shadow creeping over London, she finally knew what she desired to do with her life.

She had proven she was not useless, and she was willing to do whatever it took to prove she was capable. She was willing to bow out if it became obvious she wasn't, but she was also willing to be trained like any other man.

And like any other man, she was willing to risk herself to stop Jack and the group behind him, to protect the people she cared about. She was already deeply involved in this. She wanted to fully commit. She wanted to be of use.

She had never felt so strongly about something. She had felt passion for her hobbies like her gardening and her archery. She had felt fleeting excitement at her clandestine visits to be taught knife-fighting by Keriah's Gypsy friend. But this felt like something she was *made* to do, as ridiculous as that sounded.

She had to convince him.

But first, she wanted to free herself.

Chapter Twenty-Four

As Laura ascended the steps toward the front door of Sol's townhouse, she realized that she and her two companions were all equally uneasy, for wildly disparate reasons.

Keriah seemed even more nervous now than when first talking about Mr. Ackett's injuries, which made Laura think her anxiety was not related to his well-being. And yet, Keriah's interactions with Mr. Ackett during the Seasons in town had been so fleeting, according to what Phoebe had told her, that Laura wondered at the source of the girl's strong emotions.

Phoebe had spoken to Laura this morning, so she knew the reason for her niece's disquiet. And yet, the uncertainty hadn't caused the young woman to falter in her steps. She walked taller now, with more confidence than Laura had seen in her before. During all the years she'd lived with her father and focused her efforts on trying to please him, she had carried a burden that sagged her shoulders, which she had now shed.

Phoebe had deliberately not told her about the shot from her arrow, but Calvin and Clara had been more than willing to share. Laura had gone to see them, armed with candies, to ensure they were both well despite the harrowing events of the night before.

While the shot should have sent her into hysterics, it had not. Perhaps because she had always known she could not control

Phoebe, nor had she desired to since her father did quite enough of that himself. In fact, Calvin's raving about the difficult shot made her feel rather proud that her blood flowed through the girl's veins.

She wondered if she would have felt differently if Phoebe were her child and not her niece. Would she have been a terrible mother, allowing her daughter to embark on such dangerous escapades?

And yet, they were not escapades. They were missions carefully planned and executed by the man she was about to visit, whose purpose was guided by his sense of justice. Despite their differences, and the secrets she still kept from him, she trusted Sol. She knew she could trust him with Phoebe's and Keriah's lives.

She also did not want to snuff out the sparkling that had begun to show in her niece's demeanor. Not silly excitement or a sense of recklessness, but a deeper maturity that yet shone with brightness. Laura ought not keep her wrapped up in cotton wool and protected, but instead enable her to do the things she excelled at, to discover and fulfill her purpose. This morning, Phoebe had admitted she wanted that more than she ever had before.

Laura was not without apprehension, but it would be best to be walking alongside Phoebe, ready to help, rather than behind her and trying to hold her back.

Laura's hand hesitated before tapping the door knocker. Her own anxiety stemmed from seeing Sol again. She had not yet determined what she would say to him.

Sol himself answered the front door, and was not surprised to see them. He treated them all with his normal politeness, so perhaps it was Laura's imagination that he avoided looking at her.

"You are not my only visitors this morning," he said as he led them upstairs to his drawing room. "Mr. Rosmont and Lady

Aymer arrived only a few moments ago."

"Have they been to see Mr. Ackett?" Laura asked.

He shook his head. "Dr. Shokes is still with the patient."

She wasn't imagining it. He did avoid looking at her. Her heart quailed even as nausea rose in her stomach.

"Will it be possible for us to speak to him?" Keriah asked.

"I am hoping you all would."

His eagerness shocked her so much that she stumbled on the next step of the stairs. So far he had been quite reticent about what he shared with them from his agents. According to Phoebe, Mr. Ackett had only spoken briefly with Keriah in the coach about Mr. Shokes. And after they fetched Dr. Shokes to treat him, he hadn't been free to speak at all about what Jack had said or done.

Sol whipped around so quickly he was a blur, and suddenly his hand was gripping her arm to help her regain her balance. He finally looked at her.

There was pain in his eyes, but she couldn't tell what had caused it. Her heart thudded a beat, two beats, and then was still.

In the drawing room, Mr. Rosmont was pacing in front of the fireplace while Lady Aymer's petite form was engulfed by one of Sol's expensively masculine chairs. She smiled and greeted them.

Today, the crease between Mr. Rosmont's dark brows was still there, but there was marked respect in the way he looked at the two young women that had not been there the last time she had seen him. In fact, his bow toward them was deeper than was technically polite.

"Are you well, Mr. Rosmont?" Laura sank into one of the sofas, hoping it would encourage the men to sit rather than pace. "I heard that the other day, you were forced to deal with rather physically taxing obligations."

The side of his mouth quirked at her circumspect question. "I am much better today, my lady."

"You may speak freely," Sol said. "The room is well sealed against eavesdroppers."

Certainly, with the work he did, he would ensure his home would be secure. Others might not have noticed, but Laura saw that Mr. Rosmont's shoulders relaxed a trifle. He moved stiffly and winced as he sat in a heavy wooden chair.

"We arrived so that Thorne could give his report to Mr. Drydale as well as to see Mr. Ackett," Lady Aymer said.

Mr. Rosmont nodded, and his mouth drew into a grim line.

"It was a bad business," Laura said gently. "I thank you for all you did to support Miss Sauber and Miss Gardinier."

He did not respond immediately, and when he did, the words were drawn slowly out of him. "To be honest, they supported me quite as well."

Keriah's mouth dropped open, especially when Mr. Rosmont turned to her. "The sedative you created saved many lives, including that of my friend Michael Coulton-Jones. I had been *told* about a man who had gone mad on the Root, but it is quite another thing to *fight* with him."

"You were very gravely injured for our sakes," Keriah said softly. "And for Mr. Ackett."

"At the time, the situation was so overwhelming that I thought the only option was the more permanent one. And yet you fought against that, and it was only later that I realized that if you hadn't, my friend would not be alive."

Keriah was clearly uncomfortable with his gratitude, because she responded tartly, "You can thank me if he wakes up in his right mind."

"I regret that we couldn't have saved Nick and Mr. Shokes."

"There was nothing that could be done," Sol said. "I certainly would not have wanted you to try to stop Silas from taking Nick."

"Now Jack will surely find a way to counter my sedative

paste," Keriah said.

"You shall simply prove yourself smarter than he is," Laura told her. She eyed Sol. "That is, assuming you wish the young ladies to continue to assist you?"

He looked slightly uncomfortable to be put on the spot in such a way, but his answer was firm. "Frankly, there is no one else in all of London whom I would trust with the Root more than Phoebe and Miss Gardinier." He scratched his cheek as he turned to Mr. Rosmont. "We were just discussing Mr. Rosmont's plans when you arrived."

Mr. Rosmont's face grew stony as he replied, "Jack killed Richard. Of course I will stay and continue to help."

Phoebe and Keriah looked confused, but Laura thought she knew to whom he was referring. "Lady Aymer's older brother?"

Pink studded Mr. Rosmont's cheeks. "Should I not have mentioned him?" he asked Lady Aymer.

Sol had looked uncomfortable again, but Lady Aymer answered, "Mr. Drydale informed us about it, so it is right that we should tell these ladies also." She explained about Mr. Coulton-Jones's investigation into the poisoner of their brother's club last year, and how it seemed to point to Apothecary Jack.

"Was your brother Richard involved in all of this, then?" Laura asked, incredulous. "That would be quite a coincidence."

"He could simply have been a victim along with the other men who were killed. But if Jack did target him and his friend Albert Freeland, it was for a reason we have yet to uncover."

"The Coulson-Jones's country estate neighbors yours, does it not?" Laura asked Mr. Rosmont.

"We grew up together," he said. "I have always been good friends with Michael, but I loved Richard, too."

"I am glad to have your help," Sol said. "You have proven yourself more than capable."

Mr. Rosmont grew pensive. "I apologize about that girl ... Hetty. It was an accident."

After all he had done for them, he still thought about the young prostitute whose arm he had accidentally broken. It caused a strumming in Laura's heart as she looked at him. He would not appreciate being compared to a lost puppy, but that was how he appeared in her eyes.

Perhaps she was simply getting old.

"I have taken care of her," Laura told him gently. "She is being sent into the country as a maid to a very kind family I know."

In actuality, Laura had used third parties to enable Hetty to be hired by Lord Meynhill, who was unaware of the woman's connection to Laura. She had secretly asked Hetty to keep her eyes open and to send a note to Laura if anything strange happened, or if a stranger came to the village.

"Hetty asked me to give a message to you," Laura continued. "She thanks you for saving her, and she wanted you to know she doesn't blame you for injuring her."

The words hardly seemed to comfort him. His jaw was locked tight as he stared at the floor. Lady Aymer reached over to touch his arm, and he glanced at her, his gaze softening, but the guilt was still writ across his features.

Once Hetty's broken bone had been set and she'd been rested and fed, she had been distraught about Mr. Rosmont, because he had been so horrified by what he'd done. Laura added, "She told me that she knows the difference between a man who deliberately wants to hurt a woman, and an accident."

His jaw eased its rock-hard tightness slightly, but his eyes returned on the floor.

At that moment, the door to the drawing room opened and Dr. Shokes came into the room.

He looked exhausted, and Laura wondered if he'd slept at all in the past two days. The few stray brown hairs left on his balding pate were sticking out in every direction, giving him a bewildered appearance. Keriah's face grew pinched as she saw him, and her lips trembled.

But he gave them all a gentle, if tired glance. "Ah, it is just as well you are all here. I needn't repeat myself."

"How is he?" Sol asked as Dr. Shokes sat down on a chair with a weary sigh.

"Just as badly injured as when you asked me yesterday."

Sol gave a small, rueful smile.

"He'll mostly recover," Dr. Shokes continued. "However, the knee is in a very bad way. He may not regain the same strength and flexibility he used to have."

They were silent. Sol had confided to her that Mr. Ackett was mostly used for secretive, inquisitive work that was highly demanding of his limber joints and wiry strength. She ached for him if he could not regain his ability. She silently prayed for healing for him.

Dr. Shokes lightly slapped his hands on his knees. "Considering he also has a couple broken ribs and he's almost entirely black and blue from the beating he received, he's not doing too badly."

Laura blanched.

Dr. Shokes took a deep breath, then looked to Keriah and Phoebe. "I am giving you everything in my brother's stillroom. Do you think you could come and take it?"

Keriah was stunned into silence. Phoebe asked, "Everything?"

"Minus the tinctures and medicines I'll need. Will you be able to find another place to do your work?" He looked to Sol, understanding who might be in charge of that.

Keriah asked in a small voice, "Mrs. Shokes ...?"

"She's taking the children to live with her family in the country." His face creased as he said it, but then he set his jaw and looked up at them all. "I'm staying in London. I feel responsible for my patients here."

"At the shop?" Keriah asked, alarmed.

"No, I'll move to another place where it'll be harder for Jack to find me." He said the name almost defiantly. "I don't think he'll be interested in me since I'm not an apothecary, but he doesn't know what my brother might have told me."

"I can help ..." Sol began, but Mr. Shokes shook his head.

"I thank you, but that isn't necessary." He wet his lips, then added, "I am more than willing to help you if needed, to make up for what my brother did."

"You needn't feel that way," Sol said at the same time Keriah said, "Dr. Shokes, it isn't necessary."

Ignoring them, the doctor said, "I want to help rid London of Jack and the Root. It's only causing the evil in men to grow like yeast in bread and turn them into entirely different people."

No one quite knew how to respond to that. Sol finally said, "We shall be glad of your help, and we thank you for helping Septimus right now."

Dr. Shokes nodded and stood. "Come by the shop to collect the stillroom things today or tomorrow. I shall send a note when I have found a safe place to stay."

"You may remain here," Sol said, also rising.

"No. Jack never discovered Mr. Ackett's identity, but my presence might alert him. I'll visit like I did today, from the back door."

Sol and Mr. Rosmont shook his hand, and Dr. Shokes stopped to take Keriah's hand and squeeze it, giving her a fatherly smile. And then he was gone.

Sol led the way upstairs to the guest bedroom where Mr. Ackett was recovering. As they walked, Laura asked him, "What did you tell Mr. Ackett's mother?"

"I said that we were looking at a horse that suddenly became agitated, and Septimus was accidentally kicked a few times. I brought him here since it was closer and called Dr. Shokes to attend to him. She visited immediately after receiving my note, but I suppose, having eight children, injuries don't upset her quite as much as I'd have expected."

"Oh?"

"She looked in on him, admonished him not to be a bother, and then thanked me and left."

Laura blinked. "I suppose it's preferable to a woman having hysterics over her bruised son."

"It helps that I bandaged several of her sons' injuries when they were children." They reached the guest room, and Lady Aymer breezed through the doorway but Phoebe and Keriah paused at the threshold. Both Laura and Sol nodded to them, despite the impropriety of their presence in a man's bedroom. After their actions two nights ago, propriety hardly mattered at this point.

He lay in bed, his face calm and expressionless as usual, but his complexion pale. His gaze flitted across all their faces before riveting to Keriah's for several heartbeats.

Interesting, Laura thought.

"Well, you're looking better," Sol said as he pulled chairs close to the bed for the women to sit. He and Mr. Rosmont stood at the foot of the bed.

Mr. Ackett gave a slight grimace. "Dr. Shokes spoke to you?"

"Yes, he said you're a whining bull chin."

Even thought she was used to her servants' cant, Laura didn't know what he'd just said, but a reluctant smile pulled on Mr. Ackett's serene face. However, it was quickly erased when his dark hazel gaze fell to the lump under the covers that was his knee.

"If Dr. Shokes said you will recover most of your strength, you may believe him," Keriah said fiercely, but then after a moment, she sat back in her chair and looked away from him. She didn't seem to notice she was rubbing her left knee.

Laura remembered Phoebe once speaking about Keriah's old injury. Phoebe had met her in seminary the year after the incident, but Keriah's Aunt Carmelia had once told her that she used to be so active before the attacker who injured her leg and killed her sister. Some of the life in her died that day.

Did she see herself in Mr. Ackett? Perhaps she was uncomfortable because she knew he might be feeling the same kind of pain she experienced. Or was there another reason she would steal glances at him with those intense gray eyes?

"Are you feeling up to speaking with us?" Mr. Rosmont asked.

Mr. Ackett nodded. "Jack thought I was going to be turned into a Berserker—it's one of the names he calls them—so they were indifferent about what I overheard."

"They?"

"There was a pale-eyed man with Jack." Mr. Ackett's gaze went to Phoebe. "Perhaps the same man you saw at Mr. Farrimond's party."

She shivered. "He had a voice that was smooth and yet like ground glass."

Mr. Ackett nodded. "He didn't quite hold power over Jack, but he was more controlled. If Jack is one of the leaders of the group, that man is one, also."

"Did you get his name?" Sol asked.

Mr. Ackett shook his head. "Jack never mentioned it, but I don't believe it was deliberate. He was only there until just before you arrived. They argued about the Root. The man said it was tainted and Jack took offense."

"Tainted? How?" Keriah asked.

"Compared to his other batches, it caused men to become Berserkers rather than simply giving them superior strength."

"I wondered if it might be a different formula," Keriah muttered to herself. "But perhaps not ...?"

"He said the batch was tainted because the well was too close to the river." Mr. Ackett's words had become slower as he tried to remember exactly what had been said.

"Well water?" Keriah said. "For making the Root elixir?"

"Or for the plants?" Phoebe asked. An understanding look

passed between the two women.

"He didn't say," Mr. Ackett said. "He did mention that there were dancing girls who complained about the well water."

"A play-house near a well, near the river?" Mr. Rosmont said.

"The pale-eyed man was almost threatening to Jack," Mr. Ackett recalled. "So Jack promised to do more experiments first rather than trying to move."

"To move his stillroom or his greenhouse?" Sol asked.

"His greenhouse," Phoebe said confidently.

"He wouldn't need large amounts of water for creating the elixir," Keriah said.

"But he'd need to be near a well in order to water the plants," Phoebe said. "We should try to find his greenhouse. It would be helpful to grow the special plant Jack is using."

Laura noticed Sol's eyes flickered toward Phoebe at this statement, but she knew the girl had no other motivation than to try to find a more effective sedative. Those words from most other men would make anyone question if they wanted to recreate the Root for their own gain.

Sol shook his head as he said, "Septimus escaped, and Jack tends to move locations often. In fact, we checked, and he had already left the theater where Mr. Coulton-Jones placed the orders for poison. He might have been indiscreet about what he said in front of Sep because he could simply move to a new place."

"He and his men can move often, but he can't move a greenhouse often. It's too specialized in what he needs."

"What sort of place would he need to grow his plants?" Sol asked.

Phoebe's brows knit as she tilted her head and stared off into space. "Sir Harvey Farrows, from the same botanical society meetings I attend, renovated his London townhouse to create a greenhouse on the top floor. It is composed of as many windows as his builder could install, and he has a stove to strictly control the temperature. If Jack has something similar, he would want somewhere on the top floor of a house where it will receive the most sunlight, and it must be a building a little taller than those immediately around it."

"Another play-house would fit that description," Mr. Rosmont said.

"I doubt that he would have the top floor specially renovated," Laura said slowly.

"But wouldn't he want the best possible space for his plants?" Phoebe asked.

"I recall Sir Harvey's renovation," Laura said. "It was the talk of the town for months. It was extraordinarily expensive and inconvenienced the neighbors. Everyone knew about it, and everyone was talking about it. Which is *not* what Jack would want."

Sol nodded agreement. "Phoebe, what could he do instead?"

"Hiring a builder to install more windows wouldn't cause anyone to wonder at it," she said. "The building he uses for his plants would have lots of windows in the attic or the topmost floor, and perhaps windows cut into the roof. Or would that cause gossip?"

"Unusual, but it could be done quietly," Sol said.

"And, as I mentioned before, near a well so he needn't cart the extra water very far. Somehow I doubt he would have many servants with access to his secret greenhouse to water his plants for him."

Mr. Ackett's eyes had become bright as they followed this rabbit trail. "He also mentioned wanting treacle buns. I think there must be a shop that sells them near his greenhouse."

"Treacle buns?" Phoebe had sat up straighter. "Miss Tolberton served us treacle buns."

Mr. Ackett blinked at her blankly, so they told him what had happened in their search for him.

"I could call upon her and ask about them, since the church

wasn't far from the stable where Jack took Mr. Ackett."

Sol nodded to her. "Please do so as soon as possible. We must make the greenhouse a priority since we don't wish Jack to move his plants, improbable though that might be."

"I still feel as though Jack is always one step ahead of us," Phoebe said. "He managed to get a sample of the sedative when he rescued Nick."

"I'm sure he hoped to also capture all of you," Laura said, "so he did not accomplish everything he might have wanted."

"He captured Mr. Ackett rather easily," Lady Aymer said slowly. "Especially since Thorne mentioned that he was still frantically looking for him in the early hours of the morning before."

"According to Miss Tolberton, the pale-eyed man and Silas went directly into the basement of the church," Phoebe said. "They knew Mr. Ackett would be there. Since Mr. Brimley was waiting outside, perhaps he led them there?"

"But how would Mr. Brimley know? Does he attend services there?" Laura asked.

"Even if he did, there hadn't been any services in the time after Mr. Ackett arrived and before we did."

"Who knew you were there?" Sol asked Mr. Ackett.

"The curate, the midwife he called to treat my injuries, and one respectable woman, possibly one of the women from the charity group. She seemed disapproving of me for some reason. However, others could have seen me while I was unconscious."

"If it was someone from the charity group, we must be cautious," Sol said. "They spoke to Phoebe and Miss Gardinier, and they might remember Mr. Rosmont's face, even though he was posing as a servant. Miss Tolberton …"

"She had her comeout in the same year I did, and has known Keriah since her comeout, also," Phoebe said. "We could not ignore her."

"Nonetheless, be discreet when you speak to her."

"Would it be wiser not to ask her about the treacle buns?"

Sol thought for a moment, then shook his head. "Her information might be useful. You mentioned she has been involved in that group for some time?"

"Yes. They have acquainted themselves with the residents in that area, so her knowledge is likely extensive."

"I will also use my contacts to look into that group and into the church," Sol said.

"You heard from the twins about the church's history with … Shepherd Willie?" Laura asked.

"Yes, but we don't know if Jack knows Shepherd Willie funded his emergency hospital."

"It doesn't appear Jack is funding it now," Keriah said. "It looked to be in dire need of money."

Sol then looked to Laura and held her gaze. It was not a question, nor was it asking permission, but it was a statement of what he intended to do. She looked down at her hands and found them clasped tightly together, and feeling numb from the pressure. Had she been this way for the entire time?

Sol then told them all about Mrs. Jadis, and the pendant Laura had seen. Mr. Rosmont and Lady Aymer especially seemed uncomfortable at the mention of Wynwood's mistress. She again felt that old familiar shame at her husband's infidelity, as if it were somehow her fault.

She pressed a hand to her stomach. After what her husband had done to her, she had rejected him, and she had known he would find other beds to warm him. She had made her decision so that he would not harm her or another innocent again.

Perhaps out of respect for her, Sol skimmed over what she had done when confronting Mrs. Jadis, but he could not smudge over the clear lack of decorum of a lady visiting her husband's paramour. Even Phoebe and Keriah, who were supposed to be blissfully unaware of such seedy topics, had red cheeks and ears as Sol related the tale.

But at the end of his telling, Lady Aymer spoke, perhaps to dissipate the discomfiting atmosphere. "We must find the original jeweler's order to verify if the pendant had the symbol etched inside of it. If it did not have the symbol, it could be that Mrs. Jadis knew nothing about this secret group."

"But if it did have the symbol, what can be done?" Phoebe asked. "My Uncle Wynwood and Mrs. Jadis have been dead for over ten years. How would we find anything about their activities?"

"I am looking through old papers that belonged to Wynwood," Laura said. "I have also asked friends to return letters I wrote to them during the last year before he died, in hopes there was some news I related about him. In lieu of something as convenient as a diary, it is the best way to revisit the gossip from town that year."

She didn't mention an idea that had begun swirling in her mind, because it involved a person whose assistance she could not depend upon.

"Was there nothing else in the hidden spot where you found the pocket watch?" Mr. Rosmont asked.

"Nothing. However, I will continue to search in the house for any other hiding places. Wynwood wouldn't have had only one."

Mr. Ackett's face had formed deeper lines, so Sol straightened and gestured toward the door. "We should leave Septimus to rest now."

As they filed out of the room, Laura plucked at Sol's sleeve and gave him an even look. He closed the door, glanced at the backs of his visitors as they headed back downstairs, then asked in a low voice, "Yes?"

"I must apologize to you, Sol." She had been so apprehensive about meeting him again, but after the awkwardness of what he'd had to reveal to everyone, she found she was no longer agitated.

He seemed genuinely surprised. "I had rather thought it was

the other way 'round."

He was such a kind man, and a good friend. It was why she had been so ashamed and kept the secret from him. "I kept information from you because the entire sordid tale exposed the cruel things that I did to Mrs. Jadis. I was trying to deny this sinful part of me. I didn't want you to know this side of me."

"My dear Laura." He picked up her hand and held it between both of his. "I cannot imagine what you suffered at Wynwood's hands. In my heart, I cannot blame you for anything you did connected to him."

She shook her head. It had been Aya, who loved her enough to tell her the truth, who had convicted her of her shame. She would always remember her anger at Mrs. Jadis, no matter how she tried to rid herself of it. Only Christ could do that. She had prayed and relinquished her feelings to God.

"I still beg your forgiveness for not telling you about Mrs. Jadis and the pendant when I told you about the pocket watch. But I no longer wish to be afraid of the truth. There are few people you can trust because of the secrecy required by your superiors, but I can help you."

She had expected him to perhaps resist her, but he smiled and kissed the back of her hand. "I have realized that there are things you can do which I cannot. I would be glad of your help."

It was as if a claw had been squeezing her heart that now released it. Her heart still felt a bit bruised, but she was glad to again be on the same footing with Sol.

The hallway was empty now, and the others would wonder where they were, so they headed downstairs. They found only Phoebe and Keriah in the foyer, collecting their outerwear from Sol's butler.

"Mr. Rosmont and Lady Aymer beg you to excuse them," Phoebe said. "She had an appointment at the dressmaker's with her mother."

"I certainly would never permit Mrs. Coulton-Jones to be

kept waiting," he responded in mock gravity.

Phoebe smiled at him, and while she had intended it to put him at ease, instead there was something in that smile which immediately made him stiffen.

"Uncle Sol," she said in the sweetest tones Laura had ever heard from her, "I wish to become an agent."

"Absolutely not." His answer came out faster than a bullet.

Laura had predicted what he would say to her.

But Phoebe kept gazing steadily at Sol, her smile placid, her chin firm.

After a long minute, he finally sighed gustily. "I'll think about it."

Laura had predicted he would eventually say that, too.

"While you think about it, can I ask a favor of you?"

His expression became wary. "Possibly."

"Could I borrow one of your agents?"

Chapter Twenty-Five

Phoebe snuck into her father's home like a thief.

And yet, she was not here to remove anything that did not already belong to her.

However, she was accompanied by a man who admitted to theft in the past, so perhaps she deserved to feel like a criminal as she slipped into the mews behind her father's townhouse. She'd dressed plainly again so that any neighbors would not recognize her, but she saw no one who would pay the least notice to a tall maid and a tall footman, and the darkness cloaked them more completely than any disguise.

As they entered the mews, the only response was a whicker from her father's horse, but no alarm from the grooms. They were alone.

"It's too early," Mr. Rosmont growled beside her.

"What are you talking about?"

"It would be better to sneak into the house after everyone has gone to sleep," he explained.

"I will refrain from insulting your professionalism by asking how you'll sneak past the grooms in the mews," Phoebe said, "but the scullery maid sleeps in the kitchen nearest the fire. She would surely hear when you had to ... do whatever you would have to do to unlatch the back door."

They crept past the coal shed toward the back door to the

townhouse. Although it was shut, the sounds of loud merrymaking could be heard behind it.

Phoebe smiled. Earlier that day, she'd had eight bottles of her father's favorite whiskey delivered to the house, but it included an order slip that clearly indicated only six had been requested. She'd counted on the servants—including the grooms —enjoying themselves with the extra two bottles while their master and future mistress were away.

The door was not locked until later in the evening, so it opened easily under her hand. They entered as she had before, winding through the narrow passageways and up the servants' stairs to the second floor.

However, as they walked down the carpeted hallway, a pealing giggle shot up from the main staircase at the other end. She and Mr. Rosmont both froze.

He reached for the door closest to them, but she pulled at his sleeve and tugged him toward the second door, even though it drew them closer to the giggling. The soft thud of steps indicated at least two people were heading up the stairs toward this floor. They would spot Phoebe and Mr. Rosmont in moments, but she had a reason to dash for the second door.

They made it inside just as a woman's voice floated toward them. "La, we mustn't be here with the master and mistress away, but isn't it deliciously exciting?"

It was Agnes, her former maid. Phoebe didn't recognize or clearly hear the male rumble that responded, but it made the maid giggle again.

Phoebe let out a low breath. Although she did trust Aya's information that her father and Mrs. Lambert were expected at a very important party tonight, she'd still been a bit apprehensive.

She and Mr. Rosmont had entered her old bedroom. She saw Mrs. Lambert's hand over it already, with furniture moved and a few new pieces replacing old ones. The wardrobe in the corner was still there.

She opened the wardrobe but was nearly clouted by a mass of ruffles. After dodging a beribboned sleeve, she stared through the dimness at the masses of gowns that were not her own. *Mrs. Lambert strikes again.*

She hoped she could find something that would appease Agnes and allay her suspicions.

"What are you doing?" Mr. Rosmont hissed.

She ignored him and dug through the wardrobe toward the back until she found the gowns she'd been looking for. Three old ones from her come out years before. She'd outgrown them within a few months when she'd suddenly shot up three inches, but she hadn't liked them much—they'd been gifts from some of her other relatives—and so she hadn't bothered to adjust them. She snatched all three now and hurried to the door, which Mr. Rosmont had left cracked open. "Stay here," she told him.

Phoebe boldly swung open the door and stepped out into the hallway.

Agnes and the footman were entwined in an embrace like two snakes, but Phoebe had made sure she was loud enough to be heard through their passion. Agnes shrieked and jumped away from her swain, although he only looked dazedly at her.

"Agnes!" Phoebe hoped she looked shocked as opposed to the revulsion she actually felt.

"Miss Sauber! What ... what are *you* doing here?"

The question was rude, but Phoebe hadn't expected anything else from Agnes. She'd been counting on it, in fact. "I ... I'm retrieving some gowns I left behind." She lifted her chin, but her eyes darted about.

Agnes's gaze flattened. "That's the mistress's room now."

"These are *my* gowns!" Phoebe shook the dresses at Agnes, then hesitated, biting her lip. "If you won't tell her that I was here, I'll give this to you." She held out the least offensive gown, one colored vomit yellow but which might be lightened to a more acceptable shade if she applied enough attention to the fabric.

Agnes didn't even hesitate. She reached out and snatched the gown from Phoebe's hands, shaking it out in front of her to study it. While the color was unfortunate, the fabric was a fine muslin and the ribbons were silk. She gave Phoebe a sly smile. "Very well."

"I have only a few more to pack and then I'll be gone." Phoebe inserted a slight tremor of fear into her voice.

"What about me?" The footman's mouth formed a sulky pout that really didn't look very well on him.

She hadn't any money on her. "I'll send 'round some ale," she promised.

He seemed to doubt her, but Agnes elbowed him to get him to shut up and told Phoebe, "That'll be fine."

Then Phoebe pursed her mouth and gave a significant look to the door on the opposite side of the hallway, then to Agnes and the footman. "My father's bedroom needs airing. You should get right on it."

Agnes's smile widened, and she dipped a mock curtsy to her. "Of course, miss."

Phoebe returned to her bedroom and closed the door but left it open a crack. She listened until she heard her father's bedroom door close firmly with the soft sound of another giggle.

She let out a long breath and met Mr. Rosmont's gaze in the dimness of the room.

"How did you know they would respond that way?" he asked.

"Since I've run my father's household, I know these servants and what would sway them. They never respected me since I was away in the country for most of the year, but I knew I could use that to my advantage by pretending to need their silence."

He nodded. "You did well. The way you remained calm and clear-headed in the situation reminded me of Michael, Miss

Sauber."

She felt the heat across her face, her chest. She was unaccountably pleased by that.

"Will the servants keep their word?" he asked.

"For at least an hour or two."

"That's all we need."

They hurried down the main staircase to the ground floor and the small library at the back. As they lighted candles, she told him where she'd searched before. "Do you think you can find the key?"

"I've done something like this before."

He scanned the room, seeing the neat and rarely-used desk, the bookshelves thick with dust, the dust-free table with the decanter. He checked under her father's chair and with her help tipped the small sofa in front of the fireplace to look underneath. They did the same for the small, low table in front of it.

"My father is unimaginative and lazy. He'd hide it somewhere he'd easily remember, but not too difficult to retrieve." She thought a moment. "Perhaps the dining room next door?"

"Does he use it often?"

"Yes."

"Not there. He wouldn't want it in an area which is often used by servants, such as the sideboard or wall sconces." He looked around the room. "Is there anything new?"

She scanned everything. She hadn't had much time to look the last time she was in this room. "A new crystal decanter, but everything else on the table is the same. No new paintings. No new books." That much was obvious by the excessive dust.

She turned to the desk. "This is new. In fact, it wasn't here when I last looked for the key." She picked up a heavy, ornately decorated silver candlestick with three branches and a wide oval base, obviously only for use by the master. She tipped it upside down.

The base was partially hollow and stuffed with a handkerchief. She removed it and found it wrapped around the safe key.

Mr. Rosmont nodded. "Anyone unfamiliar with the room might not have noticed it."

She moved to the bottom shelf of one of the bookcases and emptied it of books, trying to remain quiet. It was the only shelf that didn't have dust blanketing it, and she knew he had opened the safe recently. She removed the wooden shelf entirely to reveal the safe set into the floor, then unlocked it, wincing at the metal scraping noise.

There was a velvet pouch at the top which she didn't recognize. When she lifted it, she felt the shapes of small stones.

Inside were diamonds. Hundreds, all round but in a variety of sizes. They had been recently cleaned and sparkled even in the dimming afternoon light from the partially-drawn windows.

Her heart stopped. Because she recognized these stones.

She closed the pouch and looked frantically inside the safe, finally finding a slim square case. She flipped it open with fumbling fingers and her throat caught.

The case held a necklace setting in old, almost bronze colored gold, entirely empty of the diamonds that it had once displayed. The diamonds now in the pouch.

This had been given to her by her mother. It had belonged to her maternal grandmother, and while the setting was old-fashioned and too impressive-looking when compared to modern jewelry, it had been valuable because of the quality of the stones and of the love she had felt whenever her mother let her play with the necklace.

She rummaged in the safe again, and found the boxes that contained the tiara and the two wide bracelet bands, all of them empty of diamonds.

Her hands shook as she laid the boxes down on the dusty carpet. Her father had had the stones removed and cleaned, which meant he intended to have them placed in another setting. *Except that these stones did not belong to him.*

And while she was an indifferent gambler, she would be willing to bet that the new jewelry would not be given to his recalcitrant daughter.

She closed her eyes and swallowed hard, trying to keep from vomiting the burning acid that rose from her stomach. Her hands curled into claws and dug into her thighs, crushing her gown and petticoat.

"Miss Sauber!"

The sound of her name brought her back to herself, and she started when she saw Mr. Rosmont squatting directly in front of her. She hadn't even noticed. He must have called her name several times.

"Are those the jewels?" He asked tentatively, sensing there was something wrong.

"Yes." And no. She had to regain control of herself. She still trembled with rage, but she pulled from a pocket in her gown a sack she had thought to stuff inside when she first decided to sneak into the house. She moved swiftly to pack the boxes of empty jewelry settings and the pouch of diamonds.

And she had wondered if she were being a thief? The true thief lived here.

She hadn't intended to take anything else besides her mother's jewelry, but the enormity of what her father had done made her suspicious. She searched through the safe.

Most of the contents were what she had remembered from the last time she had accessed the safe. She set aside the bag of gold, and some property deeds she remembered seeing before, and then she found the money transfer agreement.

She didn't understand what it was at first, but as she forced her whirling mind to focus on the words, she realized it was an agreement to transfer the funds of her dowry to her father.

Her dowry had been given to her by her maternal

grandmother, and he shouldn't have been able to touch it. But at the bottom of the document was a line for "Phoebe Sauber." A scrawl approximating her signature had been inserted.

Her fingers clenched again, and she nearly crumped the agreement. She forced herself to relax and read it again to be certain this was what she thought it was.

She had always hoped to one day marry. Her dowry was respectable enough to attract a respectable man, but not of the dizzying heights that would have attracted a fortune hunter. She remembered her desire mere days earlier, during that fateful breakfast, to find a man to marry this Season who would enable her to escape her father's household.

She would not have found any man. This legal document relinquished her dowry to her father in its entirety, and it was dated two weeks before she had arrived in town for the Season.

Phoebe tore the document in two.

She couldn't remember a time she had felt so infuriated. The edges of her vision were clouding until all she could see were her hands holding the torn paper, which trembled with her rage. Her heartbeat pounded in her ears, muffling all other sounds from the house—the creak of someone walking down the hallway toward the kitchen, the clopping of horses passing the house outside. She felt as if she were hearing everything from under water.

"Miss Sauber!"

Rough hands grabbed her shoulders and shook her. And in an instant, her hearing returned, her vision sharpened, focusing again on Mr. Rosmont's concerned face. Her next breath brought a whiff of old books and the musty carpet.

"We must leave," Mr. Rosmont said once he knew he had her attention again.

She nodded numbly and began putting items back into the safe. She hesitated over the large money bag, wondering if she were entitled to take it in lieu of the dowry money he'd taken from her. But she felt a quailing in her heart and knew that it would be stealing, despite the fact that her father had already stolen her money from her. She could also see her father calling down justice upon his daughter for the theft, and then having her transported without a second thought.

Phoebe stuffed the torn document into the sack with her jewels and the settings, then returned everything else to the safe as it had been. If her father had intended to reset the stones for his new wife, he would likely reopen the safe in the near future, but he would not know they were missing until then. If he wanted to report them stolen, he would have to prove they belonged to him, and he had no means to do so.

She was grateful to Mr. Rosmont for being with her, because he guided her back out of the house the way they had come, avoiding running into any of her father's servants on the way.

Her mind wanted to retreat into a shocked numbness, but she regained her wits when they entered the darkened mews. She turned away from Mr. Rosmont, hiked up her skirts and tied the jewels around her waist to keep them safe from cutpurses, then followed him out the door and away from the house.

They walked in silence in the darkness, but she drew close to him. She felt cold from the shock, and yet inside, she felt like a furnace.

She no longer had a dowry. She and Aunt Laura had wondered why her father hadn't wanted her to stay with Laura but had insisted she go to Bath. Now she understood.

If by some miracle she found a man to marry her, he would expect her dowry, which she no longer possessed. She had a greater chance of meeting someone while staying with Aunt Laura in town for the Season than when staying with Aunt Bethia in the more sparsely populated Bath, out of fashion especially at this time of year, and surrounded only by Aunt Bethia's cronies.

Mr. Rosmont somehow flagged down a hackney and pushed

her inside. She couldn't see his expression in the darkness, but his voice was gentle as he asked, "What happened?"

She told him, in a leaden voice devoid of feeling. She didn't know why she sounded like that when inside she was raging, like a storm of fire and ashes instead of rain or snow.

Her father's actions shocked him. They rode in silence for several minutes while she tried to grab hold of her thoughts, tried to pull herself together rather than flying to pieces as she wanted to do.

He opened his mouth, then closed it again. A few minutes later, he did the same thing. He likely didn't know what to say to her. She wanted to tell him that there was nothing, but she couldn't make her mouth move anymore.

When he finally did speak, the words came rushing out, as if he hadn't intended to say them but couldn't help himself.

"Don't let the anger turn you into a monster."

She didn't understand what he meant by that, although from the way he spoke, it was as if he was trying to convey something from personal experience.

She wanted to ask him to explain, but they suddenly pulled up in front of Aunt Laura's home.

He helped her down from the hackney and the brightly lit house enabled her to finally see his face clearly. There was a strange sort of empathy in his eyes, and yet there was self-loathing, too. It only further confused her.

He knocked on the door for her, and after Graham had ushered them in, he declined to stay. Before he left, it seemed he was about to say something, but he changed his mind and simply bowed to her.

Graham knew something was wrong, because after taking her pelisse, he personally escorted her to the library. Aunt Laura looked up from a desk full of papers and drew in a breath upon seeing Phoebe's face.

"Graham, tea in my bedroom, please."

"Very good, my lady."

Aunt Laura's bedroom had been redecorated directly after Uncle Wynwood had died, and she had not changed anything since then. The room was like sitting at the bottom of the ocean. The silk covering the walls was a cool, soothing blue, painted over with green swirls like waves that rolled over the pearl-colored fireplace. Aunt Laura led Phoebe to sit in one of the comfortable chairs upholstered in a milky coral color with blue and green throw pillows.

Phoebe wondered if she would burst into a fiery conflagration before the maid brought the tea, but it came swiftly since Laura's chef always had hot water ready at a moment's notice. Minnie must also have heard something from Graham, because Phoebe's favorite jam tarts accompanied the tea, despite the late hour.

And yet she couldn't eat. Her stomach was roiling.

Instead of sitting in the chair across from the tea tray, Aunt Laura sat next to her as she poured her a cup. Then she grasped Phoebe's hand and simply held it, waiting for her to be ready.

The tears came slowly, burning her skin as they trickled down her face. She swiped impatiently at them and told her aunt in a wooden voice what she'd discovered. Her aunt's grip on her hand grew tighter and tighter, until she'd explained everything.

She pulled up her dress and untied the sack from her waist, dropping it on the low tea table with a careless *thump*. She had worked and schemed to recover these jewels, and yet she was so staggered by her father's theft that she couldn't feel triumph at her successful endeavor.

Aunt Laura was thunderstruck. "I had no idea he was capable of such a thing."

"Perhaps it is best if I attempt to be logical about everything." Phoebe's voice only quavered slightly. She brushed at her tears, and they dried as if blown by a hot wind. "It wasn't as though I was planning to marry anyone right away, since I have laughably no prospects. And this way, I know any man interested in me will not be a fortune hunter."

Her aunt looked as if Phoebe's words pained her. "My dear, I don't think logic will—"

"My logic has always supported me." Her voice was harsher than she intended. "It helped me in growing roses. It helped in fighting the mortification of my first Season, and my lack of popularity in the Seasons since."

"You hardly wish to emulate your father, who did this motivated by cold, hard logic."

She had nothing to say to that, but it made her feel bleakly frozen. And yet ablaze at the same time.

"You needn't worry about where you shall live," her aunt said. "You are more than welcome to remain indefinitely with me, and I will gladly support you."

"But I don't like being a burden on you this way. I shouldn't *need* to be a burden on you at all." Her throat began to spasm. "I feel ... as if my body has been violated. We are commanded to honor our parents, but now I find I cannot do that."

Her aunt's face grew hard. "Honoring your father doesn't necessitate respecting him. I certainly have lost all respect for him."

Phoebe shot to her feet and began pacing in front of the fireplace. "I feel so powerless. And I detest feeling this way. I have only recently discovered what I wanted to do with my life and what I wanted my purpose to be. I found confidence in skills I had previously disregarded. But this ... but *he* has reminded me that ultimately I have *nothing,* I am *nothing.*"

"That is not true—"

"That proves otherwise." She stabbed her finger at the sack on the table, which contained the forged agreement. "My father controls me. He owns or has stolen all the things I thought belonged to me."

Just speaking the words made the rage seethe and foam inside her, burning her like acid. She had thought she had begun to extinguish the anger at his betrayal, but it was apparently still kindling beneath her facade of calm and righteousness.

"You must calm yourself." Aunt Laura's voice was firmer now. "We can find a way to resolve this."

"There is no means of winning against a man who deceives everyone with his false front of respectability. He has fooled everyone into believing he is honorable and admirable, and yet underneath he is as bad as Jack!"

Her aunt was shocked. "Jack is deplorable."

"And yet he has never been dishonest about who he is." She stopped pacing and glared down at her aunt, her chest heaving. She was so filled with rage that she felt hotter than the fire. "Why is my life being controlled by a man who doesn't care about me? I am his property. His slave. And I hate this feeling. I hate it!"

The words came out in a scream. She had never raised her voice to her aunt in this way. But all she saw was red, like blood or fire, and every muscle was taut and shrieking.

Aunt Laura shot to her feet, came up to her and slapped her. "Control yourself!"

The pain was nothing to the pain inside, but it was the harsh rebuke in her aunt's eyes that shook her out of her madness.

She suddenly remembered to breathe. She forced air into her lungs, and it cooled her temper.

Aunt Laura suddenly moved to her dressing table and returned with a hand mirror, which she held in front of her. "Look at yourself, Phoebe."

She was shocked by what she saw. Not by the red blotches, since she was always unattractive when she cried, but by the ugly anger still simmering in her eyes. She looked like a feral beast, one that only wished to tear apart the next being it encountered.

She cried again, but this time they left cooling tracks down her cheeks. "I'm very sorry, Aunt Laura." She was a small child again, being reprimanded for a tantrum. That was precisely how she had been acting.

Her aunt inhaled deeply, which drew her chest and her chin up, and then released it. The warmth and gentleness was back in her face. She took the mirror and laid it on the table. Then she placed her hands on either side of Phoebe's face. "My child, you are letting someone else's actions *infect* you."

Phoebe realized her emotions did feel like a sickness.

"You cannot control what he does, but you can control your own behavior. Do not allow him to have control over your emotions, also."

She nodded dumbly. Inside, she was still a riotous jumble, but her aunt's words were a thread of calm.

"I am not disregarding your feelings. You have every right to be upset. But your extreme rage has no use in solving the situation, and it is not a godly response."

She led Phoebe to sit back down on the sofa and handed her a handkerchief. "I have been concerned about your anger since your father first betrayed you, and now I worry that it will consume your good sense."

Phoebe wiped her eyes and loudly blew her nose. "I don't know what to do." Her words were muffled by her stuffed nose. "I don't like myself this way, but at the same time I want to lash out at the circumstances."

Aunt Laura rose and went to the table by her bed, then returned with her Bible. It was not like the massive family Bible in Phoebe's father's library, but a smaller one, and far more well-worn with use. "In times like these, I find it hard to offer words of comfort or wisdom, because circumstances appear so bleak. My words would seem hollow if I told you to simply persevere."

She flipped through the pages. "So I turn to the words of this book. The Hebrew King David had great injustices in his life. Men were constantly attempting to kill him, and he was being slandered when all he desired was to do justly. He wrote this psalm." She handed the book to Phoebe.

She had opened it to Psalm 13.

How long wilt thou forget me, O LORD? for ever?
How long wilt thou hide thy face from me?
How long shall I take counsel in my soul,
having sorrow in my heart daily?
How long shall mine enemy be exalted over me?
Consider and hear me, O LORD my God:
lighten mine eyes, lest I sleep the sleep of death;
Lest mine enemy say, I have prevailed against him;
and those that trouble me rejoice when I am moved.
But I have trusted in thy mercy;
my heart shall rejoice in thy salvation.
I will sing unto the LORD, because he hath dealt bountifully
with me.

The words of despair gripped Phoebe's heart, reflecting everything she was feeling. The writer understood suffering and despair—they were not simply pretty words of poetry.

But the words of trust in God near the end of the psalm seemed foreign to her.

Her aunt perhaps understood what she was thinking. "He trusted in the Lord's goodness. He trusted in the fact that he belonged to the Lord." Her hand smoothed over the page. "He realized there was no one to help him except for God. He could not save himself, and others could not save him. Only the Lord. And God is always faithful to come to help."

Aunt Laura exhaled, and her breath shook slightly. "This psalm, and also the Twenty-Second Psalm, were the passages I read the most right after your uncle died."

Phoebe remembered the uproar downstairs that night. She

remembered Jane's trembling arm as it wrapped around her, comforting her. She remembered her aunt's ghastly face the next day.

Except that now she understood the darker undercurrents of what had happened, of who her uncle had been, of how her aunt had been feeling. She also realized with a start that they had argued that night about Mrs. Jadis, whom her aunt had just visited, and who would be found dead the next day.

"I was consumed with anger at Wynwood and Mrs. Jadis when I heard about the baby."

"Baby?" Somehow the word seemed strange in the midst of this conversation.

Aunt Laura explained what Uncle Sol had not mentioned, the reason she had gone to visit Mrs. Jadis that day. "My anger made me do terrible things to her, which I later regretted. But regret does nothing when events have already occurred. Wynwood was dead. Mrs. Jadis was dead. And I was alone with my anger. But more than that, I was alone with the person I had become."

Phoebe felt as if she, too, had become a different person. The one she saw in the mirror. And in light of this startling revelation, she suddenly saw a different facet of her aunt and that argument with Uncle Wynwood that night.

Her pain was not lessened. But she was nonetheless comforted because her despair was shared by a woman who also knew despair, and yet had found strength in her faith.

"I do not wish to make light of your heartache," Aunt Laura said. "But I am telling you, from experience, that you must try to trust in God as David did."

She was feeling so flayed, so tormented, that at first she didn't quite understand what her aunt meant. "Trust in God to do what?"

"Trust in God to save you. The Twenty-Second Psalm is also about suffering, but it is quoted as referring to the suffering of

Jesus Christ. And in the midst of Christ's sufferings, God had a grander plan that involved saving the entire world. When your uncle died, I had to struggle to trust that God had a grander plan in mind. And I am telling you to try to do the same. He will do a marvelous thing if we trust Him and watch."

She nodded and took her aunt's hand. In her heart, she prayed, *Father, please forgive me.*

And yet the words did not make her anger magically disappear.

"Aunt Laura, I can't simply quench this anger."

"Of course you can't." She smiled at her. "But God can help you do so eventually. It involves more than a simple decision, but if you commit to working to become a better person, God will be pleased. And I know God will help you as He helped David in the psalm."

"I wish these feelings would simply go away. I am in so much pain." She had thought she was done with tears, but more flowed down to drip off the end of her nose.

Her aunt wrapped her in a strong embrace. "Sometimes it's the struggle through these feelings that makes us shine more brilliantly." She leaned back and stared into Phoebe's eyes, and it was as if she was trying to touch her soul.

"At the end of this, I know you will sparkle."

Chapter Twenty-Six

She was getting too old for this.

Laura squeezed her eyes shut and rubbed them with weary fingers. When she opened them, the candlelight wavered in her vision.

She sighed, breathing in ink, and paper, and the faint lilac scent from Lady Relford's perfume in the letter she was reading. She barely remembered writing these words to her friend, and yet in between the falsely cheerful lines, she could see the thread of rancor toward Wynwood.

Had his betrayal and her anger caused her to form this stranglehold control over her circumstances and the people around her? She felt a constant need to manage everything so that she could not be surprised, or hurt, or feel uncomfortable. So that she could pretend she was lovely and unbroken and the poised Lady Wynwood she presented to polite society.

Perhaps she was becoming maudlin because of her task, to read these missives and try to track Wynwood's actions and acquaintances. Echoes of emotions toward a dead man formed a sort of putrid scent in the air.

The sudden rattling sound startled her, making her drop her pen and splatter ink across the page. She looked around the room in confusion, then heard the sound again. It came not from the library, but from the adjacent room.

She rose and walked through the open door into the drawing room, which was dim without the candles that she'd gathered in the library. The sound pattered again, and she realized it was gravel against the window. The drapes were not completely drawn, and she needed only to nudge them aside to see the street.

Sol stood in the street, looking up at her. Behind him stood his carriage.

She automatically turned to look at the clock on the mantle, but it was too dark to see. She knew it had been past one o'clock when she last looked, and she'd sent the servants to bed.

The front door echoed in the foyer when she opened it, and Sol entered swiftly. "Hullo, Laura."

"How did you know I would be awake?"

"I didn't, but I took a detour on my way home. I noticed the light through the drawing room windows."

As he removed his cloak and set it carelessly on the side table, she saw that it was plain and made of rough wool. His clothes, also, were plain and dark. She had set down her candle to let him in, but now as she picked it up again, she could see that his face was as grim as his clothes.

They returned to the library. She offered him the last of her tepid tea, and all of the spice cakes Minnie had made for her before retiring. Sol handed her a sheaf of paper and began wolfing down the spice cakes.

The sheets were old, with the musty smell of something stored in an attic. The top sheet was a work order from the jewelers, Gildow and Sons.

The order was for two items, a pocket watch and a pendant. The signature was Wynwood's.

Her hands began to shake, but she deliberately set down the sheaf to sip cold tea. Then with a sharp exhale of resolve, she picked up the papers again.

The second sheet was made of different paper, finer and

whiter despite the age and poor storage conditions. Inked upon it was a drawing of the ancient Glencowe crest, and an unfamiliar hand had written at the bottom, "provided by the customer for the design of the items."

The third sheet was the same finer paper, but the drawing was the five-flowered, five-leaved symbol. Scrawled across the bottom in Wynwood's writing were instructions to put this symbol inside the back cover of the outer casing of the pocket watch.

Below that was another line, "Also place symbol inside pendant."

She drew in a sharp breath.

There was a fourth sheet, this one the same paper as the work order. In a faded ink were curious drawings of the pendant. The Glencowe crest was not drawn on the front, but she recognized the shape and the unusually shaped crown on both the top and bottom. The pendant had been drawn from several angles, including the mechanism to open it, which was a difficult process and would only be done by someone who knew the proper method. It could not be opened by accident.

She dropped the papers as if they burned her.

Sol paused in the act of finishing the last spice cake. She stared hard at him, and he asked, "Did you want one?"

"Of course I didn't want one," she snapped, then sagged back into her chair, suddenly feeling as though her legs had turned into jelly. "That's the pendant she was wearing when I saw her."

Sol wiped his mouth, sipped cold tea, and grimaced. He also sat back in his chair, meeting Laura's tired gaze. "Then Mrs. Jadis was like Wynwood—belonging to that group."

The shadows suddenly seemed darker. She turned to the fireplace. It had died down to embers, but she hadn't the inclination to build it back up again.

She shouldn't be surprised. She had already suspected Mrs. Jadis was involved in the group, from the moment Sol had explained about the symbol inside the pocket watch, because that ugly Glencowe crest had been displayed prominently on the woman's pendant.

But this symbol was a brushstroke of black across the canvas of her life, casting suspicion on the woman's suicide.

Both of them had been part of this secret organization. For the first time, this truly hit her in all its significance. She had been connected to both of them in tenuous ways, and they had both likely been killed. The group could have killed her also, if they had wished it.

Why hadn't they?

Perhaps it would cause too much fervor for Wynwood, his wife, and his mistress to die. Perhaps they had realized she posed no threat to them.

But she was suddenly convinced that God had protected her when she hadn't even realized her life was in danger.

His hunger was sated, but Sol still looked unsatisfied. And perhaps even embarrassed and frustrated. "I have never told anyone this, but my superior personally selected me for my position in the Ramparts, almost twenty years ago."

She had suspected he had been doing this for a long time, but she had no notion it had been that long. It would have been during his time in the army.

"He said he chose me because I was intelligent and had foresight. I was a good judge of character and could tell when people were lying to me. Although," he added with a rueful glance at her, "I am not as skilled as some."

She dipped her head in acknowledgment, although she wondered where his tale was wandering.

"I prided myself on making sound judgments. Perhaps that was why ..." He closed his eyes and rested his elbow against the desk, rubbing his forehead with his fingers. "When investigating Wynwood, I purposefully chose to disregard Mrs. Jadis. I had looked into her and decided she was simply a grasping prostitute out to fleece Wynwood of his money."

To Laura, she had been the woman attempting to depose her.

He set down his hand and looked her in the eye, his expression almost pleading. "I'm sorry I grew so angry with you when you kept the knowledge of Mrs. Jadis's pendant from me. *I* was the one who had information about your husband, and *I* was tasked with investigating the people he associated with. I had thought I was so knowledgeable and discerning, but in reality … I was simply proud."

"Sol, you have nothing to apologize for."

"You're wrong." He frowned, but it was a gesture full of regret. "I had no right to be upset when *I* was the one who failed *you* ten years ago."

"I think you are being too hard on yourself, Sol."

"Am I? Why shouldn't I be hard on myself? I didn't realize until later, but it must have pierced you so to face this after all these years." His eyes flickered away, and his jaw grew tight. "I know that five years before Wynwood's death, you were very badly injured, but I hadn't quite known the extent of your wounds."

She stiffened, then turned her face away from him. She couldn't look at him, couldn't see his pity and his sympathy and his care. The loss was still a hole punched inside her that refused to fill up again or be healed. But she managed to say in an even voice, "I am sorry I let my shame keep secrets from you."

A silence fell between them that was a touch awkward. She wished the candles a little less bright so that she could retreat into shadows and not see his face, nor have him see hers.

When she had regained her composure, she gave him a small smile. "But I appreciate a man who is humble and willing to apologize."

He took her verbal olive branch and returned her small smile, although his was tinged with sadness. Then he reached over to grasp her hand, cradling it with both of his, and he bent over it to kiss the back of it.

The touch of his lips was warm, as were his hands. She allowed her eyes to close briefly, to savor his gentle touch, but opened them before he could see her reaction.

The tender moment could not last. There was too much at stake outside these softly candlelit walls.

Her eye fell on the letters she had been perusing. "I don't know why a group like that would have wanted anything to do with someone like Wynwood. I thought of him only as self-indulgent and dissipated."

"A group like that would have a complex but compelling reason. I had thought we would never learn why they had killed Wynwood, but now that we know Mrs. Jadis belonged to them, also, there might be something we can yet uncover after all these years."

She steeled herself. This would only dredge up more grievous memories for her, but they needed to look into Mrs. Jadis. She shuddered with dread.

He gestured toward the closest letter. "These will be more important than ever, but they only speak of Wynwood. I don't know how to ferret out information about Mrs. Jadis."

She swallowed and faced him.

"I know a way."

Epilogue

He was drowning.

No, he was no longer in the middle of the Channel with Sep. And yet waters pulled at his legs, filled his lungs. He struggled to breathe.

It was too hot. His body was being roasted in an oven. Except that the heat came not from around him, but from deep inside him.

It was boiling, this heat. Not simply hot, but caustic and hungry, seeking to devour, longing only to destroy. It consumed him until he became the heat, he became the devourer, he turned into the destroyer.

It hurt. It hurt all over. He only wanted to burn up and disappear.

And then he saw it. A white face he recognized. Soothing sea-foam green eyes looking directly at him.

Phoebe.

He had never said her name aloud, but it formed in his mind as if planted there.

She walked through the flames surrounding him, beating them back by the beauty of her face, the reassurance in her eyes. If he followed her, she would stop the burning. She would close the jaws of the devourer. She would destroy the destroyer.

And so he chased that small flickering light. All the while, the

LADY WYNWOOD'S SPIES, VOL. 2: BERSERKER

burning inside of him demanded that he destroy, crush, smash.

Her light called to him. *Come.*

He was powerful, and yet he was also helpless. And so he followed her.

And now he was drowning. Not in water, but in darkness that wrapped around him, and the darkness was colored with pain.

Every muscle, every joint, every bone was enflamed with pain. His brain throbbed, something was trying to squeeze his eyes out of his head. His throat felt closed up, but he could still breathe, a thin stream of cool air.

He heard muffled voices that he didn't recognize. The clang of pots. The soft steps of shoes.

The smell of bread.

Maybe it was the bread that cut through the darkness and the pain. His sister had accused him of having his brain situated in his gut.

He tried moving his fingers. They twitched.

He thought he opened his eyes, but he still saw only darkness.

No, it was dimness, not darkness. He was lying down. He was still in pain. But he was awake.

Michael Coulton-Jones was awake.

Connect with Camy

I hope you enjoyed *Lady Wynwood's Spies, volume 2: Berserker*!

I really hadn't intended for Thorne to become such a prominent character in this book, but I guess it was inevitable after the events of *Lady Wynwood's Spies, volume 1: Archer*. The poor guy has had a lot of really awful things happen to him, but Isabella is determined to help him overcome them all. I didn't show it in this book, but she prays for him a lot! And eventually I'll be able to reveal more about both of them.

The story continues in *Lady Wynwood's Spies, volume 3: Aggressor*, which you can buy on Amazon (https://amzn.to/3lqnY7E).

If you haven't yet, I invite you to sign up for my email newsletter (https://bit.ly/lady-wynwood). After a few welcome emails, I send out newsletters about once a month with a sale on one of my books, a freebie, or news about when my latest release is available.

Camy

Made in the USA
Middletown, DE
30 January 2024

48845317R00175